"Sex changes

Josh continued, "You should really think about what you're proposing we do tonight."

Angela had come so far, and his bedroom was just a few feet away. Her body was protesting loudly. It knew what it wanted and it was sitting right next to her.

She glanced around his living room, and for a second focused on an electrical cord that was dangling from a fish tank. She then gave the arm of the sofa an appraising look.

I could tie him up.

She grinned.

He moved closer to her and began stroking her side in what she guessed was supposed to be a comforting gesture. But the feel of his broad hand moving down her body elicited a warmth that was now quickly spreading within her.

"Intimacy isn't just something you rush into," Josh warned. His mouth pushed on hers gently. "Kissing...maybe we could make do with just that."

Angela leaned away from him then and slipped her dress over her head. "Sure," she said in mock agreement. "Just kissing it is."

Blaze™

Dear Reader,

I can't tell you how excited I am to be writing for the new Blaze series! This line gives authors the opportunity to mix mind-blowing passion with tender romance in the best possible way!

I've always been intrigued by how people view sex and love differently—and how some people think they can keep the two separate. Take Angela and Josh, my characters from *The Driven Snowe*. Angela Snowe thinks that she can "experience" the passion of sex without being bogged down with the commitments of a relationship. Ordinarily Josh Montgomery would agree with her, since he'd been practicing that very belief for years. But with the right people, sex is not only an integral part of a relationship, but can be a doorway to the kind of love that most people only dream about.

I hope you enjoy reading this book as much as I've enjoyed writing it. Better still, drop me an e-mail at catyardley@aol.com, and let me know what you think! And check out the Blaze Web site at www.tryblaze.com.

Cathy Yardley

Books by Cathy Yardley

HARLEQUIN DUETS
23—THE CINDERELLA SOLUTION

THE DRIVEN SNOWE

Cathy Yardley

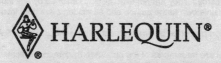

HARLEQUIN®

TORONTO • NEW YORK • LONDON
AMSTERDAM • PARIS • SYDNEY • HAMBURG
STOCKHOLM • ATHENS • TOKYO • MILAN • MADRID
PRAGUE • WARSAW • BUDAPEST • AUCKLAND

To my Mom, Yen Duong Yardley,
who taught me how to survive,
and my Dad, James Vincent Yardley,
who taught me how to plan.
I love you both.

ISBN 0-373-79018-X

THE DRIVEN SNOWE

1

"HOW DO YOU *DO* THAT?"

Josh Montgomery didn't look up from his Palm Pilot until he'd finished jotting in a name and phone number. In the notes section, he added: *Melissa. Redhead from Cable Car. Likes waterskiing.* With that done he tucked the gadget back into his pocket. "Sorry, Adam. How do I do what?"

Adam, his best friend and business partner, was grinning. "You only talked with her for five minutes, and she acts like she's ready to jump you behind the bar—but classy about it." He shook his head. "It's like this everywhere I've ever seen you. Even here in backwoods Northern Cal."

"Manzanita is not backwoods," Josh demurred. Granted, a stuffed moose head overshadowed the jukebox, and the Corona he was drinking was still looked at askance when perfectly good Bud was available, but a lot had changed since he'd grown up in the small town.

Adam huffed impatiently. "You know what I mean. City or hicksville, you've got women lining up. What's your secret?"

"No secret." Josh took a swallow of beer.

Adam's eyes narrowed. "It's the rich thing, isn't it?"

Josh laughed, gesturing at his khakis and denim shirt. "Yup. I just scream millionaire."

"Well, then, *what* is it?"

Adam had joked about this before, but tonight, he sounded stubborn about it. Josh thought about an answer. "I think it's because I'm a nice guy."

"Oh, shut up."

"No, really." Josh considered it a few more minutes, then said slowly, "My dad once said if you ever want to sell something, don't talk about what it is that you're selling. Ask about what it is they want to buy."

"That's catchy," Adam said. "I don't see the point, but it's catchy."

"The point is, if you want women to want you, you don't advertise what *you are*. You find out what *they want*." He grinned as Adam rolled his eyes. "My mom would actually agree with that."

"You may be the only man I've ever met who isn't insulted by being called a nice guy." Adam's voice expressed a mix of disgust and curiosity. "You're also possibly the only guy I've ever met that is a 'nice guy' and still manages to get laid on a regular basis. Normally, women just toss out nice guys like garbage." He looked cheered by this. "I don't suppose you've been dumped?"

"Um, not really," Josh said, grinning even more at Adam's look of disappointment. "I am also—well, *nice* enough to be completely honest with the women I spend time with. I don't promise them a bunch of stuff, and then not deliver it. So there you have it—honesty and attention." He paused. "It's just like sales, now that I think about it."

Adam smirked. "Think your patented nice guy sales approach would work on that blonde over there?"

"Depends on what you're selling." Josh glanced over to where Adam was staring. The woman in question had brilliant platinum hair that stood out like a beacon against the dark wood paneled walls. "Happy hunting."

"Nice guy. I'm a nice guy," Adam muttered as he walked away. "God. My fraternity would tar and feather me."

Josh watched as Adam made his way to the blonde's corner, easily striking up a conversation.

Josh turned back to the bar. He'd already collected three numbers that night. He pulled out his Palm Pilot and glanced at his schedule. No late meetings or out of town business next week, which meant that he'd probably be making dates with at least two of the women he'd met. They'd go out to a restaurant. Maybe a club in Sacramento. As far as anything more, well, *physical*— he considered his prospects with an almost clinical detachment. The redhead seemed like a candidate. As had the young Asian woman he'd met an hour before.

Or was that last night?

He took another swig from his Corona. He could predict the future already—he could practically type it into his Palm Pilot just sitting there. *Two weeks with redhead—dinner, dancing, partying. Go back to her place/ my place. Two more weeks, maybe three, of some really romantic interludes.*

He sighed.

Figure out that I'm getting bored with her. Very gently disengage contact. Repeat cycle with new candidate.

He was getting into a rut.

"Josh Montgomery?"

He barely glanced over his shoulder, still stuck in his own thoughts, but the soft, lyrical voice gave him pause. "Yes?"

It was another woman. She was just over average

height, maybe five foot eight, with a well-proportioned build. A bit on the lean side, but she had curves in the right places. She was wearing a black dress that would have looked a lot better if she'd stop tugging at the hemline. She had luxurious mahogany hair that was pulled back in a severe ponytail at the nape of her neck. Fortunately, she had the kind of face that could pull it off, with high cheekbones, aquiline nose and huge, wide-set doe eyes that surveyed him with velvety brown seriousness.

"Well, hello," he said, with more enthusiasm.

She didn't smile. Her lips, which looked full, were pulled taut with obvious strain. "I was hoping I'd find you here," she said, her voice a musical rush. "Can I, er, buy you a drink?"

He glanced at his beer. It was half-full. "I'm doing all right," he replied.

"Oh."

She stared at him.

He waited for her to shift the conversation into something else, likely some other sort of come-on. *Haven't I seen you before?* or *Don't you know so-and-so?* or even *Come here often?* But she just stood there, clutching at her little beaded purse.

"Can I buy *you* a drink?" he finally offered, smiling.

"Oh. Okay. Thanks." She glanced at the list of drinks posted above the bar. To his amusement, she pushed at the bridge of her nose, then blinked with a startled jolt. *She wears glasses,* he thought. *She's not used to her contacts.* "I'll have an Amaretto and orange juice. Not too strong," she added with emphasis.

The bartender quickly poured her drink, and Josh motioned to add it to his tab. She still stood, staring at him.

"Why don't we find someplace to sit?" Josh said.

He wasn't sure why he was doing this. She was pretty, but she wasn't stunning. Not to be immodest, but he'd been around enough stunning women in his career to know. Still, there was something about her that intrigued him. Maybe it was because she seemed so out of place.

"So. You were hoping you'd find me, and here we are," he said, as she settled herself in her chair. "Don't take this the wrong way, but I don't know you, do I?"

"You don't know me," she confirmed, taking a sip of her drink. It had very little alcohol, but he noticed her wince.

Not a big drinker, either. What's she doing in a bar?

"Actually, I don't really know you, either. Well, other than by reputation."

Groupie. Knows I'm rich. He smiled, even as his interest in her ebbed. "Oh. Then you know my company, Solar Bars."

"Of course I know Solar Bars. You've turned the economy of Manzanita around with it." She didn't sound impressed, and waved the comment away with her hand. "That wasn't the reputation I was referring to, though."

"It isn't?" He frowned, and dammit if that intrigue didn't creep back into his consciousness. His mind shuffled through the possibilities for a minute. "Not the football thing. I'd like to think I was a good quarterback when I was at Manzanita High, but that was how many years ago?"

She grinned, took another quick sip and made a sour face. "No, it's not that. I did live here then—I remember you from high school." She smiled shyly.

Now he was baffled and just bordering on aroused. "I guess I'm just going to have to ask," he said, with a note of seduction in his voice. "Which reputation are you talking about?"

She smiled, brightly, taking a deep breath.

"I picked you because you're a sure thing."

I MUST BE OUT of my mind! Even as the words left her mouth, Angela Snowe felt like grabbing her bag and tottering on her big stupid heels out of this meat market.

His eyes blazed at her. *"I'm a sure thing?"*

"That is, I had heard you would be very likely to— well, I was *hoping*..." She stammered, and tried for another deep breath. This wasn't working the way she'd planned. "I really need help with a situation. A, uh, *sexual* situation. I thought your stance on, um, things like this was common knowledge."

"It's common knowledge that I'm the town slut?"

She could feel her skin heating with a blush. "I wouldn't have put it that way."

"You just did." His eyes narrowed. "So you're propositioning me, is that what's going on here?" His voice was whiplash sharp, and each word cut. "You just need to get *serviced*..."

"I'm a virgin."

The simple phrase stopped his righteous tirade cold.

She felt nervousness bubble through her, and took a bracing sip from her drink. "I'm twenty-nine years old, and I'm a virgin. *That's* why I came looking for you."

He stared at her as if she'd escaped an asylum. Then he smiled, slowly. "Okay. This has got to be some kind of funniest videos show. Who put you up to this?"

It wasn't a person that had put her up to this. It was more like a thing. Not that she was about to explain it to him. "This is far from a practical joke, believe me."

He sat there as if silently weighing what she'd told

him, then shook his head. "If you're serious...no. I'm sorry," he said, in a tone that didn't really sound as if he was, "but I just couldn't."

She was surprised at how crestfallen she felt. This man was notorious for his number of conquests. The fact that he *would not* sleep with her spoke volumes. "Why not?" she blurted.

"Why not?" He shot her a look of disbelief. "Because despite what you might think, men don't just... perform. And contrary to 'common knowledge,' *I* sure as hell don't. Were you planning on paying me when we were done, too?"

"Um," she chuckled weakly, "would that change your mind?"

He shook his head, blue eyes flashing like lightning. "Lady, you're killing me."

"Honest, I was kidding," she mumbled. "I'm sorry. I didn't mean to make you sound like some sort of gigolo, or something."

"Well, that's a relief." His sarcasm could have cut glass. "I suppose you were kidding about the whole virginity thing, too."

"No, I was serious about that. I'd really like you to help me with my, well, *situation*. Tonight, that is. I don't really have a lot of choice about that." She shook her head, her fear and embarrassment warring with her determination. "I know it's a bizarre request, and I can't explain it to you. I'm...it would mean a lot to me." She glanced down at the tabletop. "I had to at least give it a try."

He studied her silently. She felt as if she was drowning in the humiliation of it.

His hand reached out, stroked her cheek, and she felt

a shuddering ripple through her body. His eyes got low-lidded, and he leaned toward her.

"So I'm a *sure thing*. What else would a modest woman like yourself call that? A man of questionable morals? Of ill repute?" He laughed mirthlessly at himself, then looked at her, his eyes suddenly turning intense. "And you're a *virgin*, huh?" he murmured, moving closer. "Only one way to find out, I guess. That is, for a guy like me."

His lips covered hers. They were soft, yet firm, and quickly molded against her mouth. After a second of shock, she became curious and pressed forward. It felt like…like eating jalapeños, she thought after a moment. The initial sweet, then a ring of fire burning her lips. She pushed forward a little more, putting a hand against his chest.

He cupped the side of her face. She felt his tongue run along her lips, causing the faintest tickle, before parting them and tickling her tongue. Her heart pounded heavily in her chest.

Just as suddenly as it had started, it seemed, it was over.

Startled, she opened her eyes, breathing raggedly. His breathing was also uneven, she noticed. His blue eyes sparked like sapphires and flame. "What's your name?"

"Angela."

"I'm sorry, Angela," he said. "I'm not going to sleep with you."

TEN MINUTES LATER, Josh had dragged Adam outside in front of the bar. "I have to talk to you. Now."

"I was about to close the deal with that blond chick using your patented nice guy technique." Adam looked decidedly surly. "This had better be life threatening."

"Oh, it's life threatening, all right," Josh promised with his own brand of menace. "I'm going to kill you for this little prank."

To his credit, Adam's face was blank. "What little prank?"

"Don't play stupid." The incident he'd just experienced in the bar still coursed through him, and he was angry at almost being taken in by it...at how affected he was by Angela and her fake soulful plea. Hell, his body was still affected by her, protesting his refusal with a vicious throb. "The really low thing was the setup. A *virgin,* all serious and scared, calling *me* a 'sure thing' and asking for anonymous sex!" He growled. "This is low, even for you."

Adam was silent for a long moment. "Buddy, I have no idea what you're talking about, but I am suddenly very, very curious."

Josh felt a sinking sensation in the pit of his stomach. "You mean, you really don't know? You didn't set this up?"

"No, but you're starting to make me wish I had." Adam's obvious humor and interest convinced Josh that he was telling the truth. "Who *is* this woman?"

"I have no idea." Josh rubbed his face. "Who else would set me up like this? What kind of a sick prank..."

"How do you know it's a prank?"

"She said she was a virgin, but I don't buy it."

"Why not?"

Because Josh couldn't figure out what the hell else she could be. Because he couldn't figure out what the hell she *was,* period. It had to be a prank. She couldn't be for real. "For one thing, she's twenty-nine."

Adam burst out in a short bark of surprised laughter.

"Get out!" He quickly headed back to the bar to peer into the darkened room, but Josh stopped him.

"I'm not kidding. Not that she looks it, or anything, but I get the feeling she would have yanked out her driver's license if I had asked her to."

Adam squinted at him. "So why do you think she's lying about being a virgin?"

Her kiss. His bloodstream was carbonated, and his body was on fire. No virgin could kiss like that.

He tried to focus on more tangible evidence. "Well, for another thing, she was insistent—she wanted to lose her virginity *tonight*. Like it was some sort of mission, or something. That's where the whole 'sure thing' came in."

And didn't that comment still sting?

He could tell Adam was getting plenty of amusement from the statement. "So what'd she do? Go home?"

That made Josh pause. He had been keeping an eye out for her. "She's still in the bar." The fact made him uneasy.

"Really?" Adam's voice was gleeful. "Maybe she wasn't kidding. Maybe she's looking for another taker. Heck, maybe *I* should go back inside..."

"No. She said that she was looking for me in particular."

She also said that she was going to lose her virginity tonight. Like she didn't have a lot of choice in the matter.

A chill washed over him. It took him a second to realize it was fear. She might be tall for a woman, but she could easily be overpowered by any of the men that were sitting in the Cable Car, right this second.

What if she were telling the truth?

"Josh? You okay?"

"Adam, do me a favor. Get lost for a good fifteen minutes. I don't want you to witness this," Josh said, not quite sure what he was going to do. Thinking about it, he growled, "If you breathe a word of this to *anyone*..."

"I won't, but I'm going to harass you bright and early tomorrow, and you'd better fill me in." Josh knew he wasn't kidding. "Happy virgin hunting."

Josh didn't dignify the comment with a reply. He was striding back into the bar in two heartbeats.

A big man in a red-checkered shirt had taken Josh's earlier seat, and now leaned over to talk to Angela. She looked totally uncomfortable. She was sitting on the edge of her seat. Josh could sense the tension in her body from across the room. He couldn't imagine she was willing to sleep with the man she was sitting with, but something about her determination, her strange practicality, kept setting off unreasonable alarms in his head.

I don't have a lot of choice...

Dammit! What she was doing was *dangerous*. Didn't she realize that?

"Angela."

Her head whipped around, her eyes wide and surprised. And relieved, he noted. "Josh."

"Me'n'her were having a little talk," the bullnecked guy protested.

"Not anymore," Josh replied. "The lady has a situation, and I promised her I'd help her with it. Tonight."

He saw hope flare in her eyes, and, to his surprise, fear. "Will you excuse me?" she said, not even looking at Bullneck. She got up and let Josh put his arm around her. The man grumbled and lumbered back over to the bar.

"You're following me home," Josh said, his voice

tight. "Then we're going to take care of this little 'situation' of yours."

And I'll show you what can happen when nice girls go looking for trouble.

ANGELA SAT, PARKED in Josh's driveway, watching him as he got out of his black Infiniti.

This may be the single most stupid thing you've ever done.

Her hand fumbled on the seat belt release. If she were this clumsy on the belt buckle, how was she going to be when she had to...when they were...

No "may be" about it. This is definitely *the most stupid thing you've ever done!*

She glanced at the car keys in her hand. All she would have to do...

A knuckle rapped on her window, and she gasped, dropping the keys.

"You okay in there?" He was still grinning, as if the whole thing were some sort of fraternity dare.

If he'd been menacing, or even overeager, she would have driven off. But his obvious amusement kept pushing buttons she didn't even know she had. Oh she'd do this, all right, she thought as she threw her keys in her small purse. Even if she mangled him trying, she'd lose her virginity tonight.

She got out of the car, closing the door with a slam. "So. This is your house?" she said, sounding as casual as her anger and nervousness would allow. "It's nice."

"I like it. Lots of privacy. You could make all sorts of noise—" he looked at her suggestively "—and nobody would hear a thing."

Ignoring the statement, she followed him in the house. He turned on the lights. *He doesn't live like a hedonistic* bachelor, she thought, then almost laughed at the primness of her own observation. What had she expected? Empty beer cans, bras hanging from the chandelier?

The furniture was modern, but not harshly so—clean lines, and a subtle styling she appreciated. Windows opened up to the trees beyond. A large octagonal fish tank illuminated the corner. "It's great."

"So. Should we go at it on the couch, or what?"

Her high heel caught on his carpet, and she stumbled. "Sorry?"

"After all, you're here for sex, right?" He sat down on the couch, patting the cushion next to him. "I imagine you're in something of a hurry."

"I see." She didn't, but then, he was the expert. "So...the point of this is to just dive in there, and be as fast as possible? I mean, is that normal for you?"

"Hardly." He looked insulted, though that wasn't her intent. He stood and faced her. "If you want slow..."

He went to her and took her mouth and her breath in the same instant. He moved languorously, seducing her lips.

Oh my, can this man kiss!

It was the last coherent thought she had for several minutes. Soon, the slow seduction became a building need. He went from sampling her lips to devouring them. She felt his kiss wash over her in waves, like a relentless storm. She was helpless to do anything but give herself over to it.

When he released her, it took her a moment to get her bearings. "Well. That was better than I expected."

He let out a burst of sharp laughter. "How would you know what to expect—being a virgin, and all?"

"I read a lot." She took a calming breath, nerves fluttering in her stomach. "But you're right. I'm out of my depth here…'' She paused, registering the smug smile that was spreading across his face. ''And *you knew it*. That's the point you're trying to make here, isn't it?''

She snatched up her purse. ''If you just brought me here to prove something,'' she whispered, her voice shaking, ''then maybe you should have left me at the bar.''

He went and stood between her and the door. ''And then what would you have done?''

''I don't know.'' She felt deflated. She wished she could take off her shoes. The pinching made it hard for her to think. ''It took me all day just to get the guts to ask you. And I know this will make you angry, but after all I'd heard, I didn't think that you were going to say no.''

''Angela, what the hell *have* you heard about me? I mean, I've had a lot of fun in my time, but I'm hardly the Casanova of Manzanita.'' He smiled when she giggled, a real smile this time, not a smug, challenging one. He sat down and patted the sofa again, with no suggestive overtones. ''Sit down for a sec.''

She did so, feeling the heat coming off his body. She paused, then kicked off her shoes. He grinned at the action.

She studied him. His black hair and cobalt blue eyes. The way his grin curved, the way his chin looked like it was carved out of granite. The small scar over his right eyebrow. The kindness of his smile, one of the first things that had struck her, and the gentleness in his voice.

She had made the right choice.

''Why are you doing this? Really.'' His voice was low. ''Are you sure you even want to?''

"Oh, yes," she breathed. "I'm sure. Scared or not, it's definitely what I want."

"It's the scared part that concerns me," Josh muttered. He tilted her chin up, looking her square in the eye. She closed them, anticipating another delicious onslaught.

He chuckled, and her eyes flew open. "No, not yet," he said. He pulled her against his chest and put an arm around her shoulders. He smelled good, like something spicy. A vague scent of sandalwood, maybe…

"Still with me?"

"Hmm?" She looked up to see his blue eyes glowing down at her. He'd obviously noticed she was paying attention to something other than his conversation. "Oh. Yes."

"Why are you doing this now?"

She tensed against him. "Why?"

He frowned. "Nobody just decides to lose their virginity overnight, Angela. What set you off?"

She shifted uncomfortably. "I don't think you'd understand…"

"Try me."

"I have a pretty good life," she started, thinking quickly. "But I sort of…well, I realized I was going to be thirty. I'd kept putting off the big stuff I'd always meant to do. I've never been to Europe. I've never gone skinny-dipping, I've never eaten a seven-course meal…"

"So," he said, grinning. "You've got a really full night ahead of you, huh?"

"Well, I figured that I was the most nervous about sex, so I'd just start with that," she said, with an embarrassed laugh. "If I can do this one, I can do anything."

It wasn't the whole reason, but it was close enough. Even brushing past the true reason made her feel queasy.

"Do you always make decisions this way?" She could feel the rumble of his voice under her ear. It tickled the side of her head, and she nuzzled him a little. He moved her so he could better look at her face. "Well, do you?" he repeated.

"Pretty much."

He laughed, and something in his eyes shifted. "Sex changes things. Even when it isn't supposed to mean anything. Maybe especially when it isn't supposed to mean anything," he said. "Believe me, you should think a little more about all of this."

She'd come so far, her body protested. Was he going to send her *home?*

She glanced around, and for a brief second glanced at an electrical cord that was draped by the fish tank. She then gave the arm of the sofa an appraising look.

I could tie him up.

She giggled. Oh, she was in trouble when ideas like that made even a modicum of sense.

He smiled at her, stroking her side in what she guessed was supposed to be a comforting gesture. The feel of his broad hand moving down her body was anything but, and she felt warmth spreading up from her abdomen.

"I mean it," he repeated. "It's not something you just want to rush into."

"Josh," she said, "I've been 'rushing into' this for about twelve years or so now, don't you think?"

"You know what I mean."

"No, I don't think I do." How was she supposed to explain this? she wondered. "I've wanted this for a long time, and to be honest, I want you. I'm sure you think that I'm going to have all these regrets tomorrow—or worse, that I'm going to have this incredible night and then think that it's going to mean happily ever after. I'm twenty-nine, not seventeen," she chastised gently. "I know it's not going to be like what I'm expecting, but I also know that I can live alone quite comfortably. I might be unhappy, but in a way, I've been unhappy for years already. I'd rather take the misery *and* the sex."

He laughed. "Angela, I don't know who the hell you are," he said, his voice gruff. "But I like you, you know that?"

"I like you, too," Angela said with a broad grin. "I wanted to do this—and when I first got here, it all hit me, the reality of it. I *wanted* to, and I *didn't* want to. Now, I'm sure that this is what I want. You're making this so much easier for me."

He was being so sweet and considerate, when he could have been so horrible. Without thinking about it, she leaned forward and kissed him.

It lasted a little longer than she had intended. When she pulled away, his eyes were half-lidded. "You're not bad at that."

She blinked. "At what?"

"Kissing," he replied, and his voice was husky-rough. She felt her stomach clench, and her heart pound. "I know I shouldn't sleep with you, no matter how ready you think you are. But maybe we could make do with that kissing of yours."

She couldn't help but feel disappointed. "Just…kissing?" Was he kidding? What had she just said she wanted?

The smile grew hotter, it was the only way she could describe it, and his eyes suddenly glowed. "Trust me. Kissing will be more than enough."

He moved toward her face, and she closed her eyes.

His mouth pushed on hers gently, a dry handshake of a kiss.

Save me from men who think they know better than I do, she thought with aggravation. *Has all this been for nothing?*

With a slow movement, his tongue flicked across her lips, then retreated. She could feel the movement of his mouth like a slow dance against her own. It was different than the rushed assault of a kiss he'd given her when he was trying to prove his point. This one was a pure, slow seduction of the senses. The sigh she gave now was anything but disappointment.

He still wasn't really touching her. He was just teasing her, with these breathed kisses, his tongue every now and then tracing her lips and retreating, caressing her tongue and then disappearing. She felt restless, and her own mouth began to move. Hesitantly, she moved her tongue forward until it touched his.

He growled with approval.

She moved her hands up to this chest. It felt rock hard beneath the thin cotton shirt he was wearing. She ran her nails down it, and the kiss deepened. His hands moved to her waist, fingers clenching her hips.

She felt her heart racing, and she was having trouble breathing. Every nerve ending seemed to pulse to the pounding beat of her heart. She felt an intense throb in the pit of her stomach and between her legs.

With a low moan, she barely realized she was moving until she pressed closer to him, winding her arms around his neck, burying her fingers in his hair. It felt cool, silky beneath her fingertips. She tugged his face closer, darting her tongue against his, following his lead, copying his actions as best she could.

They were sitting side by side on the couch, an awkward, high-school necking angle. They weren't close enough. She could feel the tension building in her, thought she might explode with the new emotions that were tearing through her like a freight train. She tore her mouth away, breathing in gulping gasps. "Oh, Josh. Please..." She felt like she'd taken some drug that heightened all of her senses. Her bra, which was ordinarily just an annoying garment worn out of habit, now rubbed against her oversensitized breasts. They felt heavy and almost ached. Between her legs was a strange ache as well—a slightly different ache. She trembled with energy she didn't know how to release.

"It's only kissing, Angela," he murmured, the rumble of his voice against her only intensifying the pleasure.

"*Josh,*" she whispered on a startled moan. He was kissing her throat with a suction that stung with slight pain, multiplying all the rest of what she was feeling. It was sensory overload. She closed her eyes, unable to handle more input, and drowned in the pure sensation of his touch.

She let herself be lowered to a reclining position on the couch. He now propped himself over her with one arm, and she felt the length of his body pressed against her side. She tried to push up against him, but he gently resisted, instead moving to the hollow of her neck and nibbling gently, moving out to stroke with his tongue. She felt a shudder roll through her body, like a power surge. She whispered his name under her breath like a chanted prayer.

He moved to one sensitive breast, and she quickly started to slide her dress up.

"Now, now," he said, and she opened her eyes to see

him laughing down at her, not with amusement but with delight. "Just kissing, remember?"

She was dying with need. The man was insane, some sort of sadist. With surprising strength, she pushed him away. "I remember."

She yanked the whole thing over her head. Lying there in just a bra and panties, she shot him an innocent look.

"We'll just be kissing," she reiterated.

She could feel his eyes caress her body. He hesitated for only a moment before lowering back down to her. She could feel the damp tip of his tongue through the silky material, and her body rocked against him. Her back arched, and he took more of her into his mouth. Her hands moved awkwardly to her back, undoing the clasp to her bra.

"Angela," he breathed. "We shouldn't..."

She ripped the garment out of her way. "I can take it," she rasped, "honest. I know I can."

He stopped, and his eyes gleamed. "Well, if you're so sure of it." He reached for the edge of his own shirt, pulling off the denim shirt with ease.

For a second, she ignored the jolting pulses of desire ringing through her body, and just thought: *My God.* She traced her fingers over the chiseled muscles of his arms, and felt the satin over corded steel of his chest. Slowly, she leaned up and traced the hollow at the base of his neck with her tongue, then moved to feel the texture of him beneath her lips. She edged across his chest, feeling the slight tickle of hair grow thicker as she moved down toward his waist. He took a hurried breath as she got to his pants. She smiled, noting the bulge there. Impishly, amazed at herself, she leaned down and traced it with her mouth, just like she'd once read in a book.

Something happened, as if she'd thrown a switch. He groaned, tugging her up to his mouth. He pushed her deeper into the cushions, and she reveled in it. The feel of his bare chest against hers seemed to intensify the feeling of his lips and tongue meshing with hers. He wasn't so careful this time, and she could feel his weight unintentionally shifting over her legs.

She spread her legs, angling away from his body, drawing him on top of her. He did not seem to notice, only pursued her mouth more diligently, stopping to dip low and take one breast between his lips. She cried out as he moved his weight between her legs. He was still trying not to crush her. Having him press against her sensitive ache was just what she needed, she realized, and her hips bucked upward, feeling the bulge in his pants pushing against her, desiring entrance.

He was breathing like a long-distance runner. "You're no virgin," he said, his eyes wide with disbelief, as he allowed himself one long push against the apex of her thighs.

"I don't feel like a virgin," she admitted, wrapping her legs around his waist and reveling in his low moan. She reached up and dug her fingers into his muscular shoulders, bringing him down against her, loving his weight and his strength and the feel of him crushing her into the couch. "Make love to me, Josh."

She was ready. She was sure she wanted this. She was *going* to do this, now, with this man.

She waited.

"*No.*" He untangled her limbs from his, then retreated to the far end of the couch. "Dammit, Angela. You don't know what you're getting into, and I do. Don't you want your first time to be with someone who means something to you?"

She didn't know whether to kiss him or kill him. Need lanced through her like a bolt of electricity. "*You* mean something to me," she breathed. "What other man would have treated a stranger this…this wonderfully?" She stood up, gathering what was left of her courage. She reached for the thin straps of her silk panties. "Josh, *I trust you.* Please."

With that, she inched the panties to the ground, stepped forward, and waited.

He stared, like a starving man suddenly placed in the main dining room at the Four Seasons—a combination of naked, almost primal hunger and stunned disbelief. He looked up into her eyes.

"I trust you," she repeated, and closed her eyes.

His touch wasn't the fierce taking she was expecting. Instead, she heard him stand up, felt his arms embrace her and then gently cradle her against him. She could feel the heavy beating of his heart against her ear as he stroked her hair, and despite the clawing need she felt, her heart suddenly ached for an entirely different reason.

"Your first time is not going to be on my couch," he said in a rough drawl.

She barely registered him gathering her up, naked against his bare chest, as he carried her down the hall. Didn't notice the neat masculinity of his bedroom as he pulled back the covers and placed her reverently on the cool sheets, as easily as if she weighed nothing. She watched as he undid his pants, pulling them down with his boxers in one fluid motion. His erection emerged, huge with need.

She was taken aback. She hadn't seen one of these things in real life. For pity's sake, she'd rarely seen pictures of one. It was…well, *odd.* She stared at it.

He half chuckled on a deep exhalation, taking a step forward. "Change your mind?"

She shook her head, then reached out with curious fingers, only to stop abruptly. She glanced up at him. "Can I..."

He closed his eyes, as if begging for strength. "Gently, now. You've got me more worked up than I ever would have believed."

Her fingertips reached out, cautiously, and skimmed over the surface of his penis. He groaned, and she pulled her hand away as if he were an open flame.

"No, go ahead, honey," he said, but his eyes didn't open. "You won't hurt me. You might kill me, but you won't hurt me."

She bit her lip, feeling the aching intensify as she traced him. It was amazingly soft...amazingly hard. The skin was like heated velvet. Her fingers circled him for a moment, fascinated. He let out a low, rippling growl. She took him into her hand with a slightly firmer grip.

He rocked toward her, then exhaled slowly. He moved her hand away with a light touch. "Okay, now that's enough. You'll have to explore later." He stretched out on the bed next to her, and her heart rate tripled. She could feel the heated tip of him brush against her thigh, and moaned, her body moving forward to meet him. She felt the tight ache of her body melt in a rush of wetness.

He kissed her deeply, so deeply that she was surprised when his fingers reached the curls between her legs. She took in a startled breath when his fingers brushed against her, tenderly pressing into her.

"Josh," she murmured, pushing harder against his palm. She could still feel the rodlike hardness of his body, now between her thighs, as his fingers moved slowly, deeper into her. It hurt, but his movements were slow, flicking against her, lovingly stroking her, gradually widening her. She felt the wetness again, and closed her eyes as the pressure built.

"Josh." She was all but sobbing now, dying for release.

"Shh," he said, licking at her breasts and inching her temperature up yet another notch. "I want to, too, but I don't want to rush. I might hurt you."

"Hurry. Please hurry!" She moved against him rhythmically, feeling an increasing tension surge through her.

He groaned against her, and she felt a drop of wetness against her thigh. He moved away, and she heard the ripping of foil. "I hope you're ready. I don't think either of us can wait anymore," he said on a vehement whisper.

She felt his weight on top of her again and almost wept with gratitude. She felt him brush against her, his hardness tracing her entrance the way his tongue had traced her lips. She started to move, but he stilled her.

"Slowly," he cautioned, and the feel of his stomach against hers, his hips against her inner thighs, was enough to hold her for a second. "Slowly, then it won't hurt so much."

She could feel the slow movement of him inside her, filling her by inches, retreating, stroking the now insanely sensitive flesh between her thighs. Pain blurred with intense, consuming passion.

"Josh," she whispered, in harsh, panting gasps.

"Angela." With a smooth, gradual motion, he filled her, pushing in until he was buried as far as he could go.

She felt him brush against her clitoris, and she shuddered. She felt...filled was the obvious word, but at the same time it was woefully inadequate to describe what she was feeling. She felt like her body was on fire...like it was brimming to the point of exploding. She was breathing in quick inhalations. Her body started to move of its own accord, moving sinuously against him, feeling the stroke of his erection as if it were a lever that activated waves of pleasure across her whole body.

She was moving faster, mindlessly, and she felt him pushing harder against her. With each joining, she felt closer to him...felt the repeated brush of him as a new shock of sensation ripped through her. She was hurtling toward something. She didn't know *what* she was experiencing, but at this point, it was so overwhelming that she didn't care. She couldn't process. She could only hang on for the ride.

Suddenly, a sensual wave hard as a punch flooded through her body. She felt the muscles between her legs clench as she wrapped around him, trying to draw him even deeper into her. *"Josh!"* she screamed, clawing at his back, flooded by the pleasure of it.

He drove into her, and the wave redoubled, shaking her to the core. *"Angela,"* he responded, then drove into her again, sending echoing pulses with each pounding movement against her body.

She felt like she'd had the wind knocked out of her. Her body was one quivering nerve. He collapsed on top of her, and she cradled him, stroking his back, comforting him even as she felt overwhelmed with...awe. There wasn't any other word for it.

After a few moments, he leaned up heavily on one elbow. "Angela?" His voice was tentative, and he moved a wayward lock of hair away from her sweat-soaked forehead. "Are you all right?"

All right? She wasn't sure. No, all right was too tepid a phrase for what she was feeling at that moment.

"I'm..." She paused. Then she brought her arms up around his neck again, pulling him down to her. She pressed her lips against his, trying to say with the most tender kiss possible what she didn't have words for.

"Thank you," she breathed.

Now I won't have to die a virgin.

2

JOSH SNUGGLED deeper into the blankets. Every breath he took was scented with her…a mix of some floral fragrance and baby powder. *Eau de Girl,* he thought with a smile.

She'd been incredible last night. He hadn't had a bout of pleasure that powerful in he couldn't *remember* how long. He clutched her a little tighter, marveling at her pliancy, the softness of her body…

Wait a second.

He did more than clutch. He *squeezed,* hard. Then he sat bolt upright, and turned on the light. After a second's blindness, he looked down to see he'd been holding two pillows in a comfortable embrace.

"What the…?"

Here he was, fantasizing, while the woman he was dreaming about wasn't even there in his bed!

Shaking his head and chuckling at himself, he got up, intent on looking for her and bringing her back to bed. No way was he letting her go that easy. He didn't bother with any clothes. He didn't have any close neighbors to peer into his large floor-to-ceiling windows, so it was a common enough practice for him. Besides, he was too intent on finding Angela to waste time on modesty. He wondered if she had put on one of his shirts to go around his house, or if she'd been brave enough to walk au naturel as well. Just the thought started to make him hard.

He was definitely awake now.

He wandered over to his bathroom, but the door was open and the light was out. Maybe she was fixing him breakfast, he thought, making his way down the hall and past the living room to the kitchen. No, the kitchen light was out, too.

He frowned. He doubted she went outside...it was March, and from what he could see, it was a cold and gloomy day. Why leave a perfectly warm bed to go out naked in...

He walked into the living room, looking intently, and his thoughts immediately derailed.

Her clothes were gone.

So was the small purse with her car keys.

He went to the front door, throwing it open. Adam was there, a box full of doughnuts in one hand, the other hand obviously poised to knock.

"Well, good morning, stud," Adam said, laughing. "Thought I'd bring you and your, er, guest some breakfast."

Josh ignored him, walking past him far enough to glance out in the driveway.

Her car was gone.

"Dammit!" He stalked back into his house. Adam followed him in. Josh went directly to his bedroom, where he pulled on a pair of sweats and a T-shirt. Still cursing under his breath, he then went to the kitchen, where Adam had already settled himself comfortably at the glass-topped kitchen table. "You have lousy timing," he said to his friend, reaching for the doughnut box.

"I know. I should be sorry," Adam said, grabbing a

glazed doughnut. "But after last night's mysterious adventure that interrupted *my* romantic interlude, I figured, what the hell. I warned you. After the buildup you gave me last night, you're lucky I waited until nine. So, where is she?"

Grabbing a glazed doughnut and biting off a mouthful viciously, Josh snapped on his coffee machine. With an easy motion, he pushed himself up to sit on the countertop next to it. "She left."

"Details," Adam prompted, sprawling back in the kitchen chair, a rakish grin on his face. "I want details."

"I don't have any details," Josh snarled. "I don't know when she left, myself."

Adam sent him a look of impatience. "I meant about last night."

"Suffice it to say that I broke my word to myself, and slept with her anyway." Josh was silent, then took another bite of doughnut. "And now she's gone."

Adam didn't razz him for a change. He just studied Josh. "She was really something, huh?"

Josh scowled at him, not trusting his friend's solemnity. He waited for the punch line. "What makes you say that?"

"Because I haven't seen that look on your face in...well, ever."

"What look?"

Adam smirked. "It's sort of a cross between seeing a really beautiful naked woman and stubbing your toe."

Reluctantly, Josh laughed. "Why did she leave is what I want to know." He poured himself a cup of coffee, then put the pot back to brew the remainder. He took a fortifying swallow, almost burning his tongue. "Last night was incredible. Then next thing I know, she leaves without even a goodbye."

"Did she write you a note or anything?" Adam asked. "Maybe she had to do something early this morning."

Josh felt a burst of relief. Of course. She struck him as a morning person, anyway...she probably had something she had to do, first thing. He quickly went to his bedroom. He looked over the nightstands, at his dresser. Nothing there. Well, maybe she'd left it someplace else. He quickly went over to the living room. Maybe she hadn't wanted to wake him, and wrote it there.

No luck.

After searching practically his entire house, he went back to the kitchen. "No note, no phone number, no nothing," he grumbled, running his hand distractedly through his hair and sitting down opposite Adam at the kitchen table. "What's up with *that?*"

"Did she leave a twenty next to the bed?"

Josh glared at him. "Pretty funny. Get out."

"Whoa, easy. Relax," Adam said, putting his hands up in defense. "I brought Krispy Kremes. Had to go two towns away to get the dumb things. That's got to be some kind of defense."

"I don't want goddamn Krispy Kremes. I want Angela back here. Now."

"Angela, huh?" Adam smiled, ignoring Josh's tirade. "So call her. Maybe she's listed."

Josh took a deep, beleaguered breath. "I don't know her last name," he said.

Adam laughed. "You don't know her last name?"

Josh glared at him. "Look, I'm not proud of this, okay? I wound up having sex with an incredible virgin, and now I have no way of seeing her again."

"There's always a way," Adam said, smiling but wisely refraining from taunting his friend further. In his current mood, it was clear that Josh didn't feel like joking around. "Let's think this through logically. How did this whole thing come up?"

Josh told his friend the entire story, from when he met Angela in the bar to just before the intimate details of what had happened last night. Not that he was ever a proponent of locker room talk—he figured as long as women knew you were good in bed, what was the point in bragging about it to men? But he wanted to guard his experience with Angela. It was too special to be discussed with even his closest friend. "She was just so determined," he finally said. "She was going to have sex last night, with me. Period. She was a woman on a mission. It was fairly crazy…and, like I said, pretty amazing."

Adam was frowning, rubbing his chin thoughtfully. "So this girl knew you in high school, right?"

"Yeah," Josh agreed, "but I don't remember any Angelas in high school. It's not like we were friends or anything."

"Well, she's twenty-nine, and you're thirty-three," Adam reasoned. "She wouldn't have been in your grade, anyway."

"You're right," Josh said, thinking about the math. "In fact, we only would have been in high school together for a year…I would've been a senior when she was a freshman."

"Exactly. So find out who the freshmen were when you were a senior. Voilà."

"And how, exactly, am I supposed to do that?"

"What, do I have to do everything for you?" Adam chuckled. He got up and grabbed a mug out of the cupboard, pouring it full of coffee. "You've got a yearbook, don't you? Look through it. See who the Angelas are."

He sipped some, made a face, then rummaged for sugar and milk.

Josh felt embarrassed. "Why didn't I think of that myself?"

"Because you're in no condition to think right now. At least, not above the waist." Adam shot him one of his trademark smirks. "So get your yearbook, and let me see who this mystery woman is. If she's as incredible as you say she is, maybe she's got a sister or two."

"I don't have it," Josh said, thinking about it. "It's at my parents' place, in San Diego."

"So call them."

"They're in Europe. Three-week vacation."

"That won't do," Adam said. "You wait three weeks to figure out who this woman is, and *I'll* kill you because I know you're going to be driving me up the wall. Where else, where else..." He thought for a minute, then snapped his fingers. "Try the library. It's closed today, but it'll be open first thing Monday."

"That's brilliant." Josh grinned at him. "Thanks. I owe you one."

"One question. What if Angela *doesn't* want you to contact her?" Adam asked. "Granted, your charm is legendary, but last I heard, women have gotten into the one-night stand scene, too."

The question took Josh aback. "It's not like that," he said decisively.

"How do you *know?*" Adam persisted.

"Because you know me. When I want something, I get it." Josh smiled, already thinking about the scene ahead. "Believe me—this is not going to be a one-night stand."

Adam looked at him, then clinked coffee mugs with

him. "Happy hunting, buddy. Poor girl doesn't stand a chance."

ANGELA SAT IN A semidarkened office, staring at the torturous device that was the mammogram machine. She'd already endured the gooey mess of the ultrasound. Then she'd been pressed like batter in a waffle iron—except this had been a freezing cold waffle iron, she thought, crossing her arms protectively over her chest. Now she was sitting in the thin flannel robe type thingy they'd provided her with, waiting for the radiologist to give her the news. She tried to breathe deeply, but found herself forgetting to inhale altogether, then breathing in quick, shallow, nervous gasps.

It's probably not cancer.

She tried telling herself, over and over. It wasn't quite working.

It probably would have been easier if she could have talked with somebody, let them know. She'd left several e-mails and a phone message for Bethany, her best friend in the world. She hadn't heard back yet. Knowing Bethany, she was on a shoot somewhere. Being a fashion photographer managed to indulge Bethany's love of travel, but made it next to impossible to ever get a hold of her in any sort of emergency situation.

Frankly, there wasn't anybody else Angela felt comfortable in telling. The girls at work—she shook her head just thinking of it. No, she couldn't tell them. What would she say? *Hi, I know we've had the occasional lunch and we've known each other for two years but I'm scared to death that I'm dying, would you listen to my worries and let me cry for a second?*

Not likely. Her mother had raised her better than that. *Her mother.* She hadn't called her, either, Angela thought, shifting uncomfortably. Telling her would only make them both panic. Her grandmother had gone in for a mammogram six years ago. The doctors didn't understand how it could have gone to stage three so fast, was the comment Angela remembered hearing most often. They were still commenting on that when they buried her, not long after.

No way was she telling her mother. Not until she knew for sure.

A nurse came in, and Angela's heart jumped into her throat. "Yes?"

"Oh." The woman seemed surprised. "Sorry. Didn't realize you were still in here. I'm sure the doctor will be back in a minute." With that, she hastily left, shutting the door behind her.

Angela sunk disconsolately back in her chair. It was the waiting that was doing this to her. She'd been waiting since Friday to find out something definite.

Friday had started in a cold, antiseptic smelling room like this, too.

She remembered her ob-gyn appointment vividly, like one of those nightmares that haunt you the whole next day. She had been in a paper robe and no underwear, lying back, trying to think of what she needed to buy at the supermarket instead of focusing on what was happening as the doctor performed the pelvic exam. After the initial unpleasantness, the doctor stood up. "You're doing self breast exams, right?"

Angela thought for a second. "Well, off and on."

The doctor frowned. "You need to do them every month," she said, moving up toward Angela's chest. "You know how, right?"

"I'm pretty sure I do."

"Not good enough." The doctor lifted the paper gown. "You need to…"

The doctor then proceeded to demonstrate on Angela's breast. Angela felt herself withdraw, back to her grocery list. *Red peppers, shallots, I think that there's salmon on sale…*

"You need to work inward, gradually, in concentric circles."

"Okay." *Maybe I'll get some more rice, I think I'm low…*

"And then you…" The doctor paused. Angela remembered that pause, remembered not paying attention to it. "Angela, how long has this lump been here?"

Some brown sugar for cookies… "What?"

"I said, how long has this lump been here? This one, in your right breast."

Angela felt her body go clammy and cold with shock. "I don't know," she said distantly, as if it weren't really her voice saying it. "I honestly don't know."

She had taken the rest of the day off, a rarity for her. The soonest mammogram she could get was Monday, first thing. She had taken the appointment. And then she had waited.

It had given her time to think.

I haven't been to Italy. Haven't been to Europe, period. She flipped through the travel magazines she had strewn around her house. She had always meant to. She had been so busy working after she'd graduated, and then, when she'd finally snapped from all the pressure, she had moved from New York City back to the calm small-town atmosphere of Manzanita. She was just regrouping, she'd told herself. She'd get to all those adventures she'd been putting off. Now, she wasn't sure what she was going to hear on Monday. Didn't know how bad it was. How long did she have, really?

I haven't made a stained glass window. Never learned flamenco dancing. Haven't been to a club in years. Never learned Mandarin cooking, never painted a self-portrait, haven't seen Hawaii…

Good God. What had she been doing with her life?

I haven't even had sex!

For some reason, that struck her the hardest. She'd never had any interest in having a lasting relationship with a man—she'd seen what it had done to her mother. But she had still thought of experiencing the act of physical love at some point, by whatever fantasy she had conjured up. She figured the situation would arrange itself at some point…when the stars aligned, or when some gorgeous Greek-god-type got a serendipitous flat tire outside her house. However it happened, it would happen without her worrying about it.

Now what was she going to do? Go to the grave, a lonely, closed-off virgin who had never left North America?

She'd paced around her house. She didn't have time to go to Europe. She wasn't going to make a stained glass window in a weekend, she wasn't going to learn flamenco dancing overnight. But she was going to do something to redeem herself, and she was going to do it that weekend. With grim determination, she'd thrown on her sexiest dress, her most ridiculous heels, and had gone to the Cable Car, a place her co-workers had dubbed "the only pickup joint in Manzanita." And she had tracked down Josh Montgomery, a man she knew only by what little she'd remembered from high school, what she'd heard, or the brief glimpses of him she'd caught in town.

The Josh Incident, as she was now calling it in her head, seemed like a dream, something too amazing to be true. Sitting alone in this cold, dim doctor's office, she knew she was right. Comparatively, the Incident wasn't real at all.

"Miss Snowe?"

Her head swung toward the door. "Yes?"

"I'm Dr. Jones." He was tall, lanky, with pale blond hair and dull blue eyes. He looked like he didn't smile a lot, and he wasn't smiling today. "Just had your mammogram done, right?"

"Yes," she said, clutching her arms around herself. "Am I…that is, is it…"

He glanced down at his folder. "Hmm. Nope. It's not cancer."

"It's not cancer," she repeated. She let out a breath she didn't realize she was holding.

"No. It's just calcified tissue. Ultrasound gave us a pretty good idea, but the mammogram—it's pretty conclusive. You should still do self exams regularly, especially with your family history." He frowned as he said that. "But otherwise, you're good to go."

She sat there, numb with relief. "Thank God."

"You can get dressed." He had already mentally moved on to the next patient, and left without another word, closing the door behind him.

It's not cancer. I'm not dying.

She got up and put on her clothes, her shaking hands making it hard to button her shirt. Finally fully dressed, she put her glasses on, grabbed her purse and walked out. It was March, but the day was clear and the sun shone magnificently, while the cool air made everything smell clean and fresh and new.

I'm not dying. She started her car, and carefully pulled

out of the driveway. She would go in to work, of course. The car automatically took the streets that headed to the Manzanita Public Library. She noticed how beautiful the trees were along the street, the way the new houses and stores changed everything so dramatically. She noticed small boutiques, shops she'd never even realized existed, showing pretty wares in their glistening windows. The Dress Barn had been replaced by The Gap. Joe's Burgers, which had sat on the same lot for as long as she could remember, was now flanked by a Blockbuster Video and a trendy-looking hair salon.

She hadn't noticed, she thought, as she nudged her glasses higher up on her face. Why hadn't she paid attention before?

I'm not dying.

She had plenty of time.

Then again, she thought, as she paused at a stoplight, she'd been under that same impression before all this started. She had a second chance here. Damn if she was going to waste it.

I'll sign up for classes. She noticed that she was stepping on the accelerator, and moving much faster than the speed limit for the residential roads she was now traveling on. Pretty houses were rushing past her window. She slowed the car down, but her mind continued to speed ahead. *I'm going to take a trip somewhere. I'll see if I can go out with the girls on Friday night, to that club they always go to. Maybe even go with them to coffee more often, make regular lunch dates.* She pulled into the parking lot, seeing the same large brick building she'd been driving to for the past two years. She smiled with determination. *I'm not going to make the same mistakes.*

She'd been given a reprieve, and more important, she'd been given a chance.

She had Josh to thank in large part for this, she thought as she shut off her car, all but floating down the paved walkway toward the double glass doors. She had been honest when she told him that she was more afraid of sex than anything else—getting that close to anyone, after all of these years, seemed so much more impossible than learning another language or taking a worldwide cruise. If he had been horrible to her, she might have given in to her apprehension and crawled back into her cocoon of daydreams and excuses.

After her unprecedented but successful move in prop-ositioning him, she could probably bungee jump naked down the Grand Canyon with relative ease. From here on, she was going to do everything she'd always dreamed of. He was a starting point. She had a long way to go from here.

Too bad she'd probably never bump into him again to tell him, she considered with a grin. He'd probably never realize how he had, by helping her with her situ-ation, changed her life forever. She wondered if he'd even think of her again.

Well, even if you don't...thank you, Josh Montgom-ery, for being my sure thing.

With a little grin, she stepped into the library.

HE OUGHT TO BE in a meeting going over last quarter's sales figures and tearing apart the capital equipment budget, Josh thought, not going on a research mission to hunt down a one-night stand. *That is, an attempted one-night stand.* He smiled. He'd change that status soon enough.

He walked through the glass doors of the Manzanita

library. In the five years since he'd been back, he didn't think he'd been in the library, ever. He'd barely gone to his old library as a high-school student. He guessed most libraries were the same. There were cheerful posters and childish drawings, each signed in a youngster's scrawled hand. There was the familiar paste-and-dust smell of books, and his shoes made a conspicuous shuffling on the floor. It had the sort of silence you could feel.

He was in luck. The old man behind the reference desk pointed him to a dark alcove, in the back of the library. He guessed it was a sort of local history archive. There were bound magazines, and black-and-white photos on the walls of the relevant events of the town—the local Almond Festival, or that fire that swept through town hall back when he was in grade school. He went past all the early yearbooks, straight to his year: 1985. The cover was a deep navy blue, scuffed from handling. He flipped it open.

Had he ever been this young? He grimaced as he saw his own face in several candid photos. And who let him dress like that?

He thumbed to the black-and-white photos of the freshmen. The self-consciously grinning faces all resembled mug shots. After a few pages, the faces blurred together. He glanced down at the names instead...Amy, Abigail, Alexandra, Angela, Adriana, Andrea...

Wait a second. He flipped back a page.

Angela Snowe.

He frowned, then kept flipping. He got all the way to the sophomores, then went through the section a second time.

That can't be her.

He scrutinized it. The girl in the photo had a dreamy expression—or at least, she looked rather dazed behind her glasses. Her hair was frizzy, standing up in a tangled nimbus around her head. He thought he could see the slight glint of braces in the small photo.

It took a few minutes, but the more he stared, the more he could reconcile the images. While her face was rounded with a little baby fat, he could see hints of the high cheekbones and strong, determined chin. He could understand how he might not remember her from high school, surrounded as he was with cheerleaders and other hangers-on. Hell, he'd been an 18-year-old football star. Back then, any girl with a D-cup was downright riveting. A freshman with glasses and frizzy hair would not have caught his eye.

He was a lot more discriminating now.

He turned, ready to ask the librarian where the phone book was, when he stopped dead in his tracks.

Angela?

It was her. She looked different than she had that night at the Cable Car, but he recognized her just the same. She was wearing a straight skirt that was worn discreetly below the knee, and a crisp white shirt. She was wearing her glasses this time, and her hair was in the same severe ponytail it had been…at least, before she'd removed the holder that trapped it, and let that glorious mahogany mass tumble across his pillows. Even her low pumps made her legs look delicious, and he knew exactly what that body was like beneath the demure outer wrapping.

He smirked in self-deprecation as his own body went hard. *Well, damn. You really can find whatever you're looking for at the library.*

So he'd found her. What was he going to do now?

Well, wait for the, er, swelling to subside, he rationalized. He put the yearbook down and wandered back into the darker corners of the stacks, waiting.

He didn't even have to hunt for her. His quarry came to him. Bearing a pad of yellow legal paper and a slightly bemused expression, she didn't even notice him there as she studied the numbers off the spine of some ancient-looking book.

He cleared his throat. "Miss, perhaps you could help me find something." His voice was barely above a whisper, and he deliberately made it low and almost scratchy.

She didn't even look up from her notepad, still scribbling down a number. "Just one second, sir, and I'll be more than happy to help you find what you need."

He grinned. *I certainly hope so.* He walked up behind her, his breath tickling the nape of her neck. "I'm looking for a book that might tell me how to track down a missing person. I met someone on Friday night, and she vanished on Saturday. I don't even know her last name. Do you think you could help me out?"

Before Josh had finished saying "missing," she'd spun around, her eyes wide behind her glasses. He smiled.

"It's you," she said, looking dumbfounded.

"In the flesh," he said, smiling and taking a step forward, getting closer to her. He noticed that she clutched the notepad to her chest like a shield. "Did you miss me?"

"I...that is..." She cleared her throat. Her eyes looked a little wild. "Why are you here?"

He laughed. "I'm here because I wanted to see you again. I would have told you that on Saturday, but, well..." He gestured, helplessly.

"You wanted to see me again," she said, as if repeating a foreign phrase.

"Exactly."

"Why?"

He blinked. "Well, ah…" He thought about it, then shrugged. "Why wouldn't I?"

He had her there, it seemed. She chewed thoughtfully at her lower lip. "You're not a relationship person," she said finally, with a slight smile, like someone finally remembering the answer on *Jeopardy*.

Not the "sure thing" reputation again. He grimaced. How long was he going to be paying for that one? "Maybe not," he admitted, "but that doesn't mean I don't want to see you again."

"Hmm. Well." She backed up against the bookshelves behind her, hitting them with a low thump. "I thought we'd agreed that it was a one-time occurrence."

"I wasn't expecting it to be as incredible as it was when I agreed," he replied.

Suddenly, her eyes looked dreamy. "I didn't, either," she admitted.

He saw his advantage, and immediately took it. He leaned close to her ear. "Just think what it could be like next time."

She put her hand flat on his chest, and gently pushed him a step back. "You're making it hard to think," she accused him breathlessly. "I understand what you're saying. I just don't think it'd be a good idea."

"Sounds like a great idea to me," he said. "You said you wanted more experiences. Why not with me?"

"I want lots of different kinds of experiences. I don't need to necessarily focus on, er, that kind." She blushed, something he found continually charming. When was the last time he'd seen a woman blush like that? "But I appreciate it," she added, polite to a fault.

"Angela," he said, ready to pull out the big guns. "I've gone through a lot of trouble to find you. I've been thinking about you constantly. I'd really like to see you again, and all modesty aside, I think you really enjoyed seeing me, too." He smiled, the most deliberately charming smile he could muster. It wasn't hard—just being close to her made him feel like smiling. "Can you give me one reason why—after you got up all the courage to ask me to help you, after the spectacular night that we had—can you give me *one reason* why you think we shouldn't see each other again?"

"Well," she said, then blurted out, "I'm not dying anymore, that's why."

"You're not *what?*" He blinked. He couldn't have heard that right.

She cleared her throat. "It's a long story."

He *had* heard her correctly. "I've got time," he ground out.

She looked at him, her eyes clear and direct. "I thought I might have cancer when I came to you. That's why I picked you."

He grimaced, completely disconcerted. "Funny. I thought you picked me because I was a sure thing."

"Well, there was that, too," she said, then frowned at him. "And I've already apologized for that. But the bottom line is, I'd always meant to have sex at some point. The scare brought the fact that I didn't have as much time as I'd thought sharply into focus. So I looked for you. I'm not sorry I did." Now she smiled. "In fact, I can't thank you enough."

"Thank me?"

"Well, yes. I want to experience life *now,* in the present, and enjoy everything I've only talked about. You helped make that possible," she said, her brown-eyed gaze soft and gentle. "I've signed up for all these classes today, I'm looking into traveling. For pity's sake, I'm even going to Club X on Friday night with the girls."

She smiled again, her tone both embarrassed and delighted. A man could grow to crave that smile. "If you knew what I was like before, you'd understand what a big step all this is. And I really feel like I have you to thank for it."

He was speechless. He'd had a lot of women appreciate their time together, but he'd never had it viewed as a life-altering experience before.

"Thanks, again." She kissed him on the cheek, like a blessing. "Who knows? Maybe I'll see you around."

"Wait a second," he said. "I still don't see why we can't see each other again."

"Because that would constitute a relationship." She said matter-of-factly, shaking her head. "That won't work."

"Maybe I don't have as many problems with relationships as you think," he said. Then he blinked. *Did I say that?*

"Maybe you don't," she said. He caught the slight Mona Lisa smile she gave him, both sad and mysterious, before she turned away from him. "But either way, I'm afraid that I do."

3

"ARE YOU HAVING a good time?"

Angela smiled at Ginny, who had yelled the question to her over the booming bass of the loudspeakers. "Just great," Angela said. Ginny smiled back encouragingly. Tanya and May, two of her other co-workers, were dancing with different men on the crowded dance floor. Ginny wandered back to them, motioning Angela to join her. Angela pointed to the bar, pantomiming getting a drink. All three women nodded back at her.

Actually, she wasn't having a great time, or even a good time. The music was literally loud enough to reverberate through her chest, making her ribs rattle like a xylophone. She was wearing a pair of jeans and a tank top, and felt like she might as well have been wearing a suit of armor next to the skimpy little nothings that the younger women were wearing.

Angela had approached them Monday, as soon as she walked into the library. After some small talk, she said to Ginny, "I was wondering…don't you guys usually go out dancing on Friday nights? To some club?"

Ginny looked at her, grinning. "Every Friday, rain or shine. All of the single girls, anyway, and some of the marrieds when they can get away." She winked at May, who nodded emphatically. "It's a lot of fun. Want to come?"

"Yes," Angela said, then looked at their faces. "If it's okay, I mean."

"Of course!" Ginny grinned at her encouragingly.

"We'd have asked you before," Tanya explained, pouring Angela a cup of coffee, "but you always seemed so...well, you never really seemed interested when we mentioned it."

"I'm planning on going out a lot more from now on," Angela said, a point she reiterated when she went out to lunch with them. She promised she'd go out with them more often. If the club was half as fun as their lunch outings, Angela felt she would have definite plans almost every Friday night.

Of course, now that she was actually at the club, she realized it wasn't her scene. For one thing, she liked dancing, but she was used to doing it while dusting her living room—not moving in a thick crowd of people who stepped on her toes or spilled drinks on her. Angela dodged to one side as a long-haired woman narrowly missed hitting her with her long ponytail. The woman didn't even turn or apologize.

So maybe dance clubs aren't my thing. Still, she was out, she was doing something different. It was definitely a step in the right direction.

A young guy stepped in front of Angela, preventing her from reaching the bar. "Hey, gorgeous," he yelled, his voice faint over the music. "Want to dance?"

"I'm here with my friends," she yelled back, pointing to them.

"They look like they're doing fine," he said, and proceeded to dance in front of her. After a second, she gave up, swaying a little, trying to figure out what rhythm he was dancing to. She saw her co-workers looking at her encouragingly. *When in Rome,* Angela thought, suppressing a little sigh. The man was good-looking, she guessed, in a blond, surfer sort of way. Maybe she wasn't giving him a chance.

She danced, but after a second or two he started to move in on her, getting uncomfortably close. He was trying to grind on her, she realized, taking a hasty step back and promptly getting smacked by the ponytail. She glared at the woman, who was still dancing blithely away. Surfer-boy kept moving in. Angela raised her hand, putting it on his chest and moving him back with a none-too-gentle shove.

He grinned. "Just dancing," he said.

She didn't like it, or him. "I think I'm tired," she said, glaring at him and still trying to keep a watchful eye on the flailing ponytail. "I'm going to sit the rest of this one out."

"Can I buy you a drink?" He fell into step with her, and she groaned.

"No."

"Why not?"

"Because…I'm…" She racked her brain for some kind of polite answer, and quickly gave up. "You're not my type."

He frowned, but obviously wasn't dissuaded. "What is your type?"

"Tall, dark and handsome," she said glibly. "Sorry." She quickly dodged through an opening in the crowd and left him there. When she finally made it to the bar, she looked back. He seemed to have focused in on the ponytail girl, like a heat-seeking missile. *More power to you,* she thought. She ordered another bottled water, and leaned against the bar, dabbing at her forehead with a napkin.

Maybe it was the atmosphere, but she couldn't help

but notice the vast variety of men that swarmed through the place. She had observed men previous to this, but it was somehow different tonight. She was more alert, for one thing, and she picked up on different details. She noticed everything from different heights to eye colors to varying scents of cologne. She seemed to be testing for something—weighing each man on some indefinable scale. Without fail, each man seemed to come up wanting. Had she always done this, and just started to recognize it tonight? Or was it something she had just started doing?

Tall, dark and handsome. Maybe she was being more truthful than she realized. The blond men were definitely leaving her cold, obviously. It was as if her body were humming with a low, repeating message: *Not a match…not a match…not a match…*

She looked around the room. At the end of the bar was a man who was easily six foot two, with jet-black hair and broad shoulders. Her heart rate picked up a little, and she walked over to him slowly, like a cat approaching a mouse. She took a deep breath.

He turned, then noticed her and smiled.

Not a match.

She let the breath out with disappointment.

His eyes lit up as he gave her a once-over. She fought the urge to squirm. "Can I buy you a drink?"

"Er, no, thanks." She made a quick wave of her hand. "I thought you were somebody else." She hastily retreated, moving back to her end of the bar. What in the world had she been thinking?

Angela frowned at herself. Tall, black hair, broad shoulders. Everything but the blue eyes.

You know exactly who you were thinking of.

She sighed, moving back out to the dance floor with her friends. She moved into step with May. "Are you having a good time?" May asked, echoing Ginny's question.

"Great," Angela said. "Just great."

"HEY, JOSH." The bartender, a hulking giant whose idea of a smile usually struck fear in grown men, sent him an appraising look. "Business must be doing good. Haven't seen you in months."

Josh shook the bartender's beefy hand. "I know, Danny. Been a long time."

"What can I get you to drink?"

"I'll just have a soda."

Danny's eyes narrowed curiously, but he poured Josh a Coke. "Lot of honeys out," Danny said, gesturing to the crowded floor. "If you're looking for some companionship, you picked the right night."

Josh took a sip of his soda and immediately spotted who he was looking for. She was dancing with a group of people, wearing a snug pair of black jeans and a black tank top, her hair in her customary ponytail, no glasses. He smiled.

There was only one "honey" he had eyes for tonight.

"Thanks, Danny." Josh took his soda, and retreated to a shadowed corner, to figure out his next move.

Ordinarily, he would be out there, having a good time, blowing off steam—possibly with a date, or maybe just for fun. Not tonight. He wasn't there to dance, to party, to close the place down. He was there to convince. Specifically, to convince Angela that she hadn't quite made the right decision.

What you're doing is stalking the poor girl.

Josh shook aside the thought. He'd been grilling himself since he walked out of the library, dazed and amused by the fact that she'd turned him down and walked away from him for the second time in three days. The amusement had worn thin in a short period of time. The desire he felt for her had not diminished in the slightest.

It wasn't that he was trying to force her to do anything she didn't want to do, he reasoned. Of all the men he knew, he was one of the biggest supporters of the "no means no" concept when it came to women. If Angela had told him that she didn't want to ever see him again, that she had no interest in him, then he would have shrugged it off and moved on with his life.

But she hadn't said that. She had given him one of the most gracious kiss-offs he'd ever received in his entire dating career. She hadn't been playing games, trying to make herself a challenge in order to pique his interest. She'd been honest and disarming, and…and wonderful, he realized. Consequently, she had piqued his interest considerably. Furthermore, she hadn't said that she didn't want him. In fact, it seemed that on some level at least, she wanted him as much as he wanted her. It was *relationships,* she'd explained in that cute and earnest tone. She just didn't want to get involved.

What she didn't seem to realize was that her very disinterest in trapping the male of the species made her *perfect* for him.

He saw a man scoot up behind Angela, a predatory gleam in his eyes as he moved to press his body against hers. Josh felt his blood pulse as his muscles tensed in anger. He put his drink down with a muted clank on the nearest table.

Before he could walk over to where they were, Angela had already spun, and given the man a stern frown and a little half shove, like someone reprimanding an overly frisky puppy. The man was not amused. Josh, however, couldn't stop grinning.

Damn if he didn't enjoy that woman. And damn if he wasn't going to show her how much she could be enjoying him, too, if she'd just recognize that she wasn't in danger of getting into a relationship with him.

Angela was looking tired and uncomfortable. He guessed she didn't go clubbing that often. She leaned over to her friends, speaking slowly, her eyes apologetic. The other women were nodding with understanding, pointing slightly to the door. Angela was shaking her head, smiling, then distributed those women-type good-bye hugs.

She's leaving.

He saw his opportunity, and walked with purpose toward the door.

"I'm going home," Angela told Ginny.

Ginny looked at her. "Are you okay?"

"Sure. Just a little tired. It's been a while since I've been out." She smiled gamely, but her mind felt numb. She wanted out of this whole atmosphere of sexual availability, scoping out and being scoped. "I'll see you guys on Monday."

"Okay, Angela," Tanya said, giving her a little half hug. "Are you going to be all right, going out to your car on your own?"

"I'm parked close," Angela assured them, then hugged Ginny and May, and walked away.

She needed to get back to the comfort of her small apartment. She didn't realize until she was out in this crowd of hungry single people, with the music beating through her body like some tribal aphrodisiac, that she had woken up to the sexual world. Worse, she realized that her body now refused to be relegated back to its hibernation.

The biggest problem was, it was not a general sexual hunger that coursed through her. Apparently her body craved one person only. She glanced at every black-haired man she walked past, and felt increasingly impatient with herself.

You're developing an unhealthy obsession with Josh Montgomery.

She had understood that there would be fallout from Friday night, especially once she no longer had the looming specter of cancer keeping her mind occupied. She thought she'd been rather successful at keeping thoughts of him at bay, especially after he had surprised her by showing up at the library. She'd been busy with the new classes she'd signed up for, she'd been hanging out with her co-workers. But the nights...she'd woken up from feverish dreams, feeling frustrated to the point of madness.

At least there was one good thing that came from all of this. She knew that if she continued seeing Josh, that she would definitely have done something foolish like getting involved with him—or getting *attached* to him. She'd just gotten to the point where she had the courage and the momentum to expand her horizons. How far was she going to go if she wound up spending her time mooning over a gorgeous love-god in a denim shirt and khakis? Better to concentrate on herself—on her own personal growth.

Of course, that's not going to keep you from waking up with a jolt, hyperventilating and sweating.

No, she told herself sternly. She didn't need the complication. She'd made the right decision.

Angela had not gone more than ten feet when she felt

a hand on her arm. She sighed. "I'm going home," she said firmly, then turned and gasped.

Josh smiled at her. "But it's so early," he said close to her ear. The brush of breath against her earlobe and neck made her shiver, and she put a hand on his arm to steady herself. He took her hand. "I'd hoped I could talk to you. Stay a little while longer?"

She tried to think logically, but it was hard to override the continuous loop of her body, all but screaming *Match!... Match!... Match!*

"I'm sort of tired," she stammered, but didn't take her hand away.

"I can see that. Maybe it's the heat," he suggested, tugging her toward a dance floor that was closed off, the lack of strobe lights and empty bar showing that it was not in use. He steered her toward a darkened corner. "Maybe you just need to sit down for a second."

She ought to pull her hand away. She really ought to leave, go home, get out of the way of temptation.

I wouldn't want to be rude. She knew it was a lie before she even finished the thought. *Besides, I really ought to find out what he wants to say.*

JOSH FIGURED HE'D be a lot more capable of persuading this woman in a logical and compelling fashion if she'd just stop turning him on like a floodlight every time he talked to her. He wanted her in his bed, *now*.

"I just want to talk with you, if you're amenable," he began carefully. He continued to lead her over to where some couches had been pushed pell-mell. He was in luck—no one else was hiding out in the deserted area. "To start, I wanted to apologize for our conversation on Monday."

Her eyes widened…he clearly had her attention. Now he just had to see how long he could keep it.

"You've got no reason to apologize," she said, with obvious surprise. "I've already told you…I can't thank you enough."

"You shouldn't thank me, Angela. I should be thanking you." They sat down on one of the couches. He noticed she sat as far away from him as possible, and stiffened slightly when he moved a little closer. "Friday night was incredible."

She smiled, her doe eyes large and thoughtful. "I know." She seemed to sit up straighter. "I appreciated your help, believe me."

He laughed. She made it sound as if he'd helped her do her taxes. "So I guess you had a good time?" He lowered his voice, leaning even closer. "I didn't hurt you too much?"

"Oh, no," she assured him, also lowering her voice and moving closer toward him, as he'd planned.

"Since I didn't have time to ask you the next day," he said, "I worried."

Her gaze warmed, and she put a consoling hand on his arm. "You didn't hurt me at all," she repeated. "At least, not really. It hurt a little, at first, but then…" He saw her eyes dilate, and her pulse beat a little harder in her throat. She stared at him for a second. It was all he could do not to yank her in his arms and kiss her senseless right there. "Then it didn't," she murmured.

"I should have asked you that on Monday, but I was too wrapped up in the fact that you left without a word. And more than that, I really wanted to see you again. I just approached it all wrong." He studied her. "Or was I all wrong, period? Would you really rather not make love to me again?"

She nibbled on her pouty lower lip, a gesture that almost had him groaning. "It's...complicated."

He grinned. "It almost always is."

She glanced around, probably wondering if her friends were watching. Then she leaned as close to him as she could. He could smell her perfume. He'd been smelling it on the pillow she'd used since she left. He blamed the amazingly vivid dreams he'd been having on that fact and refused to do anything about it. "I...it's just the fact that I haven't done—*that*—before," she said slowly. He wondered if she was trying to convince him, or herself. "So it's natural that it will take time to get used to all this."

"'All this' being what?"

She swallowed hard. "Wanting you," she said. His body tensed at the words.

"You could maybe get used to it gradually..." he suggested, but she interrupted him.

"The thing is, I know it's just my body doing all the thinking, and if I don't get a grip on it now...who knows what it's going to convince me to do."

He didn't think that sounded like that terrible a demise. Abruptly, he realized the whole reason he was on this quest to convince Angela was a result of his body— at least at first. Now, he didn't want to think about exactly why he was doing what he was doing. "I actually can understand that," he said. "Still, I think you're making a little mistake here."

Her eyes widened, obviously insulted. "Okay. Maybe not *mistake*," he corrected. "Just...a little flawed reasoning. You're afraid that if you and I enjoyed some more time together, that we would get involved."

"That about sums it up."

"Are we involved now?"

She looked at him, warily. "I don't think so."

"It wouldn't be much different, Angela. In fact, I think that spending more time with me would make it easier to get used to what your body is putting you through. It's like..." He racked his brain for an analogy that would convince her. "It's like dieting."

She smirked at him. "Is it?"

"If you deprive yourself, you're going to just lose it and binge," he said. "Better to let yourself have what you're craving—have *exactly* what you're craving," he said, and smiled to himself as he saw her eye his body, then quickly look away. "Otherwise, you'll wind up indulging in other areas, and be unhappy and unsatisfied."

He could see that her body desperately wanted to go along with his reasoning, but her deep brown eyes were still clinging to the logic she'd started with. "I can understand your point," she said seriously, "but I don't think you can separate what we've done from the possibility of having a relationship."

He always had in the past...but now wouldn't be a good time to make that point. He tried changing tacks instead. "Why don't you want to be in a relationship?"

"I have a lot of things I want to do, and see, and experience. I don't want to get that all clouded up because I'm involved with somebody. From what I've seen, and from what all my women friends have told me, men are simply too...distracting. Actually, the term they use is 'high maintenance.' If you're in a relationship, that usually takes precedence over everything else, and I have too much to do to get bogged down that way." She glanced at him curiously. "I'd suspect men feel the same way. Isn't that why you haven't really had relationships?"

"I would rather say I just haven't found somebody I can be happy with."

She squinted at him, then shrugged. "Well, that's my reasoning."

He wasn't getting anywhere with this logical debate. His body was starting to "distract" him even as she made her argument in her clear, schoolteacher tone. He didn't want to reason with her. He wanted to...

Maybe that's what I've been doing wrong. His body wholeheartedly agreed with him.

"I won't argue with you. But we do have one problem." He stroked her thigh with a gentle, barely there touch. "Do you honestly think that one night was enough?"

He heard her catch her breath as he moved forward slowly, giving her ample time to stop him, to tell him no. To his intense relief, she didn't...she simply stared at him with those deep, soulful eyes. He nibbled at her earlobe, feeling satisfied as she gradually pressed herself against him, putting her hands up against his shoulders.

"A good experiment takes place over an extended period of time," he pointed out, kissing her neck as she clutched at his back and her breathing shallowed. He lifted his head, brushing teasing caresses against her cheeks, along her jawline, down her neck. "You don't want to get involved. I can respect that. But I really think you're not giving yourself enough of a chance to fully enjoy the experience."

They were in a dark corner—away from everyone. The pounding beat showed that the DJ was mixing full force, and no one was coming back to this empty part of the dance floor. "Allow me to demonstrate," he said, tugging her gently onto his lap, straddling him.

Her pupils had dilated further, making her dark brown

eyes seem black. He noticed this as he held her there, poised over his erection, just staring at her as she settled breathlessly. She had to feel it, pressing hard at the junction of her thighs, against those jeans that fit her body like a second skin.

He didn't even have to nudge her. He just stared, as she shivered slightly, and he felt her body move against him, her thighs clenching enough to make him push up to meet her. He watched as she took a deep breath, and moved her head down to meet him with an ''I-can't-believe-I'm-doing-this'' expression.

Her kiss was surprisingly gentle for the fire he'd seen in her eyes. She started just touching velvet-soft lips to his, parting slightly, moving in that slow searching way that made him feel every movement of the muscles in her mouth. It was maddening. He wasn't sure how, but just by a slow kiss she made him wonder what it would feel like to have that gentle, moist suction over every inch of his body. His erection tensed.

He couldn't take it anymore. He teased her lips with his tongue, and the kiss exploded. She was breathing hard, meeting him stroke for stroke. She tore away to mimic him and worked on his neck. He'd never thought himself particularly vulnerable to that sort of pressure, but the feeling of it was enough to almost push him over the edge. Her hips...the rhythm she'd displayed on the dance floor was no joke. She was grinding against him in a seductive sway that was mind-blowing. He stroked her breasts, rubbing the nipples through the thin cotton fabric of her tank top. He heard her gasp as she pressed herself farther into the cups of his hands, and made out the mewling little cries of pleasure he'd reveled in when he made love to her before.

If this kept up, he was going to take her, right here in

this dance club. It wasn't the place or the time. He had to get a grip.

With more control than he thought he possessed, with more willpower than he'd ever *needed* to use before in his life, he nudged her back. To his surprise, he was breathing hard himself. She growled in frustration, something he found unreasonably sexy.

"Like I said," he whispered, panting, "there's more to this than just one night."

"I don't want a relationship," she repeated, although he could feel the wave of attraction flowing between them. "But I still want you. So where does that leave us?"

He frowned. There was no way he was going to lose this woman. "How about a contract, of sorts?"

She laughed abruptly. He loved the sound of her laugh. "Didn't you get insulted last time when you thought I'd offered to pay you?"

He laughed with her. "I don't mean that kind of contract. I meant an agreement, a clear definition of what we're doing before we do anything." He smiled, stroking a hand over her hair. "I just want you to feel comfortable, Angela. No pressure, no regrets. And I'll make sure you enjoy every single minute."

She eyed him warily. "You're not serious about this."

If he thought it would get him closer to her, he'd sign his name in blood. He threaded his hand in her hair and tugged her down for a quick, searing kiss. "Did that feel like I was joking?" he asked.

She shook her head, her eyes looking a little wild…a woman at war with herself. "How will I know that we won't get involved?" she said, in a small voice. "I don't know, Josh. This is all so sudden. I just want you so much. I'm not thinking. I can't think."

He needed to keep her in that state. At least until he could convince her that this was the right thing, for both of them. He needed to show her that she wouldn't be trapped by him, of all men. "I don't have a track record with relationships," he pointed out, hoping to reassure her.

Her eyes narrowed. "But you *do* have a track record," she said slowly.

He hadn't even been thinking of other women, so her statement caught him off guard. "Yes, I do. I can't pretend that I don't, Angela."

"Yes, but how will I know that you aren't…" She trailed off, staring at him, obviously hoping he'd understand.

It took him a second, then he sighed. "No. If you decide to, ah, spend time with me, I promise I won't be spending time with any other women. If you knew me, you'd know you wouldn't have to worry…but then, you don't know me, do you?" He thought for a moment. "I said it'd be like a contract. Let's make it semi-official then."

"You want to run this by a lawyer?"

He chuckled. "No. I mean, we can set a time limit, and I promise that during that set limit, I won't see any other women. And after that set limit, we call it quits. No harm, no foul, no regrets." He looked at her meaningfully. "Unless, of course, we agree to extend the bargain."

She bit her lip. "I…I don't know. This is all so fast. And it's strange. It's like something out of a movie."

"I know," he said, leaning his forehead against hers. She moved to press a satin-soft kiss against his temple, and he felt a tremor that wasn't purely sexual hit him in the gut. "Clubs are always sort of unreal…and the way

I met you was practically alien. Maybe this is dumb. All I know is, I want you, and I want this."

She pulled back enough to look at him, then kissed him…one of the sweetest kisses of his life. "A month." Her voice quavered. "I think I could handle a month."

"A year."

She pulled back a little more. "Are we…bargaining?"

"Like I said, it's a contract." He grinned at her shock. "I'm a tough negotiator. Ask anybody."

He held his breath, waiting for her reaction. To his relief, she smiled slowly, moving back to him again. "Two months," she said, her voice holding a hint of challenge.

He stroked her cheek. "What say we just split the difference, and go for six?"

She stayed quiet for a long time, and Josh suddenly wondered if he'd blown it for good.

"That Friday night…" She took a deep, shuddering breath, and for a brief moment, Josh ignored his need to ravish her. The shadows in her eyes, the clenched tension of her body, all made him want to just hold her until her fear subsided. She might categorize it as concern or reasonable apprehension, but it was obviously fear. "It was a wonderful blur. I had an agenda. I can still barely believe it really happened."

He waited while she paused, then finally whispered, "So what are you saying, Angela?"

"Convince me," she blurted out, her hair tumbling over one shoulder. "I mean…I'll see you one more time. If it seems like I can…handle that, then I'll agree to six months."

He kissed her, relishing the way she clung to him. Tonight wasn't going to be that night—at least, not from her point of view. Still, it was a window. He could work around it, maybe…

"If that's what it takes," he said.

She smiled…a smile so sweet, that the suggestion that they make tonight her trial run froze in his throat. "So when would you like to do this?" he asked instead.

She frowned. "I…I have a lot of classes. I'm sort of booked."

He paused. That didn't sound promising. "Until when?"

"Next Friday."

He groaned to himself. Seven days until he could hold her again?

"All right." He kissed her, lingering until her breathing sped up. "I'll see you on Friday night."

As he got up to walk her to her car, he swore to himself that he was going to make it the beginning of something incredible…a night she wouldn't forget.

4

THE FOLLOWING FRIDAY, Josh could still picture Angela, almost feel her in his arms when he closed his eyes. But he had neither seen nor felt her since their episode in the deserted part of Club X. In the meantime, he'd had plenty to focus on with Solar Bars, but the night ahead was making him as antsy as a grade school kid on Christmas Eve.

"You know, you're the only one who really *works* at working lunches, Josh."

"If I don't, who will?" Josh said, grinning at his friend. They were sitting in Joe's Burgers, papers strewn around the Formica tabletop, binders propped open on the napkin container. Their sleeves were rolled up. Joe was standing behind the counter, shaking his head, his grizzly face amused. Josh and Adam had been having working lunches at Joe's Burgers since they moved the company to Manzanita five years ago. "Besides, I've got a big date tonight."

Adam looked stunned. "You're going out on a date? Tonight?"

"So what?" Josh looked up from the report he was rifling through. "It's Friday, isn't it? Lots of people go out on dates on Friday."

"Not a Friday before the auditor gets here, you don't."

Josh sighed. The auditor. Not that Solar Bars had done

anything wrong, but the way they'd posted earnings, and the growing size of the company—they were due, he'd figured. They'd been lucky to get away without an audit for this long.

Ordinarily, he'd be sweating it out with the accounting team, checking over every figure they came up with. "I trust Bill," Josh said slowly, referring to his corporate controller. "He and the accounting staff can handle it." He felt his shoulders tense, and forced them to relax.

Adam stared at him.

Josh finally put the report down in disgust. "All right, *what?*"

Adam shook his head. "Nothing. It's just that—well, this isn't a critique, you understand. It's just that you like to get involved in every little aspect of *everything.*" He broke into a grin. "Remember that time, when you would have fallen headfirst into the granola mixer if I hadn't stopped you?"

"Are you kidding? You never let me forget it."

"But you still do stuff like that—work with the line crew every now and then, check in on accounting, pester my R and D people, hunker down in the trenches with the marketing team. You like to be hands-on, all the time. It's what's made Solar Bars the company it is," Adam said seriously.

"Thanks," Josh said. "But what does that have to do with my social life?"

"That's just it. You've never put anything from Solar Bars on hold for a *date*. This is unprecedented." Adam sounded more than curious—he seemed downright intrigued. "So. Anybody I know?"

"Not exactly," Josh hedged.

Adam stared at him, a broad grin creeping across his face. "You did it. You found the virgin."

Josh groaned. "I don't think you should refer to her that way," he said.

Adam's grin grew even wider. "That's true, you took care of that."

"Watch it." Josh's voice was steel-edged. "Yes, I'm going out with Angela tonight. *Angela,*" he said, with emphasis.

"Wow. *Angela* must be a damned fast learner," Adam said, laughing despite Josh's warning glance. "Girl must be a gymnast or an acrobat or something to get you to take a step back from work. What do you have planned for tonight? As if I need to ask."

"I've got plans," Josh said. "We're going into Sacramento, catching a show, dinner, the whole nine yards."

And by the time the night was finished, he was going to know everything there was to know about one Angela Snowe—and she was going to know that her next six months, perhaps longer, were going to be booked solid by Josh Montgomery.

"You're doing it again."

Josh dragged himself back from his thoughts. "Doing what?"

"That corporate-takeover smile," Adam said, his jovial tone curbed. "This is a lot more serious than I thought."

Josh made a negligent gesture. "She's different. I appreciate the different."

Adam started to say something, then stopped abruptly. "Well. Here's something *I* can appreciate," he said finally, nodding at something behind Josh.

Josh turned, then narrowed his eyes. "Shelly? Is that you?"

She had honey blond haircut in a stylish shag, and her

very full breasts were straining at the buttons of her cherry-red blouse. She wore a short denim skirt and a pair of heels. He could see how Adam would be attracted by her. He could see how any man in the joint would be.

"Josh?" she said. "Josh, is that you?"

He stood up, reaching arms out for a friendly hug. He noticed that her full chest pressed against his a little longer than he was expecting, then brushed the thought aside. "I haven't seen you since high school," he said, smiling fondly. "You haven't changed a bit."

She smiled, the same luscious smile that had his whole defensive line drooling, back when he'd played football at Manzanita High. "It's been a long time," she said, her green eyes looking at him with open admiration. For the first time, he felt uncomfortable with it, thinking of big brown doe eyes—the kind that looked at him with a mixture of innocence and longing.

I'm just saying hello. But the little pang didn't go away, and he frowned.

"So how have you been?" he said quickly.

At this, her pretty face frowned slightly, showing a spasm of bitterness that she wasn't quick enough to hide. "I've been...well, things haven't been so good." Her right hand moved reflexively to her left hand, rubbing her ring finger. "I've recently been divorced, actually."

"I'm sorry to hear that," Josh said, and meant it. Shelly had always been a pistol in high school, a flirt and a terror of sorts, leaving broken hearts in her wake.

"I've just moved in with my parents, until I get back on my feet again. It's just temporary," she assured him, as if waiting for him to judge her. "I've gotten a job at the Travel Center, as a travel agent, so it's just a matter of time before I get a place of my own."

"Planning on staying in Manzanita, then?"

She nodded, her eyes surveying him under long lashes. "That depends on whether I find anything worth staying for, I guess."

"Well then. I guess I'll be seeing you around."

She lightened up a little. "That would be wonderful. It's been such a long time, and I don't know anybody in town anymore, it seems." She looked sad, and he felt sorry for her. "Manzanita's not the little back-fence community I remembered."

"It's better," he said, patting her shoulder. She moved in for another bosom-heaving hug, and he kept it brief. "Maybe we'll do lunch sometime," he said, easily.

Her responding smile was intent. "I'll hold you to that."

She turned, moving her hips in a walk as seductive as an aphrodisiac. Josh noticed that every male in the place was riveted.

Josh sat back down in his booth.

Adam looked at him, bewildered. "So, do you know *every* fine woman in a five-mile radius, or what?"

"I'll get you a list. I'm sure I've got their phone numbers somewhere."

"Lunch, nothing. Why don't you take her out to dinner?" Adam was all but drooling. "That is one *fine* woman."

"I've already got a fine woman," Josh said, laughing, then stopped abruptly, realizing what he'd just said.

Adam heard it, too, and his eyes narrowed. "Do you, now?"

Josh pointed to the binder propped open in front of Adam. "Just tell me about those new soy bars you wanted to come up with. The carob-soy protein bars."

But even as Adam went on about the new product line, Josh went back to his statement. *I've already got a fine woman.*

He'd have to think about that.

IT WAS VERY CLOSE to dark, and Angela negotiated the winding curves that led to Josh's isolated house in the hills, her heart beating fast.

She was going to have sex. Fantastic, mind-altering sex.

She frowned.

Fantastic, mind-altering, *uncommitted* sex, she corrected.

Maybe she was a fool to try to repeat the incredible experience of two weeks ago. This time, she wasn't stressing about dying a virgin. Now she was stressing about living with the consequences. She'd been having second thoughts since she'd agreed to his crazy proposition. And third, and fourth thoughts…

Maybe she was losing her mind. Or maybe she was going too crazy with this whole "experience gaining" craze she'd stepped into.

Or maybe every time the guy gets within three feet of you, your eyes cross and your arms and legs suddenly get the intense desire to wrap around him, ninny.

She gripped the steering wheel a little harder. Okay, there was that, too. But she'd never been at the mercy of her body before, and that's just what she felt like…like her hard-won independence was being bowled over just because she'd finally introduced her hormones to real, down-and-dirty, fantastic sex.

She felt her pulse spike as her mind came up with the images and memories it had stored around said fantastic incident. Suddenly, the temperature went up several degrees in her car, and she rolled down her window to let some of the cool evening air in. It was as if her body was saying, *Yeah, we enjoyed it, we'd do it again in a heartbeat. Wanna make something of it?*

The only problem was, it *wasn't* just her body. That's what scared her half to death.

What if I somehow fell in love?

Her own mother had been much younger than twenty-nine when she became pregnant with Angela. Angela had seen pictures of her mother, happily cuddling a chubby, cheerful infant, looking much like a girl herself. Later, hugging a skinny, straggly-haired girl who gradually grew like a weed, while her mother seemed to age much more rapidly.

Her father had never been in any of those pictures.

Her mother had planned on being an architect when she met her father at a party. It had been love, at least on her mother's part…head-over-heels, crazy and out of control. They'd gotten married a handful of months later, and she had gotten pregnant. She'd worked as a secretary to help make ends meet while her father finished school. By the time Angela was one, her father had decided that he did not want to deal with a young wife and child. Last Angela had heard, he was now married, with a seven-year-old son. Apparently later in life he'd recanted his decision.

"I don't begrudge your father anything," her mother often said. "He gave me you." But Angela could still remember her mother watching television shows about old buildings, or looking through books on architecture, as she propped up her feet after a long day. Her mother worked brutally hard to keep herself and her child financially afloat. Her dreams of architectural school remained just that. Dreams.

Angela closed her eyes. This wasn't love. This was sex. She knew the difference.

She had spent most of her adult life working too hard and dreaming too often, following in her mother's footsteps. She had been too busy or too scared to get involved with a man. Now, she had a chance to make up for lost time.

What she wanted, to put it quite bluntly, was sex. Pure and simple. She wanted to ravage, and be ravaged. She wanted to feel him, naked, his skin brushing against hers as he entered her...

She focused back on the road. God, she was turned on. She didn't feel like driving into a tree just because her body was running a little overheated, though. She chuckled at herself.

She had carefully dressed in a blue silk sheathe. Basically it was just a casing for the black lingerie she had meticulously strapped on. The garters in particular had been a challenge. After cursing at them for a good fifteen minutes, she'd finally got the whole getup put together, and she had to admit that the effect was well worth it. She'd pouted at herself in the mirror as she put on lipstick in her underwear, a little sex-kitten practice, then laughed at her reflection. *I want this so much!*

Maybe he'd sweep her up at the doorstep and carry her to the bedroom, she thought. Or maybe there would be a lingering kiss, and a seductive trail of clothes through the house as they made use of every piece of furniture that came within their path to the final destination. She didn't know. She figured that was what made it all so much more exciting. To other people this might be old hat, but to her, it was an intriguing new world. She felt like somebody with a new car or computer or something, someone that had to push every single button to find out what it did.

She was going to push plenty of buttons tonight.

She parked her car in his driveway. Immediately her heart started beating faster. She tugged her black coat around her, and stepped out carefully. She was wearing heels again, more sensible ones than she'd worn when she first met him, but still sexy. She grinned. She wasn't planning on wearing them that long, anyway.

She got to the door and rang the doorbell, her skin tingling, heart racing.

Josh opened the door, and her heart stopped for a second. He was wearing a black tailored suit with a snowy white shirt and a burgundy tie. His hair was slightly damp and slicked back, with his bangs hanging rakishly in front of his blue eyes. He looked like a fallen angel. He looked like a model out of *GQ*.

He looked good enough to eat.

"Angela," he said. She felt his gaze rake over her body like a caress. "You look…damn."

She smiled at him. "I take it that's good."

He kissed her, and she immediately parted her lips, pressing against him hungrily. She felt his fingers dig slightly into her hips, pulling her to him. She swayed against him. *Let the ravishing commence.*

She was still pressing forward when he stepped away, and she took an awkward little half step. She chuckled. "Whoops."

He was breathing harder, and he stroked the side of her face. "You, lady, are dangerous."

She was about to respond to that when, to her surprise, he took another step away from her and grabbed a coat of his own. "Um…"

He smiled at her, then snapped his fingers. "Wait a

sec. Almost forgot.'' He disappeared into the kitchen for a second.

He was putting on his coat, she thought, bewildered. Where was he taking her? She liked to think she was as adventurous as the next person, maybe more so in her current jumped-up state. But still...

He interrupted her thought by returning to her from the kitchen. ''For you,'' he said, and presented her with a long-stemmed red rose.

''Oh.'' She stared at it for a second, then sniffed at the tip. It smelled...well, like a rose. ''Thank you. It's lovely.''

He grinned, with a casual shrug. ''I'm glad you like it.''

She held it awkwardly for a moment. What was she supposed to *do* with it? Put it in a vase? Take it with her?

''Come on,'' he said. She guessed she'd take it with her. ''Are you terribly hungry?''

She thought about her stomach, all but doing somersaults with nervous energy. ''Not even a little.''

''Good,'' he said cryptically. ''Come on. I don't want us to be late.''

''Late for what?''

He ushered her toward the door. ''You'll see. I'll drive. It's a surprise.''

She was surprised, all right, she thought as she walked over to his car and climbed in, settling on the cold leather seats. This was not the way she had envisioned this evening going at all. Not that she was complaining—well, not really. Maybe he was just trying to build up the suspense, she justified. He was, after all, the expert at this sort of thing.

She could breathe in the sexy spiciness of his cologne

in the car, watched the way his thigh muscles flexed as
he stepped on the gas or shifted gears. She started hyperventilating.

Down, girl.

She tried to keep up that pretense as they drove all
the way to Sacramento. He pulled into a parking garage,
then escorted her out. She walked as carefully as she
could on the concrete steps. *What was he up to?* Maybe
he was taking her to a hotel…

A crowd of well-dressed people in front of a playhouse stopped them. She immediately moved to sidestep
the crush, but suddenly, Josh's hand was on her shoulder. "No, you're good right here," he said, then grinned.
"Surprise!"

She glanced around. No, no hotels. "Surprise?"

He produced tickets from the inner breast pocket of
his coat. "I got us tickets to this Broadway revival everybody's been raving about. I thought you might like
it." He grinned again, like a flash of summer lightning.
"Front row, too."

He was looking at her expectantly. "That's, er, wonderful," she said, in as close an approximation of a gush
as she could manage. *A Broadway revival?* Her body
was in a momentary state of shock. She'd been prepared
for bearskin rugs, not musicals. She felt like an engine
that had been plunged abruptly from fourth gear to first.

He nuzzled her neck, and she felt the rev of her body
again, a quick, brutal blast. She pushed herself against
him in a fierce hug, but he pulled away.

"Not here," he murmured, and then proceeded to talk
to her. She couldn't really focus on what he was saying…small talk, the weather, how her day had been. She
felt like she'd been sucker punched.

So this is a fling, she thought, laughing at herself as

the crowd crushed inside the playhouse like well-dressed lemmings. *Funny. Somehow I'd always pictured it with a bit more sex.*

THE RESTAURANT WAS just the way Josh remembered it. The muted mauve walls, the crystal chandeliers, the snowy white linen draped over the tables. Waiters in their somber black uniforms, moving quietly. The clink of crystal and the lulling murmur of polite conversation.

This was not going as planned.

Josh was frustrated. He sat at a table at Le Bateau, one of the classiest restaurants in Sacramento, waiting for Angela to return from the rest room. He'd been careful to get the best seats in the house, then he'd taken her on a little walk through a nearby sculpture park. He'd kept up a stream of nonstop patter all night. Frankly, he was getting sick of his own voice. She wasn't taciturn—in fact, he enjoyed talking to her. She made him laugh, usually unintentionally, with her observations, and she was just generally sweet. But she was…*evasive,* was the only way he could put it. She didn't make coy remarks, didn't flirt or share intimate stories in the hope of encouraging him to do the same. She didn't make any effort to "get to know" him, or for that matter, give him any shred of *anything* to help him get to know her. He knew just as much about her as he did when he first met her—which was just about nothing.

Ordinarily, this probably wouldn't bother him. In fact, as he thought back about some of his dates, a rest from the constant unloading of past and present would be a relief. But he was intrigued more than he could remember being in a long time, and the crumbs she was tossing him when it came to her past only whetted his appetite for more.

To top it off, he couldn't shake the feeling that she was somehow disappointed. He would make comments, and she would stare at him for a second, with a sort of disbelief. He'd been treated to one of those when he'd told her they were going to this restaurant. Then she'd laughed, another thing she seemed to be doing a lot of, as if she were constantly amused by some running private joke. It wasn't like she was laughing at him...it was almost like she were laughing at *herself,* though he couldn't figure out why.

This wasn't going the way he'd planned at all.

Gerard, the owner of Le Bateau, stopped by his table. "Josh, it's wonderful to see you again!" He took a quick seat. "But strange to see you alone, and after so long. What's been happening to you?"

Josh had known Gerard for a good twenty years, since Le Bateau opened and Josh's parents were some of the first patrons. He was an old family friend. "I've been busy with work," Josh said, not wanting to explain that he hadn't felt like expending the effort of taking a woman here, to one of his special places, in several years. "And, as it happens, I'm not alone tonight," he added, as Angela returned to the table. She gave Gerard a shy smile.

Gerard stood up immediately. "I see that," he said, with an approving nod.

"Hello. I'm Angela," she murmured, offering her hand.

"Angela," Gerard gushed, then nudged Josh. "I'll send out one of our special desserts. Bananas Foster, I think." He leaned down, whispering to Josh loudly enough for Angela to overhear. "It's about time you found one worth keeping."

He thanked Gerard as the man left, grinning at Angela. "Sorry," Josh said. "He's an old friend of the family."

"He seems very nice."

"Yeah, in that pushy, romantic, meddling sort of way," Josh said with a sigh, and Angela laughed. "But he has an incredible restaurant."

"He certainly does," Angela said, gesturing to the plate in front of her. She smiled gently at Gerard's disappearing form. "The food has been absolutely fantastic. And I haven't had Bananas Foster since I lived in New York—this will be a treat."

Finally! "So. You used to live in New York?"

She blinked, as if suddenly realizing she'd said something personal. "Oh. Yes."

"When?"

"Before I lived here."

Josh waited for her to expand on this, then realized that was it—that was all she was going to say. "Before you lived in Manzanita? Were you going to school there? Working there?"

"Both." She said, then shrugged. "For a while. You moved away from Manzanita to go to school, too, didn't you? Went to UCLA or something?" She grinned playfully at him. "Hence that whole football reputation you referred to, the night I…"

She paused, then blushed. He couldn't blame her…he wasn't sure how he'd put the first night they were together, either. He felt his chest warm…among other things. He quickly picked up her conversation. "Yeah, I went down to L.A., got my degree. I only played football for two years, though. I could have been a fairly decent quarterback, but I knew I didn't have what it took to be a professional football player—an almost obsessive love of the sport. I love a lot of different sports, and it turns out I liked business a lot, too.''

''So Solar Bars was really a perfect business for you,'' she said, taking a sip of her wine.

Josh found himself telling her all about Solar Bars... how he'd met Adam, how the two of them had started making their high-energy protein bars out of a warehouse in Venice, California. How the thing had grown beyond their wildest dreams, and how, when it finally came time to open a larger factory and expand, Josh had convinced Adam to move the whole operation to Manzanita, the town he'd grown up in.

They'd finished the meal with the dazzling spectacle of Flambé Bananas Foster, and Josh realized as he walked her back to the car that she had managed to divert him from her life back to his...so neatly that he'd yet again missed finding out about her.

''Thanks for a wonderful evening,'' she said, as he drove her back to his place. ''I wasn't expecting all this.''

''Don't thank me yet,'' he said, thinking of the seduction scene he'd set in his house. ''The evening isn't over.''

She went silent for a second, then said in a low, sexy voice, ''It isn't?''

He was getting hard just thinking of it. ''Not by a long shot,'' he promised. He looked over. She had pinked slightly. She shot him a melting, brown-eyed stare. She obviously liked that answer. *It's about time*, he thought. He paused for a second. ''Where's your rose?''

She looked down at her purse, then bit her lip. ''I'm sorry. I think I left it on the table at the restaurant.'' She was blushing this time, a full-blown rosy red. ''I'm sorry. I've never gotten a flower before, and forgot that I had it. I've been a little distracted.''

Distracted was one way to put it, but she seemed genuinely apologetic. He smiled, reaching over and stroking her downy-soft cheek again. "That's okay. Really."

They got to his house. She was still quiet, almost eerily so, as if she were thinking about something. He wondered again about her "distraction." Maybe she was nervous? It had been over a week since they'd last had sex—since he'd *taken her virginity*. He had to keep reminding himself that this was all new to her, that he needed to keep control and go slowly.

He led her into the living room. He took his coat off, gesturing to her to do the same. "Can I get you something to drink?"

She took her coat off and quickly kicked off her shoes, putting them neatly in the corner by the door. "I could use a glass of wine, if you've got it." She sat down on the couch.

Definitely nervous. He smiled. This was more familiar. He went over to the wet bar in the living room and chose a bottle from the wine rack. He poured her a glass of Pinot Grigio, and one for himself, then sat down next to her. "Did you have a good time tonight?"

"Um, yes. I had a great time tonight."

Boy. Talk about ringing endorsements. He'd done everything but give her a carriage ride through the city. For an inexperienced virgin-type, she was pretty damned tough to impress!

He grimaced. "Well, I wanted tonight to be special for you." He paused. "I have to ask. You seem really distant tonight. What's going on?"

"Nothing," she said, then let out a little half laugh.

"It's just…this wasn't the way I expected this to go at all."

"It isn't?" he repeated, mystified. "What were you expecting?"

"I don't know that I was exactly expecting anything specific," she said instead. "I just know that if I *were* picturing anything, it wasn't this, that's all."

He read between the lines. "You didn't like it. Any of it."

"No, no," she said quickly. "It's not that. It's just— I guess after last weekend, I was expecting a different, er, *focus*, I guess you could say." She was blushing a deep red now. "I mean, I'm new at this. I was ready to be more—I mean, I was expecting that we would just…"

"Angela, what is it?"

"I really wanted you!" She finally blurted out.

She *wanted* him? *That* was what had been distracting her all night?

He felt like smacking his head with his hand. "Why didn't you say anything?"

"You'd gone to so much trouble, and I didn't know what else to do. It seemed rude to not go along—this was your way of convincing me, after all. I enjoyed the restaurant," she added, as if to reassure him the date wasn't a *complete* failure. "Besides, I felt like I was acting like a high-school boy who was going to, you know, get some action."

He laughed. "Having been a high-school boy, I can understand that." No wonder she kept looking disappointed! He'd been working off of his own sexual history when it came to women, not thinking of how different she was. He thought she'd want to be charmed and romanced, but what she really wanted was just *him*.

The thought charged a zing of sexual energy through him. "I'm sorry. I guess I got a little carried away."

She grinned at him, her pouty full lips quirking seductively. "As you say...the night's not over yet."

He grinned back, feeling his body stir. He held her hands, kissing her neck gently and feeling gratified by the quick gasp of desire she let out. "What did you have in mind?"

She leaned over, her breath tickling his ear. "I want you to make love to me." She sounded a combination of embarrassed and breathless.

"Now?" he said, surprised by the quickness of her hands.

"Right now," she said, turning his head with both hands. He saw her smile, a beautiful, slightly mischievous smile, just before she lowered her mouth to his.

She started to ease his suit jacket off his shoulders, and he immediately complied as best he could as they continued to tease and torment with their mouths, him nipping at her neck, her pressing kisses along his jawline and in the sensitive spot just behind his ear. Next thing he knew, she was straddling him on his own sofa, much as he'd encouraged her to do on the couch in the darkened club.

His erection went rigid in a moment. So much for taking things slow.

How in the world did I think she *was the nervous one?*

Trying to catch up, he rubbed his hands over the silk dress, cupping her breasts. She leaned back, growling low in her throat as she pushed herself up to meet his searching fingers. His hands smoothed down to her hips, matching the rhythm she was developing, stroking her along his penis, feeling the heat of her through his trousers. She gasped, and the little sound made him ache.

He pushed her down, and she gasped again, clutching at his shoulders.

She tugged his shirt out of his waistband, and he almost tore the thing off, tossing it to the floor. She smiled, even more devilishly, then reached for the hem of her dress. The smile disappeared for a second as she slowly pulled the dress up and over her head, revealing the black merry widow she was wearing, complete with matching black garter belt and stockings. Desire hit him like a club. "If I'd known what you were wearing under that dress..."

"I wasn't sure if you were ever going to find out," she said softly, stroking her fingers down his chest. She darted forward and nipped at his earlobe. "I've been waiting all night for this," she whispered huskily.

Reverently, he tugged down the cups of the merry widow, exposing her firm, high breasts. He leaned forward and teased her nipples, first with his breath, then lips and tongue. She cried out, and he felt her thighs clench around his. He went from teasing to suckling, and she clenched her fingers in his hair, holding him to her. She was panting now. He wasn't far behind.

He pulled himself away. "Don't you think we ought to move back to the bedroom?" he asked, trying for some semblance of control. After all, he was the one trying to prove a point tonight...trying to convince her.

She grinned. "No, I really don't," she said, before grinding herself gently against his erection and eliciting another moan. "I think we're doing fine right here, don't you? Except for one thing." She sent him a frown of mock ferocity. "Those pants have got to go."

She stood up, and he felt bereft without her warmth. He stood and unbuckled his pants, then watched as she tugged her lingerie off, leaving only the garters. It was a brutally sexy assault. Her body was just as perfect as he remembered, all smooth curves and satin skin. His pants dropped to the floor with his boxers, and he reached for her.

"Condom," she breathed, and he stopped. Almost bolting, he headed for his bedroom, ignoring his carefully crafted seduction scene as he grabbed a handful of foil packets. He made it back in record time to find her still standing, with a welcoming smile on her face and an even more welcoming pose.

"I want to watch this," she said, and despite her sexy tone, it was the obvious and real curiosity that made him laugh. "I wasn't really paying attention last time."

He felt somewhat self-conscious as he slipped one on, then rolled it up the length of him...he'd never been the object of scrutiny during the process. She smiled, then reached out and circled him with her hand, clenching him tightly, adding a gentle stroke.

"Angela," he muttered, pushing forward at her hand instinctively. Her responding smile was sly, as if she'd suddenly realized her own power. She moved with a gentle rhythm, first hard, then soft, then hard.

He needed to be inside of her, right now, but he wanted to make sure she was ready. She was driving him mad, but she was still inexperienced, and he wasn't. He nudged her down onto the couch, and she parted her legs easily. "Josh," she murmured, sliding her arms out to him.

He nuzzled her throat, loving the breathy gasps, then gently moved down to her breasts, devoting more attention there. Still working on them, he positioned his penis at her entrance, gently stroking up and down. She gasped some more, and he kissed her, hard, their tongues dueling amidst matching groans. He could feel her wetness increasing, easing his entrance. He put the tip in, and the tight warmth was almost enough to push him over the edge. He wanted to slam into her, to bury himself up to his hips in her warmth.

Control, he thought desperately. *Gotta keep it together.*

She was chanting his name, and her legs inched up higher on his hips, trying to take more of him in. He resisted. She'd gotten enough teasing in tonight. Now, it was his turn.

He backed out, then reentered, barely going deeper, stroking at her entrance, circling and returning. She was breathing hard, making incoherent noises of frustration and need. Finally, she opened her eyes.

"Josh, I want you inside me," she pleaded.

He smiled. "You have me inside you." He pressed in a little more. "Just a bit."

"I want all of you inside me," she countered. "I want to feel you pushing against me, deep. Please!"

He pushed in a little further, then retreated. The effort was almost killing him…her moist warmth was tight as a glove around him, and he could feel every ripple of her body. At this point, if he pushed in full he was afraid he would lose his mind and just give in to mindless passion. She was still too new, too tender…

With a growl of frustration, she wrapped her legs around his waist, pulling him all the way inside of her. She let out a harsh rasp of triumph, and he felt his control dissipate like smoke. Her breasts rubbed against his chest and her fingers roughly raked down his back before clenching at his hips. He withdrew, then plunged into her, making sure each thrust angled him against her pleasure spot, circling slightly to make sure her clitoris got just as much attention. *She's so tight, she's so…she's perfect.*

She was meeting his every thrust with a cry of pleasure, and a slight twist of her own that made her body pulse and clench around him. "Josh…I'm…I'm coming…." she breathed, and he increased his speed. Suddenly, she let out a low, rippling cry. *"Josh!"*

He felt the change in her body, and suddenly the pressure on his erection increased. He felt the waves caress him, and it sent his own system over. He groaned, and jerked against her, feeling his own orgasm rip through him like a gunshot.

She let out another cry, to his shock, and the wave redoubled…and to his amazement, he jerked again, a reverberation of his first orgasm.

They lay there for what seemed like a long time, her legs still tight around his waist, his face buried in the crook of her neck. After pulling himself together, he leaned up on one arm. She was covered in a sheen of sweat, and her eyes were closed. Her bangs were plastered against her forehead. He pushed them out of the way, then ran a gentle finger down her cheek and along her neck. Then he kissed her, just as tenderly. When he stopped, he saw her eyes open, rich as chocolate.

"Was that as fantastic as I thought it was?" she asked, in a breathy whisper.

It was more fantastic, he thought, than he would have expected…and in some ways, more than he'd like to admit. "Not bad…for a second time," he said, then laughed as she glared at him. "Angela, it was incredible for me, too."

She smiled, not the devilish smiles she'd tempted him with, but an angelic smile of gratitude. "Thank you."

He remembered the first time she'd said that…how it

had thrown him a little. "No, Angela," he said, kissing her again. "Thank *you*."

He carefully withdrew from her. "I'm going to get you a towel," he said.

He went to the bathroom, cleaning himself off. She was right…that had been incredible. And it was just the beginning. He'd rushed, and he hadn't meant to. Next time, he'd be slower, more thorough. At this rate, she'd think that every time was a speed race. And he'd get her into the bedroom, too. She probably shouldn't have sex again tonight—despite her enthusiasm and her obvious desire, she was bound to be sore—but there were other ways of enjoying each other, and he had hours yet to get her to agree to his six-month proposal.

He brought back a hand towel for her, then paused when he saw her.

"Angela?"

She had already put her dress back on, and slipped on her shoes. It looked like she had her merry widow and stockings piled haphazardly over her clutch purse. She smiled. "I know this seems really abrupt," she said, apologetically, grabbing her coat and putting it on. "But I have to go."

He didn't know what hit him harder…knowing she was wearing nothing beneath that silky little dress, or knowing she was about to leave the house in that manner. "After what just happened…you're going to just *leave?*"

She quickly ran her fingers through her hair, smoothing it down. "Unfortunately, I've signed up for an early morning yoga class at the community center, so I've got to get home, get some sleep, then get over there by *six*." She shuddered, then smiled. "I'll call you tomorrow, though."

He frowned. "You mean that?"

She walked up to him, and brushed a quick kiss over his lips. "After this, I've made my decision. I can handle the six months."

He was even more surprised. He supposed he ought to feel happy—he'd gotten what he wanted, after all. She had agreed to see him again, the night had not been a complete disaster. But he was still feeling somewhat bereft. "Six months, definitely?"

"Definitely." She kissed him again, then took a deep breath, and as he watched, she turned and walked out his front door. "I'll see you," she said, smiling, then shut the door behind her.

After a few shocked moments, he heard her car start, then pull out of the driveway. The hum of the engine disappeared into the night.

He was standing, stark naked in his living room, holding a hand towel and wondering when the hell he had lost control of the situation.

5

SHE WAS IN COMPLETE control of the situation.

"Okay. The next pose is Proud Warrior," Angela heard the tranquil voice of the yoga instructor say over the tiny sounds of a murmuring brook and some sort of bells.

Groaning, Angela pulled herself up from her inverted triangle position, where she was basically trying to bend at the waist while making her top half and bottom half point in completely opposite directions. She had always heard of the relaxing benefits of yoga. Maybe the people who had said that weren't getting up at six in the morning. They certainly weren't doing it after having a really rousing bout of sex the night before, either.

She stretched and turned, feeling the soreness between her legs as yet another reminder of what had happened the previous evening.

Angela twisted and reached for her feet. She also figured she shouldn't have any problems keeping the situation firmly in hand. It would just depend on her setting a few guidelines for herself, that's all.

She remembered the look of shock on Josh's face as she left last night. Later, as she drove home, she realized that it had probably not happened to a man like Josh all that often. Not that that was why she was doing it, but she had to admit there was a certain power in walking away. And as much as she didn't want to hurt his feel-

ings, or make him feel cheap, she had a bigger respon-
sibility to make sure she stayed safe. She felt sure he
hadn't worried about hurting people's feelings when his
brief affairs had run their course, even though she
thought he was otherwise very considerate.

Why should she sacrifice her peace of mind, just so
he wouldn't be upset with her?

She needed to make it clear to herself: this was a
sexual arrangement, *not* a relationship. She wasn't going
to be leaving a toothbrush at his house, or clearing out
a drawer for her underwear and socks.

*Rule number one: no staying over at each other's
houses.*

She thought about it some more…the brook and bell
combo the instructor was playing seemed to help clarify
her thoughts, even if the contortions didn't. The thing
is, she really *had* left Josh so she'd be ready for her
yoga class. For a brief moment, she'd considered staying
with him, of forgetting the class entirely. She'd seen far
too many women lose all their interests as a new love
affair consumed them. That wasn't happening here. She
was going to continue pursuing her growth in other areas. She still had her own life, and more recently, her
own friends.

*Rule number two, then: never cancel plans in order
to accommodate Josh.*

She would hardly impinge on his plans, after all. She
felt sure that despite his attention to her, he'd manage
to have his own busy social life. He was far too outgoing
and charming a man not to have his own social circle,
she had to assume.

She paused, midcontortion. Josh. Now he, himself,
was the biggest trouble spot. If this arrangement had
been with someone she had felt less attracted to, she

could have stuck with just rules one and two. But after she and Josh had had sex, when they'd been lying in each other's arms for those few fleeting moments, hadn't she felt that sneaking warmth, the kind that made women want to blurt out some profession of love? Hadn't she been ready to chuck rules one *and* two right out the window, if he hadn't chosen to leave the room just then?

She frowned, not just at the pretzel-mimicking position the teacher assured her she could configure herself into.

For that matter, hadn't she felt that same warmth of emotion as she'd listened to him talk about his past, when they *hadn't* been having sex…despite her best efforts to stay aloof?

Rule number three—and the most important as far as she was concerned—*she could never,* ever *say "I love you."*

Not ever.

She was still sore when she got home, not just from Josh, but from her morning. Even her head was sore, from thinking so much about the whole thing. But she felt clearer about her stance and her direction, more relaxed and at ease with herself. She had ground rules. She had definite goals. She knew what she wanted, and felt remarkably at peace about the entire thing.

I guess there's something to yoga, after all. She'd go again next Saturday.

Her phone rang, and she picked it up. "Hello?"

"Hey, you. How's life in Manzanita?"

"Bethany!" Angela smiled, settling herself at her kitchen table. "Where the heck are you calling me from?"

"If it's Tuesday, it must be Tuscany," Bethany said with a laugh. "At least the photos are going great. I haven't even turned on my computer, but I got your messages. So when are you going to come out and visit me already?''

It had been a running joke between the two of them since college. Bethany had been dying to go to Europe since high school, and had studied languages and photojournalism with equal ferocity. She'd always cajoled Angela to join her, but Angela had never had the time or the finances, or the motivation, it seemed. "I'll go one of these days," Angela said, her usual response.

"Yeah, yeah. Angela, you're too comfortable, I've often said it. Not that there's anything wrong with it, but you and I both know you want to do more with your life," Bethany said seriously. Angela smiled more…this, too, was a familiar litany. "I really mean it this time! I know you've probably got tons of vacation stocked up. Come out to Europe and visit me," she wheedled. "I'll find you a handsome, virile Italian who'll make love to you like there's no tomorrow. Not that I'm going to push you on that point, either…as usual…"

Angela sighed. "We need to talk, Bethany."

Bethany's chipper persuasiveness halted. "Well, that sounds ominous. What happened? You've got a brain tumor or something?"

"Well, there was a little medical thing…."

"Oh, my God." Bethany's voice crackled with worry. "There's never anything 'little' with you. Do you really have a brain tumor? Something else serious?" Her caring was evident, as was her increasing panic. "I can be on a plane in an hour…."

"Whoa! No brain tumor, no problem, I'm fine," Angela said, loving her for being such a good friend, but still ruing her impulsive nature. Even though it was one of the things she most admired about her friend, it was hard to contain. "I had a little jolt, that's all…lump in my breast, turned out to be nothing."

"For the love of…Angie, don't scare me like that!" Bethany scolded.

"I didn't mean to…but the whole thing scared some sense into me." She thought about her new agreement with Josh. "Okay, maybe *sense* isn't quite the right word. But it scared some courage into me."

Bethany went silent for a moment, then a tone of glee crept into her voice. "No way. Don't tell me you…"

"You're talking to an ex-virgin, pal."

Bethany crowed. "Whoo-hoo! Finally!" Once she'd finished cheering, her tone got businesslike. "Who did it, where was it, how did it go? Full report. I want every juicy tidbit."

"Well, you're not getting every juicy tidbit," Angela said. "But I'll tell you this…it's everything you said it was, and then some. And then, just a little bit more."

"So how did this all come about? You were introduced by friends? Met at a party? In line at the DMV?"

Angela bit her lip. "Actually, it was more like a decision I made. This guy is fairly well-known around Manzanita—not exactly as a womanizer, but as a…" She thought of how best to describe Josh. "A professional bachelor, let's say. I just sort of…well, I made him an offer."

"Don't tell me…you decided you were going to lose your virginity to him, and then went gunning, didn't you?" Bethany's laughter was exuberant. "If you could see me, you'd find me kneeling in front of my phone in homage to you. Don't take this the wrong way, but I didn't think you'd have the balls to just go up to a guy and ask him to jump you."

"Oh, knock it off," Angela said. "It turned out okay in the end."

"I just bet it did," Bethany said. "So, are you going to see him again, or what?"

"We've worked out a sort of…arrangement." Angela could feel her face coloring. "We, er, *see* each other, but it's nothing serious."

Bethany paused again. "Oh, my God. Angela Snowe, the virgin extraordinaire, has herself a *fuckbuddy?*"

Angela winced. "Oh, and doesn't *that* sound attractive."

Bethany obviously recognized her friend's tone, and eased up. "Sorry for my bluntness, but you know me. It's just that a couple of months ago, I was scolding you to get out more, maybe consider dating. Now, I'm talking to a flagrant libertine, and I honestly couldn't be happier." Bethany's voice was warm. "I'm proud of you, Angela."

Angela relaxed. "Thanks, Bethany. You're right. I was too comfortable. I figured I had plenty of time— who doesn't think that way, right? Next thing I know, I'm facing breast cancer and then I wasn't, and it was the push I needed. I just jumped into everything I ever wanted to try. I'm barely even *home,* I'm taking so many classes. I probably won't stick with everything, but… Bethany, I feel like a new person."

"I've got a shoot in a little while, sweetie, so I'll have to cut this short. But I've got to get one more try in." Angela could hear the smile in Bethany's voice. "I don't suppose this 'new person' has a passport?"

Angela thought for a second, still drenched in her new euphoria. And then it struck her.

In six months, my arrangement with Josh will be over. She saw her arrangement with Josh as an experiment in personal growth. She didn't want a relationship, and neither did he. Instead, he was helping her test her wings. She wasn't going to hide in her books anymore, or avoid adventures. Between her classes, her friends and Josh, she would finally start living the life she'd secretly wanted.

What better way to culminate this six-month experiment by finally doing what she'd always dreamed of—traveling to Europe?

"You know, Bethany," she said slowly. "You're on. I'll go to Italy."

JOSH SAT AT HIS DESK, watching the blink of his voice mail light on his phone. He knew there were several urgent messages from his marketing team, about the fact that the agency had made a huge mistake, and their new product launch was going to be off schedule. In the meantime, Bill had pointed out that they were going over budget in marketing anyway for the second quarter, and something needed to be done. Adam's research and development team were starting to have problems with one of the natural emulsifiers they'd been toying with for the new carob-soy bar. All in all, the day was going to hell in a handbasket.

Despite all of this, he thought with a self-deprecating grin, the thing that seemed to be popping up most on his mind was Angela. He wasn't sure how that happened.

It was the type of relationship most men only dreamed of. If some guy had told Josh that he'd be lucky enough to get a beautiful, sexy, willing woman, no strings attached, for six months, Josh would have probably bought the man a beer.

Now that he'd been experiencing it for a month, he'd probably punch the same man out.

He sat at his desk, ready to tear his hair out. He'd been "seeing" Angela for over a month now. He couldn't even bring himself to call it dating—dating was far too personal. He wasn't even seeing her that often. Between her crazy schedule of classes and her friends, he was lucky to get Friday and Saturday night with her, so he'd only "seen" her about eight times or so. And it always seemed to be the same thing. She would drive to his house. They'd engage in some small talk—if he were lucky, he could convince her to go to dinner, or if he were really lucky, a movie. She would be serene and indulgent, and would listen to his stories without sharing too much about her personal life. Then they would go back to his place and go at it like rabbits. After they'd gone two or three rounds, she would calmly smile, kiss him tenderly, then get dressed and go home.

He shut the report on his desk with a snap, rubbing at his eyes. That sounded awful. But he couldn't think of how else to put it. Any other man might consider this the perfect arrangement—"friends with benefits," however you wanted to call it. But for whatever reason, he finally figured out it wasn't working for him. At all.

The more maddening thing was, it seemed to be working perfectly for her.

If she had grown annoying, that would be one thing. He'd had that happen before: date a girl, have a great weekend, then in another two or three weekends he wondered what the hell he'd ever seen in her. But not with Angela. Despite her concentration on the physical aspects of their relationship, she was still sweet, still funny, still intriguing. Nevertheless, she was still completely emotionally unavailable. It was crazy-making. He'd have called it quits, except...

Except he wanted her so goddamn badly. Not just her body, but her—her smile, her personality, the whole ball of wax.

His phone rang, and he answered it absently. "Josh Montgomery."

"Josh? Honey, how are you?"

"Hi, gorgeous," Josh said, a grin instantly lighting his face. "I was just going to call you."

"Don't try to play me, Josh. I'm your mother. Your charms are wasted," she said, laughing. "The real question is, when are you going to *see* me?"

Josh grabbed his Palm Pilot, flipping through his calendar. His weekends had *Angela* blocked out. "I don't think I can get away any time soon. Solar Bars is in a little bit of a crisis right now."

"What about...let's see, two months or so from now? I know you're busy with work and whatnot, but check your calendar."

"I don't know..." Josh scrolled through even more dates, stopping on an entry that had a flashing reminder note. "Whoops. Dad's birthday."

"Whoops, indeed." His mother chuckled at him. "Honestly. I figured you might have forgotten. How such a brilliant businessman can't keep his family's birthdays straight is beyond me. I think it's a male thing. I honestly do."

It was a familiar tirade. Josh just smiled at it. "What can I say. We're inconsiderate scum."

"So you'll come, then? We're having the whole family over for a party."

Josh thought about it. *That's one weekend away from Angela.* Despite his problems with the way their relationship was going, he valued every minute he got to spend with her. He didn't know how much time he was going to get before she decided she'd had enough. That was a whole other problem, frankly.

Still, this was his family. Nothing was more important than his family. "I'll be there," he said.

"Good. It'll mean so much to your father. You know he's not going to want to face that sugar-free carrot cake alone."

Josh's tone became more concerned. "How's he doing, anyway? With the diabetes?"

"Oh, you know your father," she said. "It's hard on him, but he'll never let on. Stubborn as a mule, charming as the devil. This is one problem he can't attack head-on. He can't talk his way out of it, or plan his way out of it. At least he can control it by diet—he's not doing the insulin route."

Josh nodded in agreement. "He'd hate that."

"He still feels like his body is betraying him, though. The man in control of everything can't even keep his own blood sugar in line. It's an indignity." She sighed. "But he's learning to live with it. Naturally, I'm helping."

"Naturally," Josh said, smiling again. "Where would he be if he didn't have you?"

"Probably in jail or the loony bin," his mother said firmly, causing him to laugh. "Well, somebody has to take care of the man before he runs himself into the ground. Good heavens. And now I'm going to have both my girls and my son, all under the same roof!"

She obviously sounded delighted by the prospect. "Don't know how you stand it, Mom."

"Oh, I don't know, either," his mother said, and he

could almost picture the gentle smile on her rounded face. "You four are pretty tough to take."

His mother lived for her husband and her kids, and he knew it. "I'll make it up to you, I swear."

"Try giving me some more grandkids," she suggested. "Then I'll have more people to focus my attention on instead of bothering my only son."

This, too, was familiar ground. "I just haven't met…" he started, then stopped, thinking. "Just out of curiosity, what would you say if I brought somebody home for Dad's birthday?"

His mother was quiet for a second. "I'd say, honey, go get the first aid kit, I think I've keeled over."

"Cute, Mom," Josh noted. "No, really. How would you feel?"

"You've met someone, then?"

Josh cleared his throat. "I didn't say that."

"What did I tell you before? I'm your mother. You can't con me." She sounded triumphant, and excited. "So, what's she like? What's her family like? And how did you meet her?"

He was *not* telling his mother how he met Angela. "Well, she's sort of hard to describe," he hedged. "She's very special."

"She's got to be, if you're considering bringing her here. Where is she from?"

Josh frowned. "I don't know, really."

His mother paused again. "You don't *know?*"

"Well, she used to live in New York."

"When?"

What difference did it make? But these were Mom-type questions. He should have been used to them by now. "Well, she lived in New York before she lived here,'' he said. ''She used to live in Manzanita. We went to high school together.''

''Was she one of your friends, then?''

''Um, no. I didn't really know her.''

''Was she born there?''

Josh rubbed his temples. ''It hasn't come up.''

''Josh, for someone who's about to bring a girl home to meet his parents, you sound like you're picking up a stranger from the bus station.''

Josh didn't have a ready argument for that one.

''Honestly. How long have you known the girl, anyway?'' she asked, her voice thick with suspicion.

''I don't know. Two months, I guess. Maybe three.'' Three sounded better, and he didn't like his mom's tone.

''Three months, and you don't know anything about her? What in the world have you been doing?'' She paused. ''Wait a minute. Don't answer that.''

''Wasn't planning to,'' he responded. He saw Jackie from marketing making an impatient motion at his doorway before disappearing down the hall. ''Listen, I've got to go into a meeting. Say hi to Dad for me, and tell the girls I'll be there for his party.''

''Sure will. I love you, son.''

''Love you, too, Mom.'' He hung up the phone.

Like you're picking up a stranger from the bus station.

He went into a meeting to see the new ad spots their agency had been working on. As the marketing people squabbled over the report he'd read over, he thought about his mother's words.

He didn't know anything about Angela, he realized— at least, nothing that mattered to Angela. It was just like their first ''date.'' He had been trying so hard to work out an ''arrangement'' with her, of romancing her and seducing her, he hadn't even considered getting to know her better. He had to admit, he had wanted to impress her and win her over—his consideration hadn't gone further than securing their six-month arrangement. He felt a little uneasy knot in his stomach that felt suspiciously like guilt.

He'd never had to worry about women opening up to him in the past. Women with marriage on their minds always wanted to become your best friend—they told you stories of their childhood, their entire relationship history, all in the hopes that you'd break down and do the same. Then, if you did drop any stories, they'd start trying to wear you down further, with china patterns and children's names next on the list.

Angela hadn't been like that. She wouldn't be like that—from what he knew about her, opening up was not something that came easily to her. And for the first time in his life, he might actually want her to try.

He would stop by her house tonight. Not for their usual seduction, or varied and exotic sex. Tonight, he was going to really delve into the mystery that was Angela Snowe. And maybe, just maybe, their "arrangement" would turn into something much more.

ANGELA FLOPPED ON her couch. She was tired. It had been an unusually crazy day at the library, with two very irate patrons, one missing book shipment, and an on-the-spot employee resignation. She glanced at the clock. Six-thirty. She was supposed to be over at Josh's at seven-thirty. Maybe she should cancel—she was a little too exhausted to be up for their usual weekend antics.

She stretched a little, rubbing at her neck. She hadn't thought she would ever say that. It certainly wasn't that she didn't enjoy the sex. If anything, every time she was with him made her seem to want him even more than before. But something wasn't quite right, and she couldn't put her finger on what it was.

Maybe I've just been too tired. Classes four nights a week, on top of her forty hours of work, and yoga bright and early Saturday mornings was beginning to wear her down.

The doorbell rang before she could pick up the phone. Frowning, she got to her feet, moaning lightly—her feet were killing her. She didn't want to deal with solicitors. At this point, somebody with a million-dollar check could be waiting at her front door, and she wouldn't care. She'd tell him to take a hike, then call tonight off.

She glanced through the peephole. To her surprise, she recognized the man's features in the fish-eye lens. She opened the door slowly. "Josh?"

He grinned, and she smelled the delicious aroma of take-out…Chinese, maybe? "Hi there," he said, and came in while she was still too surprised to do anything. "I thought you'd be tired. I brought movies and some Thai food."

She held the door for a minute, shifting her weight from one foot to another. She'd been hesitant to have him come to her house, preferring to have their arrangement take place at his house so she wasn't constantly reminded of it when she was home. But the food smelled delicious, and she'd been figuring on just having a sandwich or maybe oatmeal for dinner, anyway. And he looked so *comforting,* standing there with his hands full of packages. "You can put all that stuff down on the kitchen table," she finally said, closing the door and locking it.

He set up everything in a matter of minutes. "How was your day? You look exhausted."

She hadn't really talked about her job before. Part of

it was her habit of not sharing a lot...she didn't want to bore him, and besides, it didn't seem particularly applicable when it came to, well, what they *did* on weekends. That had been her choice, and his as well, she rationalized. Just because she'd had a rough day...

"Angela?" Josh walked up to where she was sitting, and put a broad, warm hand on her forehead. "Honey, you're not getting sick, are you?"

The gesture was so sweet. It reminded her of when her mother used to do the same thing, checking for fever. She smiled at him. "Just beat. Had a tough day at work." Words just seemed to tumble out of her, and before she knew it, she was relaying the scene in bits and pieces. "So there I am, standing between two old men who were in a shouting match about whether or not the *Kama Sutra* should be allowed in a public institution, one yelling that it's smut and the other all but singing the national anthem and quoting the constitution, and Linda just throws up her hands and says, 'That's it—I quit' and walks out. It was a wretched afternoon." She rubbed at her temples, then jumped slightly as she felt his hands on the back of her neck. She relaxed almost immediately as his fingers gently massaged her neck and shoulder blades. "Mmm. That feels great," she said, leaning back slightly. *It's just a back rub. That's still physical, not emotional, right?*

"Man. You really did have a day, huh?"

"It's better now," she said.

They ate the Thai food, and he cleared away the dishes. "Just relax on the couch," he had said, shuffling her back to her living room. So all she could do was sit there and relax while he handled everything. She was touched, but she was also sort of disconcerted. He seemed to be looking at everything. Maybe she was being paranoid.

"Wow," he said, as he was rinsing dishes before loading them in the dishwasher's wire racks. "Lots of recipes you've got around here."

She glanced around the kitchen, trying to see where he was looking. "I'm taking a cooking course," she explained, slightly embarrassed. "I might have mentioned it."

"You said you had classes all week," Josh said. "You've never said what they were in, exactly. So... Chinese cooking, huh?"

"Um, yes."

He read over one of the recipes she had posted to the refrigerator, and another few on a book rest. "Lots of chopped vegetables involved here, huh?"

She laughed. "Yeah, that's been the only drawback. After a long day of work, the last thing you want to do is chop up a bunch of carrots and greens and bok choy and things."

"This is pretty," he said, switching gears.

"What is?" She craned her neck to see what he was referring to, but the pinching pain there stopped her.

"This little stained glass thing in your window. It looks unusual."

She felt herself blushing. "Another class. I'm taking stained glass making. That's one of my early attempts," she said, surprised at how embarrassed she was. "It's not that good."

"You made this?" He dried off his hands, then came over to the couch, bringing the movies from the kitchen table. "It's really good. I like the way it looks sort of like a rose, but in a more modern style."

"There's this architect that made roses sort of similar

to that," she explained. "Charles Rennie Mackintosh. He's one of my favorites. My mom was really into architecture..." *That sounds so boring!* What was she doing, anyway? He was there for hot sex with her, not a lesson in the Arts and Crafts movement! She tried shifting gears. "Anyway. We're just staying in, right?" She started to halfheartedly stroke the back of his neck, wondering where she'd get the energy to seduce him. She was just getting comfortable, too.

He kissed her with a very gentle tenderness, then looked in her eyes. She was surprised to see the seriousness in his sapphire gaze. "I had a little bit of a rough day, too," he said. "Tough day at work, and a call from my mom. She's doing fine, asked about you."

Before Angela could feel one way or another about that remark, he continued.

"My dad's health could be better, though. He has adult onset diabetes—just got diagnosed with it a few months ago. It's been pretty hard on him."

"Oh, Josh," Angela said, rubbing his back sympathetically. "Is he going to be all right?"

"It's not that bad, really. There's a lot they can do if you catch it early enough, and I think that in this case, they've got a good jump on it," he said, and she could sense the tension running through him. He laughed, a sort of ironic chuckle. "Still, you'd have to know my dad. This is going to drive him nuts. He likes being in control of things—he's completely and utterly driven. He likes having things his way. The fact that his body is now calling the shots, and that he has to stop doing things that he likes, is really going to drive him up the wall. Retirement was bad enough."

Angela could sense the depth of love in his voice as he talked about his father, and it moved her. Hesitantly, she rested her head against his shoulder, hoping to communicate as much comfort as she could. He leaned back against the couch, cradling her with one arm, and stroked her back with one hand absently as he continued speaking.

"My dad was my coach in junior high, did I tell you that?" Angela shook her head no, and Josh kept talking. He obviously needed to talk, and his voice, his tone, was soothing. "He was the one who convinced me that I could do anything I wanted to, if I just planned it carefully enough, worked hard enough. I love my mom, but sometimes I really think my dad made me who I am." He paused for a minute, then asked, "What's your dad like?"

"I don't know," Angela said. "He left Mom when I was a couple of months old."

There was another pause, and then she felt him hug her, a comforting, wordless embrace. Finally, he said, "That must have been hard."

She didn't want his pity, so she found herself explaining something she very rarely spoke of. "No, it wasn't that bad. I mean, my mom…you'd have to know my mom. If your dad taught you that you could have anything you wanted, if you just tried hard enough—my mom taught me that you can survive anything. And she has. She always said she never held anything against my father, because she got me out of the deal." She smiled. "She also refused to take handouts from anyone. She taught me to be self-sufficient. I guess you could say my mom made me who I am."

"Your mom sounds pretty strong," Josh said, kissing her temple gently. "Where is she now?"

"She lives in Arizona. She says she likes the climate

better. I think she still works too hard, but she seems much happier than she used to be.''

"Why was she unhappy?"

Angela paused for a minute, then slowly said, "She didn't have an easy time of it, being a single mom. She worked two jobs for almost as long as I can remember. She still has a weekend job. I've tried to help her as much as possible, but she'll only accept so much." Somehow, just saying the words made the tension between her shoulders ease slightly. She barely registered the fact that she was sharing so much with someone, but somehow she couldn't seem to stop herself. "Anyway, she's going to school at nights now, too. She always loved school...really valued education. She was so proud when I got my scholarship to Vassar."

"You went to Vassar? On a scholarship?" She could hear the quick awareness in his voice. "That must be when you were in New York."

She grinned. He sounded like Columbo or something, solving some mystery. "Yes. I got a job in New York City for a few years, too. Corporate librarian."

"I didn't even know there were corporate librarians."

"My mom didn't, either. She wasn't thrilled with me becoming a library science major—she thought I wouldn't be able to support myself, and she didn't want to see me struggle like she did. Still, I made a good deal of money when I worked in the city, even with the high rents they have there. I was living with a bunch of people, so it wasn't as bad as it could have been." The problem was, they were mostly bankers or stockbrokers. They worked hard and partied harder. She'd barely seen them at all.

"So what made you move back here?"

Angela sighed, absently rubbing her cheek against his

chest. His shirt felt soft and fuzzy—flannel, she registered. "It's a great city, don't get me wrong. I just couldn't be happy there. I was working really long hours, doing research for all these departments. I wasn't dating, because I'd been so busy in school and was just so wary of relationships that I just never seemed to get out there and do it. Besides, by the time I was twenty-two or so, being a virgin seemed to make me something of a freak. Or worse...a *challenge*." She didn't mean that to come out as bitterly as it did, and quickly changed the subject. "Besides, I missed nature. I hated being on the street in the perpetual shadows that skyscrapers seem to make. I missed Manzanita. Every so often, I'd look it up on the Internet, see what was going on in local papers. When I found out they were building a bigger public library for Manzanita and the outlying towns, I just felt like it was time. I sent my résumé, they hired me, I moved back." She shook her head, remembering. "My mom thought I was crazy. She still does, I guess."

"My parents thought I was crazy when I moved Solar Bars up here, too," Josh said, and she felt that he truly understood. "There's just something about this place."

"Yeah." She nuzzled against him, then looked around the room. "So have I bored you yet?"

He nudged her, propping her up to look at him. She could see his eyes were intense. "Angela, nothing about you bores me."

She leaned toward him, closing her eyes, and kissed him. She expected the usual conflagration of passion that snapped between them, but there was something different this time. There was heat, definitely, but something else. She melted into him, pressing against him gently, feeling the warmth of their two bodies. He stroked her gently, kissing her with a tenderness that made her feel dizzy and yet completely…

Safe.

That was the word she was looking for. He made her feel comforted, and secure. *That* was why she'd said so much.

She pulled away, unsure of what to do with that latest discovery. He nodded. "I brought two movies," he said, his voice slightly uneven.

"Okay," she said. Whenever he rented movies, it was usually just a front—something they had running in the background while they made love. She started to unbutton her blouse, but to her surprise, he stopped her with a gentle hand.

"It's not that I don't want you. I always want you," he said, in a low voice. "But I'm tired, and a little beat up today. And I'd love it if you could just sit here, in my arms, and maybe talk to me."

She paused, a vague alarm bell going off in her head. *This isn't what we'd agreed to.* Still, she ignored it. It didn't break any of her rules. Besides, the alarm bell in her mind was nothing compared to the overwhelming tug on her heart.

6

A BREAK WAS ONE THING. One month with no sex was something else.

It was bright and early on a Saturday morning, and Angela was cooking with an energy she wouldn't have believed she possessed. She chopped green onions, relishing the way the cleaver minced through the vegetables with an efficient hiss.

She was feeling edgy. It made no sense—she'd gone for years without sex before. Of course, she hadn't actually known what she had been missing, not really. Now, it seemed like she couldn't breathe without thinking of the last time she'd pressed her body against Josh's. And if that wasn't insane, she didn't know what was.

Maybe he's tired of you.

She stopped for a moment, then picked up the chopped onions on the broad, flat cleaver blade and popped it into the hot oil of the wok. It sizzled and spat. Some splattered on the back of her hand, and she sucked it, absently.

She'd been having thoughts like that since this whole period of renewed celibacy had gone into effect…since she'd been too tired to do anything, that night he'd dropped by unannounced. Josh had said that he'd always want her, when he'd held her on the couch. Then, he'd been busy with work the next two weekends, and had to fly down to his parents' house this past weekend. She hadn't altered her class schedule, of course, but she doubted he would have been able to see her even if she had. So she was getting considerably anxious.

She stirred the onions, turning the heat down a fraction before they burned.

The thing was, if she really thought that he was tired of her, she would have shut tight like a clam—just written him off, and plowed even more thoroughly into her other pursuits. But he wouldn't just disappear. He made a point of calling her every night…and several of their phone calls had gotten her heated up to the point of driving over and seeing him, even if he was exhausted. Any man that could make her sweat just by whispering a few well-chosen words ought to be arrested…especially if he couldn't make good on his promises for three weeks.

She pushed red bell pepper and chopped broccoli into the wok, stirring briskly. Strangely, it wasn't that conversation that had pushed her off balance the most. She was getting to be pretty comfortable with that whole sex thing. It was the other calls that disconcerted her.

"Hi, beautiful," Josh had said one evening, after she'd gotten back late. "How was Chinese cooking class?"

"I'd be ready to take on the Iron Chef," she joked, rubbing at her sore shoulders, "if it weren't for all the chopping. How was your day?"

"Distribution problems in the southeast, big marketing snafu, and the joy of trade conventions for the next two weekends," he said with a sigh. "I'm so tired I almost slept in the office."

"Poor baby," she crooned, then sighed herself. "You didn't have to call, Josh."

"I wanted to call," he said, in a low voice. "I wanted to make sure you were all right. I like talking to you."

She liked talking to him, too…and seeing him for the brief ten-minute snatches he could steal from his workday. He'd taken to dropping by in the late morning or early afternoon, sneaking her out of work, hustling her behind a large weeping willow in a nearby park, and kissing her senseless—then taking her back to work. He'd whisper to her, stroke her cheek in that way she loved, and smile at her with a gentleness that always disarmed her…until she got back to her desk and realized how totally turned on she was with no satisfactory outlet. The last time she'd returned to the library like that, Ginny had taken one look at her and grinned.

"I brought a peanut butter sandwich," she quipped. "What did *you* have for lunch?"

He still wants me, doesn't he?

She tossed the vegetables, then poured them into a dish and quickly stir-fried some chicken strips. Of course he still wants me, she thought anxiously.

Still, it wouldn't hurt to have sex with him today, just to be sure.

It had been an idea that had been getting more and more prevalent in her mind as she grew more edgy. In the past three weeks, she'd read every book on seduction and sexual escapades she could get her hands on, from *The Art of Sexual Ecstasy* to the *Kama Sutra*. She was a woman with purpose.

That was what this whole arrangement was for, after all. She leaned back, sighing as she rubbed her forehead. Wasn't it?

The doorbell rang, and she jumped, startled.

She checked the peephole, then pulled the door open. "Josh?" He looked wonderful. She could see the way his chest muscles flexed in his T-shirt, and the way he wore his jeans...yum. "I wasn't expecting you until later." When she could at least get some decent clothes on and get into seduction mode!

"I wanted to surprise you." He sniffed as he walked through the door. "I wasn't really expecting you to be up yet, but I guess I shouldn't be surprised...what is that? That great thing I'm smelling?"

She glanced at the kitchen, embarrassed by her comfy oversized pajamas, her glasses and her frenetic cooking. "That is, um, chicken stir-fry...and some egg rolls. And a little beef and broccoli." Her timer dinged. "Oh. And some jasmine rice, too."

He glanced at her, then at his watch. "It's seven-thirty in the morning."

"Until they cancelled yoga class, I was getting up at five-thirty." She glared at him. "Besides, I had a little trouble sleeping."

"Fair enough." He grinned, and she felt certain he realized how much he'd contributed to her lack of rest. "Well, if you're done here, you might want to get changed."

She nodded. "Just give me a minute to shower."

She bolted to her bathroom. This was just the opportunity she was looking for. She didn't even want to ask him where he was taking her, because she knew they weren't going to get there. She was going to seduce the socks right off him. And the shirt and pants, she mentally added with a giggle.

She got clean, and then quickly put her contacts in and smoothed some makeup on. Then she toweled her hair dry, letting it fall in long, slightly wavy locks down her back.

She decided not to bother with anything else.

She went out to the living room with a smile. He was glancing at a picture on her desk. "Ready?" he asked, without turning to look at her.

"Am I ever," she whispered.

He turned around, and stopped, still as a statue. She could hear his breathing quicken. She smiled, opening her arms slightly in invitation, and waited.

It seemed to take a long, endless moment before he finally spoke. "I must say I approve of the outfit," he said, and it sounded like he was choking on something, "but it'll be a little cold where we're going."

She tried not to be disappointed, and walked closer to him, pressing her breasts against his chest. He backed away until he bumped into the desk, sitting on its surface. She leaned in, kissing him teasingly on the neck. "After all this, you still want to go outside?" she murmured, in her best husky voice.

He sighed, a long, drawn-out sound of suffering. "I know what you want, and believe me, I want it, too..."

"Then there's no more discussion," she said, moving in to kiss him. He dodged, pulling his face away. She felt disappointment stab her like an ice pick.

"Angela, honey, I really think you ought to put some clothes on."

She pulled back, staring into his eyes. They were like frozen cobalt, and his chin was set with determination.

"All right, Josh." She felt numb, and horribly embarrassed. She was blushing...she could see it creeping over her chest and felt it on her neck and face.

"Honey, I don't mean..."

"That's okay," she said, although it was no such thing. He didn't want her. Obviously. He couldn't want her. What was he still doing there?

"Put on a pair of jeans and a sweatshirt," he said.

She nodded as she fled to the bedroom. She didn't want to see him…didn't think she could handle the humiliation. What was she doing? How had she ever thought this sort of an arrangement could work?

You can handle anything, Angela, she could hear her mother's voice say in her head. She wasn't going to let him know how devastated she felt. It was just supposed to be a casual relationship. If he wanted to break it off with her after three months, no big deal.

She was cool and composed when she walked back out, wearing a T-shirt, sweat jacket and jeans with a hole in one knee. She pulled on her sneakers, and tugged her hair into its customary ponytail. "So where are we going?"

He smiled, and started to stroke her cheek. She forced herself not to pull away. "It's a surprise," he said.

She let him lead her to the car. A surprise. She'd already been surprised enough for one morning.

In the car, Josh glanced over at Angela. She'd let him blindfold her, something he'd meant to be playful. But sitting there in the passenger seat of his car, still angled blindly away from him at the window, she looked more like the victim of a kidnapping than a romantic getaway.

Maybe he should have slept with her. He certainly *wanted* to. No matter how many times he saw her, having her just casually present herself naked was something that hit him like a punch in the gut every single time. He'd gone hard in a matter of seconds. He'd never reacted to anyone as passionately or as quickly as he did to Angela.

That's why I've got to show her—there's more to this than sex. That she's got to see it as more than just sex.

He drove with grim purpose. He'd tried talking to her,

but she'd given coolly polite answers and then more silence. So he drove through the winding countryside, checking his map every so often. Finally, they got to his planned destination. His tires crunched on gravel as he pulled over to the side of the road.

"We're here," he said, with enthusiasm. She merely nodded. "I'll help you out of the car."

He ran around to the other side of the car, getting the door, helping her to her feet. Despite her outward aloofness, he saw her cock her head slightly. "Is that...water?" she asked slowly.

"Just a few more minutes. Wait right here." He ran to his trunk, popping the latch and grabbing a few items, then running off a little distance. "Just stay there!" he yelled, as he made his preparations. When they were done to his satisfaction, he ran back to her. She was frowning behind the blindfold, and yet smiling slightly. "Okay, walk with me."

The crunching of gravel gave way to the soft sounds of grass. "Where *are* we?" she asked, and he grinned.

"Just a second...here." He turned her, then took off her blindfold.

She blinked a second, trying to get accustomed to the sunlight, then glanced around. He felt gratified as her mouth dropped open. "This is...this is Cache Creek," she whispered. "I haven't been here since I was a little girl."

He had taken her to a grassy cliff, overlooking rapids. The water crashed and gurgled. "I know. I saw a picture of you and your mother here, on the wall by your desk. I figured if it made you smile then..." He stopped, noticing that tears were forming in her eyes. "Whoa. This wasn't the reaction I was hoping for."

She smiled even as a fat drop crawled down her

cheek. "I...I'd always meant to come back here, but never had the time or the energy." She did a quick twirl. "It's beautiful, Josh." She turned to him, her smile hitting his bloodstream like pure sugar. "Thank you." She kissed him, sweetly, then threw her arms around him for a hug.

He tugged her over to the picnic blanket he'd put out on the soft grass. She sat down, looking amazed. "What's all this?"

He pointed to the wicker basket he'd prepared. With fanfare, he opened it, "For today's lunch—or brunch, considering the time—we have the following—French rolls, herb cheese, fresh fruit..." He listed off each item as he presented it, Vanna White-style, onto the blanket. She smiled and applauded accordingly. He went through the contents, then finished with, "And for those of us with a sweet tooth no matter what hour of the day, I have cinnamon buns and chocolate cake."

She grinned. "I can't believe this. You went to a lot of effort." She glanced at the gift-wrapped box sitting next to the now empty basket. "And what is that?"

"That," he said, wiggling his eyebrows, "is for you."

She glanced at him shyly. "You didn't have to get me a present."

"I think that's the main reason I do...because you're never expecting it." He nudged it toward her. "Go on. Open it."

She looked at it for a second, then started to gingerly tug the wrapping off at the edges.

"Come on, come on. Tear into it," he said.

She stuck her tongue out at him. "Of all people, you should know about anticipation..." she said, then stopped cold when she got the wrapping off. "It's a food processor."

"That way you won't get all tired chopping vegetables." He waited for some reaction. She sat there, and to his alarm she started to get that weepy look. He quickly scooted next to her. "Don't cry. Please. I'll never get you a food processor again…"

"I don't…open up to people. Not easily, anyway." Her voice sounded choked. "I don't *mean* to close people out, it just sort of happens. No one has ever gone through this sort of effort to get to know me—especially without me telling them. You are the most perceptive man I've ever met," she whispered. "You know me better than I ever would have guessed. Sometimes, I think you know me better than I know myself. How do you do that?"

He grinned, chuckling softly. "Just lucky, I guess."

I COULD DIE a happy woman, Angela thought as Josh skillfully drove them back from Cache Creek to his house. They had picnicked all morning, then in the afternoon they had hiked and stared up at clouds, just like she had when she was a kid. It was one of the most perfect days she'd ever had in her life. The sun was setting, a gorgeous fiery orange-red bleeding into midnight blue.

It seemed as though she had a perpetual smile on her face. She hadn't thought of her seduction plan once since he'd taken her to the riverbank and began his elaborate surprise. She could only think of how wonderful he was—too wonderful for her to be afraid of how she was feeling. The sex, incredible as it was, paled in comparison to the amazing tenderness she now felt. She didn't want to even think too much about it, and wake up from this dreamlike experience. Instead she kept talking to him, holding his hand.

They got to his house, and he carried her food processor and the remnants of the picnic inside. She kicked her shoes off, twirling a little in his living room. "So how was San Diego?" she called to him in the kitchen, flopping on his couch with a grin. "Too busy working, or did you have time to play a little?"

He was putting their picnic lunch/dinner leftovers away in the fridge. She could hear him rummaging around. "It was great. I swam a little bit, after my last meeting. You'd love it. You'll have to come down with me one of these weekends," he called back.

She smiled with pleasure. "Sure." In her current frame of mind, anything seemed possible. "Josh, I want to thank you."

He emerged from the kitchen, looking at her with surprise. "Don't thank me yet. I'm not done."

She blinked. "There's *more?*"

He smiled, and for the first time since he'd picked her up that morning, it was a devilish smile. There was nothing sweet about it. A tender smile, maybe, but even that was a stretch.

She thought she'd put all thoughts of sex away in the face of the remarkable sweetness she'd been presented with, but apparently she was wrong. Her body started to throb just at the grin. She stood up. "So," she said, her voice husky. "What else did you have in mind?"

He motioned her forward, but instead of letting her come to him, he took her out onto his patio. She noticed that his pool, normally covered, was open. She looked at the pool, then over to him, not comprehending.

"You're the one who loves new experiences," he said, with a slow grin. "I thought, well, she's probably never tried this."

She rolled her eyes. "I've been swimming plenty of times, thanks."

"Not like this, I bet." His smile turned more devilish, and he pulled his shirt out of his waistband.

She thought hard, then slowly she got the gist of what he was saying, and crowed with laughter. "You don't honestly mean…"

"You got it." He took off his shirt, and her breath caught, just as it always did when she saw his well-muscled chest and back. She was apparently a torso person. "Well, get naked, woman. You can't skinny-dip like that."

She laughed even as she felt the blush cover her. A blush he'd soon be witnessing all over her body. So silly to be shy after all they'd done, she scolded herself. Nonetheless, her fingers faltered on the button of her jeans, and she tugged off her T-shirt with reluctance. *I'm getting naked, outdoors, in front of the world and everybody!*

Everybody being a couple of squirrels and possibly a raccoon, she realized. Still, it was just the idea of it.

She was still in her underwear when he shucked off his boxers and, with a war cry worthy of an Apache, plunged into the water. He yelped, then sighed. "Thankfully, I took the time to heat the pool," he said. "I don't do it that often, so you'd better be grateful, as well. Otherwise, I'd shrink so bad that swimming is *all* we'd be able to do."

She took off her bra, gasping as the cooling night air hit her breasts, making her nipples pucker. "Were you planning on doing more than that?" She dropped her panties and got into the water, carefully. Feeling the water on every part of her was a lot different than swimming with a bathing suit, she thought after a moment.

The heated water felt heavenly, and she found herself ducking in up to her chin. It was warmer than the air, and it covered her like a cozy, comforting haze. It caressed her, enhancing her desire. She moved her limbs through it lazily, smiling to herself.

He floated over to her, and she felt his hand move past her in the darkened water. He hadn't turned the pool light on, so she couldn't see. He touched her, his hand gliding over her body like a faint caress, a current against bare skin. Her nerves quivered, and she moved closer to where he was.

"So how do you like skinny-dipping?"

His face was barely outlined by the pale light from the house. She felt that same dreamlike surreal quality she felt when she'd agreed to see him in the club, that one night, months ago. She felt him move forward, and his body slid against hers in the water. Her nipples hardened almost painfully, and she felt a wave of tightness from her stomach to between her legs. She tried to slow down and savor the sensation, but only succeeded in breathing faster, more shallowly. "I like it a lot."

She felt his erection brush against her, and the tightness redoubled. "Angela, I have to ask you something."

She wound her arms around his neck, pressing kisses against him, floating high enough to cradle him between her thighs. "Right this minute?"

"Definitely," he said on a groan. "Did you go on the Pill?"

She paused. It was hard to concentrate, given the circumstances. "Well, yes."

"When?"

Inexplicably, she felt herself blushing again. There was something about these conversations that hardly lent themselves to romance and moonlight seduction. "Actually, I've been on it for a long time. That was why they found out about the lump. They were being extra careful when I went in for my refill prescription. I've been on since I was in high school. Health reasons, not…'' She cleared her throat, a sound that wound up ending with a gasp as he pushed against her entrance. ''Not, um, other reasons.''

''Yes, honey, I know.'' He cleared his throat, too. ''I took a blood test. I'm safe. I've got the results upstairs, if you want to see them.''

She blinked at that, now completely jarred out of the mood. ''You did?''

''I know you trust me. But there's trust…and then there's *trust*,'' he said seriously, before pressing a series of scorching kisses down her neck. ''Hell. I haven't trusted anybody like that for years.''

She warmed at the idea of him trusting her, but there was more going on here. He was starting to talk in some kind of code, and her body was starting to respond in that mindless, reckless way that always seemed to manifest when he held her like this, touched her like this. Whatever he was suggesting he trusted her enough to do, she wanted to do it, and as soon as possible. But this was obviously important, too important to just accept blindly. ''What are you saying?''

''If you're ready,'' he said, ''then there's something new we can try.''

She thought about what he was saying. He'd gotten a blood test…he wanted to make sure she was safe…

She suddenly realized what he was asking.

Did she trust him?

She pulled away from him, the water seeming cool now compared to the heat they'd produced. ''You mean, sex without a condom?'' she clarified.

"That's right. Just you and me."

"Oh. Well." She didn't know why she felt nervous suddenly, and she moved aimlessly in the water, not wanting to keep still. She felt his stare, even if she couldn't see his face clearly. "I'd never really thought about it."

"I have." His voice was dark and rich with promise.

She mulled it over. She was on the Pill—he'd gotten a blood test. It was sweet, actually, if she thought about it. He cared enough to ensure that she was safe, that she *felt* secure. As sweet as it was, it was also unnerving. This wasn't about a passionate, no-strings-attached, do-as-you-please affair. This was taking it to another level, as it were.

And he was asking her. It was all her decision.

It was a matter of trust. It was a matter of…vulnerability, she thought, nibbling at the corner of her lip.

Did she trust him?

She stopped her swimming, closed her eyes. And waited a minute, to see if any alarms would go off in her mind or body.

Yes, I trust him.

She swam over to where he was patiently waiting, making no move toward her. She moved her body fully against his, reveling in the groan he produced. "I want to try," she said softly, tucking her forehead against his neck for a moment, then lightly nibbling his shoulder. She couldn't remember feeling this excited, or in a way this scared, since she'd made love to him the first time. *This man. Always with this man.* "I…trust you."

He paused. "Thank you," he said, his voice reverent.

She braced herself for his entry, but to her surprise, he didn't take her immediately. He must have noticed, because he laughed.

"I'm glad we got that out of the way," he said, nuzzling her neck. "But you're not ready enough."

"I'm not?"

"Not by a long shot." He grinned. "Also, as much as I'd love to try it from a purely scientific standpoint, I also would hate cleaning the pool afterward."

She frowned at him, then splashed water. "Okay. That ruined my mood."

"Hardly." He splashed her, and the two of them got thoroughly wet before he cornered her against the hot tub section of the pool, kissing her as she panted, breathless from laughter. The kissing abruptly turned more serious, and her breathlessness had nothing to do with humor. The feel of his body, naked and slick in the heated water, stirred up her desire, even as the cool shock of the night air seemed to only heighten her senses. She felt his tongue rub against hers and she wrapped her legs around his waist. He growled, and she felt his hardness again, dipping inside her. She gasped, disengaging from his kiss and throwing her head back. "Oh, *Josh.*"

She felt him press a little further inside her before retreating…the rush of heated water only reminded her of her own wetness. She felt a keen stab of disappointment. "Come on." He pulled her up out of the water. The coolness of the air tortured her skin, making it feel more alive, more aware.

She barely paid attention to the fact that they were dripping water on the tiles of his kitchen floor, through his dining room, down the hallway to his bed. When they got there, she headed instead for his bathroom. By the time she'd grabbed two towels, he'd lit candles.

She patted herself dry, seeing his erection in the flickering light, his body sculpted and golden. She licked her

lips nervously. This was so different, even though she'd
had sex with him before. Why was this so different?

Because it was going to be without barriers. On several levels. It was more than just protection of her
body...it was the protection that she was giving up. This
was going beyond casual, anonymous sex. This was intimacy. This was trust.

For pity's sake, this was *blood tests*. Like marriage...

She refused to think of what that normally signified,
focusing instead on the feel of the cooling air on her
body, the tingling rush. She bit down on her nervousness
and sat down on the bed, almost instantly laughing.
"Satin sheets," she murmured around a chuckle.

"Silk," he corrected. "Silver silk. But I didn't kick
down and get the magic fingers." He reached for her as
she laughed, motioning for her to lie down on the bed.
"Thought I'd provide those myself."

She looked up at him, her heart in her throat. "They
feel nice."

His blue eyes were almost black in the flickering light
of the candles. "Close your eyes. Really feel them...and
me."

Taking a deep breath, she closed her eyes, and was
plunged into a world of sensation, much as she had been
when he'd blindfolded her to take her to the car. She
felt the cool slipperiness against her back even as she
felt the almost searing heat of his body cover hers for
an instant, his lips pushing against hers with a burning
intensity.

She moved sinuously along him, and he retreated,
much to her disappointment. Instead, he pressed kisses
on her neck, and his hands moved slowly down her body
in long, gliding strokes. He was testing her, running

strong fingers in loving patterns over her highly sensitized skin. She reached for him, but he evaded her grasp.

"You need to just enjoy this. Trust me," he said. "I know what I'm doing."

She sighed, not really being able to argue with him. Before, their sex had always been this consuming hunger...somewhere along the lines of high-school kids knowing that their parents would only be gone for an hour. There was plenty of experimentation, but there had also been a quick, ravaging impetuousness about it. This was grown-up sex, she thought wryly.

Then she gasped as his lips started down the curve of her stomach. "Oh, *Josh,*" she said, and felt the heated breath of his chuckling against her solar plexus as he trailed wet kisses even lower. *Correction. This is* virtuoso *sex.*

He started to nestle lower, into her curls, and she jerked up like a marionette. "I don't know about this," she said, feeling the moment start to slip. She was anxious. She wasn't sure if she could let him go through with something so...intimate? That wasn't the word, but somehow it was different than everything else they'd done.

"Shh. I didn't know when you'd be ready for this, but it's something I've wanted to do for a while. Just relax," he said, and she felt helpless to do anything but feel her body jerk spasmodically at every new touch. When his lips closed in on her sex, and his tongue slowly explored her, she could barely breathe. It was all she could do to stay on the bed. She clasped the sheets, feeling their slickness sliding beneath her fingers. Her hips moved against his mouth of their own accord as he stroked his tongue rhythmically against her, circling her clitoris with strong strokes. She was panting, all but crying against the flood of sensation that threatened to burn out her system.

"Josh," she moaned, sitting up. "Please. I need you inside me."

He looked up, his eyes dark and mysterious. "I'm not done with you yet," he said instead, nudging her down with one arm. And he wasn't. Just when she thought she couldn't possibly take the pressure, he retreated for a second, allowing her air and a second to get her bearings. But the pressure kept increasing, kept growing notch by agonizing notch. She was chanting for him, begging him to enter her.

Unexpectedly, he did, pushing a finger inside her slowly and stroking a spot she didn't realize she had. Her orgasm exploded through her, and she screamed incoherently. After a few moments, she came back to the reality of her still quivering body.

He kissed his way back up, stopping to nuzzle her breasts and finally her neck, beneath her left ear and jawline. "So how was that?"

She blinked, breathing heavily. "Wow. After three weeks of no sex, I think I almost passed out."

He laughed, bringing her still sweat-slicked body on top of him. In the golden light his hair shone with highlights, and his eyes reminded her of an alchemist. So did his wise, small smile. "It wasn't just the abstinence, and you know it."

She nuzzled her cheek against the hair on his chest. "Still," she said, slowly, as her breath recovered, "I can't help thinking you're showing how much more you obviously know about all this—sex and whatnot—than I do. You've probably done all sorts of things that I've only read about."

He shrugged beneath her. "I like that. I like knowing you're learning with me. From me."

She felt energized, empowered. "I've been doing a lot of reading." She sent him a mock frown as he chuckled. "Hey, I'm a librarian. That's what we do when left to our own devices…which, I might add, you've done in spades in the last month."

"So," he said, making those long stroking glides down her naked body again with his fingertips, "what did you read about while I was away?"

"Oh," she said, with a mysterious smile of her own. "This and that. Are you serious about wanting me to learn with you? Because there's something I want to try."

He smiled almost ferally. He tucked his hands back behind his head, obviously completely unafraid of her fledgling attempts. "By all means. Knowledge is power."

She rolled off him. "Great." With that, she leaned down and took his erection into her mouth.

"Whoa," he said, as the breath rushed out of him almost violently. Then he hissed as she gently suckled him. He took a few quick, panting breaths. "Angela… What did you *read* while I was gone?"

She didn't want to lose concentration—all the books said to be very careful, very gentle, let him lead. She stopped long enough to grin up at him. He tasted like the rest of his body, only more so, and he was like fire and satin beneath her lips. "Did I hurt you? Was that wrong?"

"Too right," he said ruefully, and brought her back up to him. He kissed her deeply. "I keep forgetting. I keep thinking I can keep control of this. But you make me…I…" He kissed her again, passion making him rough and tender in alternating moments. He switched their positions, moving on top of her. She felt his erection, almost larger somehow, pushing against her stomach without the usual cool cover of latex. She shivered. "I don't know why it's always this way with you, Angela. But it's always unbelievable."

He positioned himself lower as he kissed her harder. She could feel him move his hand down, as he guided himself against her, stroking against her. She felt her stomach tighten and her heart beat even faster as he stroked along her already slick entrance. He stopped, just the tip inside of her, poised.

He was breathing harshly, and she could see the sheen of sweat covering him. His bangs were pushed away from his forehead, and his eyes glowed. "Angela," he said, his shoulder muscles corded with tension.

She wasn't sure, she wasn't sure. She wanted him more than she'd ever wanted anything on earth, but she knew somehow inexplicably this was going to change things. "Wait," she murmured, holding her breath, pushing her fingers into his shoulders.

He'd already started to move forward, so the head of his penis was inside her. And that pushed her over...the feel of him, the weight of him. She took a deep breath. *It will be fine,* some part of herself convinced her. *Somehow, it will have to be.*

"Yes," she said, finally, looking deeply into his eyes and committing herself. "Now."

He let out a deep, quavering breath, and slowly filled her.

It was different. There was more give, somehow, she thought as she moved experimentally against him. He was less rigid and foreign. Instead, he seemed to melt against her, the smoothness of his body perfectly rubbing against hers without the friction she'd grown accustomed to. He glided into her slowly, pushing all the way in. She didn't feel even a moment of discomfort. She sighed instead, with bliss-tinged relief.

He retreated, and she could feel the motion of him everywhere, it seemed. His breathing spiked. "Oh, yes." He pushed forward, a little faster, his hips pistoning slightly.

She could feel the familiar pressure building. "Josh," she said, with a quaver of uncertainty at the almost primal sound of his pleasuring. She was getting excited by it, by the low growling sounds coming from his throat.

"Ah." He pushed against her, rubbing against her, and the feel of his naked skin against the sensitive skin at her entrance was a gentle caress. She could feel her own pulse hammering in her chest as she started to move her hips against his, arching up, twisting her legs around his. "Ah, baby, don't move like…oh, Angela," he moaned.

Not realizing what she should be stopping, she paused, her body angled up, and she slowly twisted to find a more comfortable position.

He lost his mind then, and took her with him. He groaned, *"Angela,"* against her neck, and suddenly he started to move, with a power and passion he'd never used before. She felt assailed by it, his body pounding against hers, her body responding with an instinct she didn't realize she possessed. She thought she'd been mindless with passion before. Now they were more than making love…she couldn't even describe it. She bit his shoulder, and he sucked on her neck, the pressure stoking her pleasure as she wrapped her legs against him and cried out his name.

She was hurtling toward climax as he pumped against

her, and she felt the familiar pressure building to a heat and intensity she had never felt before. Suddenly, her whole body clenched. *"Josh!"*

"Angela," he yelled, and he slammed into her. She felt her body grip his as he poured inside of her. He pushed against her twice more, then shuddered, another low sound emanating from his throat. *"Angela,"* he repeated, on a sigh. He rested his forehead against hers.

His sweat-soaked body slid slightly over hers. She could see his long lashes, resting against his sculpted cheeks. She held him, closing her own eyes.

Something had changed, profoundly. She held him close. She was ready for something to change.

7

ANGELA WOKE UP nestled against Josh. One arm cradled her head under her pillow, while the other gathered her close to him, pressing her back against his naked front. They were a perfect fit. His breathing whooshed gently in her ear. It was hot, close, but she didn't feel suffocated. She just felt immensely cared for.

Last night…last night!

She hated to admit it, but weeks of abstinence and longing had really made yesterday's lovemaking absolutely astounding. Of course, as Josh had pointed out, it was more than that. She would not have believed it until she had experienced it for herself.

It's morning. A part of her, the part that had been ringing little alarms since she walked into the Cable Car those months ago, was not impressed with her post-sex elation. *You've just broken your first rule to yourself.*

She sighed. That was true. And the way she was feeling this morning was hardly the detached, sex-is-fun attitude she'd been sporting for the past few months.

Still, maybe she'd been too hasty when she made those rules. She didn't have any practical experience, anyway…she'd thought that being in a relationship was about being trapped, giving up your sense of self in order to gain a sense of togetherness. She didn't feel as if she had given up anything. Yesterday, she felt like she'd gained something…a sense of safety, and comfort.

Not that she was even *in* a relationship. Josh had been kind, considerate and wonderful, but he certainly hadn't made any promises. Neither had she. She was just...*enjoying,* she told herself.

As she thought about it, she noticed her left hand, the one she usually tucked under her pillow, was holding Josh's. Their fingers were interlaced. She tried untangling them. As she moved slightly, Josh made a sound of protest, holding her a little more tightly to him. He didn't wake up.

She felt her chest radiate even more warmth than their two bodies generated together. She'd just be lying to herself, and not convincingly, if she didn't accept the fact that they'd crossed a threshold last night. She couldn't see them as simply very intense sexual playmates. There was more going on here.

So what if there was? She re-laced her fingers with Josh's and stroked his thumb with her index finger. He was a good friend, different than her girlfriends, and not just in their nontalking activities. He listened to her...and like yesterday, he really paid attention to what she wanted. She'd gotten a food processor, not a dozen long-stemmed red roses. He'd paid attention to what she did in *her* life, the life she maintained when she wasn't with him. She couldn't believe the lengths he had gone through, just in order to make her happy. And he'd made her happier than she could remember being in a very long time.

So she broke one of her rules. She still had two more. She was in no danger.

He stirred behind her, murmuring incoherently. "You awake?" she asked softly.

"Barely," he muttered heavily.

"I was thinking of taking a shower, maybe making

us a little breakfast," she said, pressing a kiss on his knuckles. "Care to join me?"

He paused. "Right this minute?"

She laughed. "Tell you what. Why don't I take a shower and make breakfast, and give you a little time to sleep in?"

"Mmm-hmm." He released her, turning over. He was snoring softly before she'd even thrown his shirt on. She grinned.

Today, she was going to relax and not sweat it. She had plenty of time to think this thing through—today, she was going to just *feel.* She showered, taking her time, letting him rest…*he'd need it,* she thought wickedly. She still had chapters of erotic exercises she'd mentally filed away for later use, and they had plenty of leftovers. He wasn't going *anywhere.*

He was groaning and making noises like he was going to get up when she left, and by the time she'd made it to the kitchen, he was in the shower. Apparently he liked taking even longer showers than she did, she noticed, since by the time he was done, she'd made two omelettes, toast and coffee. She heard him come out of the bedroom just as she was pouring orange juice.

"I made coffee, but there's OJ if you want it," she said, turning, then stopped abruptly, juice glass in hand.

He was fully dressed…jeans, T-shirt, socks and sneakers. She, on the other hand, was wearing one of his T-shirts as well, and nothing else. He also was hardly wearing what she'd call an elated expression. She stared at him, stupidly, holding the empty juice glass. "Or there's always breakfast to go," she murmured, looking down at his shoes.

"I totally forgot. Adam—I told you about Adam—is

having this barbecue at his house. I promised that I'd go help him play host.''

''Oh.''

''I figured it's going to probably take me all day,'' he said, in a low voice. ''So I'm pretty booked.'' He waited as she stared at him, not quite comprehending. ''So. What do you think you'll do today? This frees up your time.''

It wasn't that his tone was harsh, or even negative. It was just very, very obvious that she wasn't included in his plans.

She sat for a moment, silent. ''Um. Well…I suppose I could work on my next stained glass project.'' She nodded briskly. ''And I have tons of reading to catch up on, and I might go shopping with one of the girls.''

''Okay. I figured I'd leave pretty soon.''

He looked at her pointedly. She frowned. ''Can I finish my eggs?''

''Huh? Oh! Of course. Of course you can finish your eggs, don't be silly.'' He fidgeted for a moment, then turned. ''I ought to go, er, check my e-mail.''

''Don't you want any breakfast?''

''I'm not usually that hungry in the mornings,'' he said, not even turning as he walked down the hallway. He promptly disappeared into the small bedroom he'd converted into a home office. After a few minutes, she heard the computer keys clacking away.

She stared at her now-cold eggs. She pushed them around on the plate. Strangely, she knew how they felt. She'd gone from steaming hot, herself, to cold and clammy with shock.

Did I do something wrong?

She toyed with her toast for a minute, then got up and threw out what was left of her breakfast, putting the dishes in the dishwasher. Suddenly, she had completely lost her appetite.

How can he go from tender and hot to cool and withdrawn, just by going to sleep?

She poured herself a comforting cup of coffee. She was new to this sort of thing, but this still seemed wrong, somehow.

She needed to get out of here. Quickly.

He'd provided her with a wonderful day—one of the best days she'd ever had. And one of the best nights, she thought, feeling the light heat of a blush. What was she trying to do…expect him to spend *all* of his time with her? Of course not.

Hadn't she just been thinking about the fact that they *weren't* in a relationship? That wasn't how their arrangement worked. In fact, yesterday and last night probably represented the best their arrangement could offer. She had no right to get pouty and feel hurt simply because he'd forgotten he'd made other plans today.

She went back to his room, tugged on her jeans and sweatshirt, and put on her shoes. She stopped by his home office door, and knocked.

He looked up from his computer screen. "You needed something?"

"I'm tired, and I thought I'd go home now," she said, smiling at him with deliberate cheer. His hair was rumpled and damp from the shower, and he was just wearing his usual jeans and a T-shirt, but he looked fantastic. She felt her resolve start to crumble a little, until she noticed he had trouble staying focused on her eyes—like he didn't want to look at her too closely. She shrugged. "I was hoping you could give me a lift."

He looked a little contrite. "I'm sorry. I didn't mean to make you rush through breakfast."

"It's not a problem," she assured him. "Guess I wasn't that hungry anyway."

He just stared at her for a moment. She shifted her weight from foot to foot. "What?"

"Don't be like this."

When in doubt, pretend you don't understand. "Be like what? I'm just tired." She smiled at him, brightly. "I'll go get my food processor. You go get your keys."

"Josh! What are you doing here?" Adam said, giving him a man's half hug and promptly handing him a beer. Josh grabbed a newly cut lime off of the bar and promptly stuffed it in the neck of the beer bottle. "I thought you were going to be busy today. You know. Involved, romantic Angela-stuff."

"Had a little change of plans," Josh replied quickly, taking a swig of the beer. The sun was high and brutally intense, beating down on the backyard like a baseball bat. He rubbed his forehead with the back of his hand.

"Your change, or her change?" Adam smirked at him. "Don't tell me. Angela signed up for underwater basket weaving, and didn't tell you until last night, right?"

"No, as a matter of fact. I just decided I wanted to hang out, that's all." He ran a hand through his hair. He might jump in the pool, if it stayed this hot.

The pool. Memories of last night's pool adventure flashed in his mind, and he gritted his teeth to prevent anything else from popping up.

"Ooh. I'm sensing trouble in paradise," Adam said, herding Josh to a more private corner of the patio. The rest of the party guests were either carousing in the pool or talking in clusters around the backyard. "What happened? She's finally stopped the vanishing act... Has she gone the other way? Is she starting to get pushy—trying to get you to commit?''

"No, she's not trying to get me to commit." Josh hadn't told Adam too many of the details of what he'd agreed to with Angela. Not that he didn't trust his friend—it just didn't seem right, somehow. He shook his head, curtly. "She's not the type. She hasn't pressured me at all. She was more than happy to let me come here. Hell. She was smiling like a beauty pageant contestant when she left.''

Adam looked at him for a minute, then nodded sagely. "I see. And that's what's bothering you. That she didn't care.''

"She cared," Josh said, sighing. "I'm getting better at reading her. She doesn't let a lot show, but I knew." He knew how much last night had meant to her. The thing that had scared him was what yesterday and last night had suddenly meant to *him.* "But even knowing that she wanted to stay with me, I came here. I hadn't planned to—I meant to spend the rest of the day with her. I just…panicked.''

Adam let out a frustrated huff. "Okay, I give up. What's really going on here? Are you breaking up or getting hitched or what?" He grinned. "The suspense is killing me.''

"I don't know. We had this incredible day yesterday, and last night…I've never felt anything like it. And then I woke up this morning, and she was still there. No excuses about an early yoga meeting or class or whatever. She was there sleeping next to me, and then she woke up, like she was happy to be there. She even made me breakfast. And all of a sudden, I thought, *what am I doing?* I'd gotten her right where I wanted her, and now I didn't know where I was in the scheme of things. And

I told her I'd promised to come here. You should have seen the look on her face when I said it. I felt like such an ass, but I had to get out of there. I had to try to figure this thing out.'' Josh took a seat on one of the chairs Adam had put out, and Adam sat next to him. "I must be losing my mind. What am I worried about? I mean, I've got it made, right? She's perfect for me. She doesn't pressure me, doesn't expect a lot, doesn't want anything from me that I can't give. She's funny, and beautiful, and I love talking to her every night. Now, she's finally coming around, and then I pull a stupid move like this." He shook his head, bewildered. "What the hell *is* going on with me?"

"I'm sorry, Josh." Adam really did look it, too. "From what you're describing—you're in love, I think."

"Shut up, Adam."

"I'm not kidding." Adam looked at Josh, and for a second, his normally smarmy expression went sober and sympathetic. "You want her to be with you all the time. You're trying to stay in control of the situation, and she's running you ragged. You want her, twenty-four-seven. You want to know that she feels the same way. *That's* what's wrong with you."

Josh looked at him. He'd known Adam for years, since college. He'd never seen this aspect of his devilish, handsome, perpetually joking business partner. "How did you figure that out?"

"Been there." His eyes looked shadowed for a moment, then he shot Josh a trademark half grin. "Worst half hour of my life."

But Josh saw the pain in his friend's face. "What happened?"

"Not worth talking about, really. I fell in love when

I was young, and stupid. When she was done with me, I wound up drinking, picking fights with random strangers in bars, and generally being an idiot. More than usual, anyway.'' He grinned, without mirth. ''She did a good enough job on me that I never fell again.''

''Man.'' The raw pain in Adam's voice was unnerving. ''What'd she do to you?''

Adam paused for a second, looking away. He shrugged. ''She left.''

It was all he needed to say. They sat for a minute, drinking slowly, listening to the raucous laughter of the oblivious party crowd.

Adam spoke first. ''So now you know. What are you going to do about it?''

''I'm not sure. I've never felt like this before.'' Josh took a deep breath, scowling. ''How am I *supposed* to deal with this?''

''I know you. You're persistent.'' Adam let out a little half laugh. ''You'll make it work. If I had to put money on anybody making a relationship fly, it'd be you. You just need to get a grip on it mentally, that's all. Decide if it's really what you want. From what I've seen, love is never easy.'' He grew more serious. ''I mean it. Really, really make sure it's what you want.''

''I don't know. I think it's what I want. I mean, why wouldn't it be, right?'' He sighed. ''I don't know.''

''When you *do* know,'' Adam said, getting up, ''get out of here and find her, would ya? Telling me your conclusions isn't going to help you a damned bit.'' He gave him a pat on the shoulder and headed back toward the crowd.

Josh watched him walk away, wearing a broad, dashing smile, tickling some brunette in a miniscule bikini while winking at the redhead standing next to her. You never would have guessed that not one minute ago, he'd been bitterly revealing the love he'd lost. Suddenly, Adam's serial dating habits made perfect sense.

A lot more sense than his own perpetual bachelordom, now that Josh thought about it.

What are you afraid of?

Several hours later, after hanging out with the crowd, socializing, he still didn't have an answer. He was doing all the things he'd done as a "single" guy…joking with the guys, talking with various women. He missed this, he realized—relaxing, hanging out with friends. He'd been too intent on catching Angela to spend time on much else, other than work.

Maybe I'm afraid of losing this—my friends, my lifestyle.

But that didn't seem right, either. He still hung out with Adam, and thanks to Angela's aggressive schedule, he had plenty of time on his own. He'd stopped going to the bar because of the women—he'd started to come to that conclusion when he met Angela, that first night. So that wasn't it.

So what *was* it?

He was sipping a soda by the barbecue, deep in his own thoughts, when he felt a tap on his shoulder.

"What are you doing, sitting here all by yourself?"

Josh looked over. Shelly was standing there, in a red bathing suit that was very low cut or high cut, depending on which end you were observing. She filled it out very, very well. He noticed that she wore lipstick that exactly matched the shade of her bathing suit. *That's weird. Won't it wear off as soon as she gets wet?*

He thought, immediately, of Angela, dripping wet from last night. She'd worn very little makeup to begin with, but he'd thought that gleaming and damp, she was one of the most breathtaking things he'd ever seen.

"Sorry?" He realized Shelly had continued talking, and he hadn't paid any attention to her at all.

"I said, are you all right? You look under the weather."

He smiled. The least he could do was to be social. He motioned to a lounge chair next to him. "Just got a lot on my mind, that's all. How have you been? I didn't realize you'd be here."

"Adam invited me. Got my own place," she said, and the pride in her voice was apparent. "So things are looking up. Now I just want to get out a little more." She shot him a sideways look. "You know, you'd mentioned we should go out to lunch. Adam's already taken me out twice."

"He always did know a good thing when he saw it. Besides, we're business partners. It's just like having lunch with me."

She gave him a sweet smile. "Not really. But it's been nice to go out, anyway."

"You're too kind." He smiled again, genuinely glad to hear she was doing so much better. "We'll have to do that, then."

"When?" Her eyes studied him, almost hungrily.

"Um, soon," he said, a little disconcerted.

She smiled, and he wondered if maybe he'd imagined the whole thing. "Okay. No pressure."

No pressure. Man, wasn't that ironic? That's what he was looking for. The ability to figure out how he felt about Angela without any pressure. But whatever he felt about her, it was strong.

"Are you *sure* you're okay?" Shelly asked again. Now her eyes looked concerned.

He nodded, slowly. "Just sort of wrestling with a problem."

"You're at a party," she said, leaning a little closer to him. He noticed her cleavage being thrust at him, and leaned away a bit. "Relax. Enjoy."

"I'm working on it."

They talked for a good half hour. Josh gradually relaxed—it was nice, he thought. A nice change of pace.

Who are you kidding? You could be at home, in bed, with Angela.

It was still nice, granted. But it wasn't where he really wanted to be. What, did he need to be hit with a signpost or something?

Shelly laughed her musical little giggle, and he tried to think of a pleasant way to break off the conversation so he could go collect Angela, and spend the rest of the day with her. And the rest of the night, he thought with a wry smile.

"I will say this—working at the Travel Center has given me hope, as a single woman," she said, still smiling at him. "There was this one woman—pretty enough, but she looked so *rigid.* She was like one of those schoolmarms in the Old West. I mean, her shirt was buttoned up to *here.*"

She pointed to a spot right at the hollow of her throat. Josh could understand her amazement. He liked Shelly, but he doubted she had ever worn anything buttoned up to *there.*

"And her hair—she had great hair, too, nice long brown hair, but she had it pulled back in a ponytail so tight, it hurt me to look at it."

Suddenly, Josh started paying sharp attention to the conversation. He felt a little nervous twinge starting up in his stomach.

"So I'm expecting her to buy tickets back East or something, to visit some sick relative. Maybe even go to a quilting convention. But instead, she tells me she wants to book a six-week trip to Italy!" She laughed, not noticing that Josh didn't join her. "Stopping in Milan, then taking the train to Florence. She'll probably wind up all over the place. I know it sounds terribly stereotypical, but I swear, to look at her, you'd never guess that she was doing all this exciting stuff."

"You know what they say. Looks are deceiving," he said. "You don't mean Angela Snowe, do you?"

Her eyes widened. "You're kidding!" she said. "Do you know her?"

"A little bit," he said, casually. "She works at the Manzanita Public Library."

"A librarian!" she said, laughing. "Oh, that's perfect!"

He ground his teeth together for a minute, not wanting to scare her with the simmering burst of temper he was currently suppressing. "You know," he said, when he could trust that his voice would stay calm and casual sounding, "she mentioned she was going on a trip, but I don't remember when."

"Oh, not till October. It's cheaper in the off-season."

"When did she book that again?" He felt like throttling somebody. "Fairly recently, right?"

"About a month ago, I guess," she said, shrugging. "I can't believe—well, I guess I can believe you know her. Even with its Blockbuster and its Starbucks, Manzanita's still a small town at heart."

"Too small," he agreed, feeling the anger beating at his head like a hammer. "Would you excuse me? I suddenly remembered something I've got to take care of. Right now."

ANGELA SAT DOWN on her sofa with a flop. She took a deep breath as she surveyed her apartment. It was spotless, and though she was tired, she was feeling much, much better. Definitely better than she had when she'd walked into her apartment that morning.

She'd been letting her housework slip a little. Not that it had been keeping her up nights, or anything—she'd barely noticed it with the breakneck pace she'd been keeping lately, between classes, her friends and Josh. But she had the whole day to herself, so she attacked the dust bunnies and dishes with a vengeance as she put on her favorite Mighty Mighty Bosstones CD and cranked up the volume. She even mopped the kitchen floor and vacuumed. Now, as she contemplated her clean environment, she finally let her mind settle on the issue she'd been assiduously avoiding.

So what are you going to do about Josh?

She fought the sudden urge to do something else— deice her freezer, say, or maybe organize her sock drawer like she'd always meant to do. She was just dodging the issue at hand, and it was a biggie.

She thought she handled this morning very maturely, but that still hadn't stopped her from being upset the whole way home. She didn't know what was going on with her. She liked spending time with him—after a day like yesterday, who wouldn't?—but that didn't mean she wanted to be joined at the hip with him. Hadn't she always made a point of keeping her class schedule, even if the temptation had been to go to a Wednesday evening movie with him or maybe dinner one Thursday night? So why was she expecting him to drop everything he was doing, just to spend time with her?

Because I thought he'd want to, that's why.

It was always *her* running, before—*she* had something

to do, *she* didn't want to get close. If he suddenly understood her desire for them to have separate lives, and chose to assert it today, it certainly wasn't something she could blame him for. She ought to be thankful he'd finally understood her point.

She groaned. Not that it made her feel better, but logically, it made a lot of sense.

She got up, heading for the fridge. She had a ton of Chinese food, so naturally she had no interest in eating any of it. She wanted something comforting, something that had nothing to do with her classes. Ideally, something that had nothing to do with vegetables. After a second's thought, she went to her freezer and rooted through (*really need to deice this,* her mind made a last ditch effort) until she found what she was looking for—a hidden cache of tiramisu ice cream. She tore off the lid, took a spoonful, and sighed.

After making a fair dent in the container, she felt calmer, more herself. She'd gotten a lot done today without thinking once of Josh. She'd gotten herself under control. She was starting to worry about how much she was thinking of him, and caring about what he thought. She was getting way too *involved.* She needed to be more careful, anyway. If she kept going like this, she'd get so involved that she'd probably wind up canceling all of her classes—or getting so emotionally wound up that she'd sterilize her entire apartment, just because he didn't call.

I am independent. I am independent. I am independent.

She smiled. She'd just have a little bit more from the carton, and then maybe hunker down with the Bridget Jones sequel. She didn't need a man to make her feel validated, dammit. She had ice cream and a clean house!

She was just getting ready to read her book when there was a knock on the door. Her heart leapt for a brief instant, before she chastised herself for the reaction. It wasn't going to be him, she told herself. She never saw him on Sunday evenings…

She opened the door, and there he was. He was still wearing a T-shirt and jeans, and still looked just as good in them. His eyes were intensely flashing sapphires, and he had just the slightest growth of beard. He looked almost dangerous—and very, very hot.

"Josh!" Her heart, the traitor that it was, started dancing a mamba in her chest. She couldn't stop the smile from spreading widely across her face, either. *Will I always react this way when I haven't seen him for a couple of hours? It's ridiculous, but it just doesn't seem to go away.* "I wasn't expecting…"

"You're going to *Italy?*"

She blinked. "Um, yes. Well, I'm strongly considering it, anyway…"

"You bought the ticket." His voice was like magma, spilling out in scorching, destructive syllables. "You bought the goddamn ticket, and you didn't even tell me. I had to find out from your goddamn travel agent at Adam's party!"

She felt her heart still, and her body went cold. She stared at him for a moment.

"Let me get this straight," she said in a low voice, ice to his fire. "You spent the day at Adam's party, found out I've made travel arrangements to go to Italy without telling you, and then drove over here?"

He nodded. "After all the time we've spent together, I frankly expected more from you than this," he said sharply. "I thought I meant more to you than this."

Oh, this is rich. She just stared at him for a minute or two in disbelief.

"So?" he said finally, all but shaking with impatience.

"So, what?"

His eyes widened. "So, you want to explain this to me?"

It surprised a chuckle out of her, causing his scowl to deepen. "Okay," she said slowly. "I went to the Travel Center. When you go to a place like the Travel Center, you get a travel agent—that's somebody who helps you with things like airplane tickets and..."

"Very funny," he snapped. "When were you planning on telling me you were going to Italy?"

"I didn't know," she replied coolly. "What apparently my indiscreet but terribly helpful travel agent neglected to mention was that I deliberately paid more to get fully refundable tickets—in case something came up, and I couldn't go. For all I know, my friend Bethany is going to have to go on some photo shoot somewhere, and I'll be out of a place to stay unless I book a hotel. You see my dilemma?"

He paused, and she saw his eyes lose some of their fire. "Oh. I didn't realize..."

"No, apparently you didn't." And yet he'd come over here, full of ire, ready to rip at her for doing something without his approval. After leaving her to her own devices all day—and after giving her such a wonderful time the day before.

She looked at him, as if she'd never seen him before. "I didn't know you'd be like this," she said after a moment.

"I'm sorry I jumped to conclusions," he said, in that surly voice that basically meant *I'm sorry you're upset by it,* not *I'm sorry I did that.* "But you might have told me you were planning on going on a trip anyway, especially one that serious."

"I think maybe you should leave."

Looking away, he said, "I really am sorry, Angela..."

"I know," she replied, and she felt withdrawn, like an observer more than a participant. "I still think you should leave."

He grimaced. "You don't need to freeze me out. I said I was sorry. We need to talk about this."

That stung. She kept her reserve up, like a bulletproof window. "I don't see that we need to talk about anything. I planned a trip. You found out, and got upset about it. You came over here and made it clear you were upset. I realized I didn't like being yelled at for doing what I'm well within my rights to do. End of story."

He glared at her. "I hate that you can be so calm about all of this. I was worried that you were leaving, dammit. I was angry that you'd keep something like this from me, after all we've been through. Can't you understand that?"

He was worried that I hadn't cleared it with him. He was angry enough to yell at me, like he had a right to.

"I still think you should leave."

"I just might leave for good one of these days, Angela. Has that ever occurred to you?"

She crossed the room and opened the door. "It's occurred to me ever since we made this arrangement, Josh."

He stared at her, with a look of frustrated fury, then stormed out. She shut the door quietly behind him.

At least I've still got ice cream, right?

She was still smiling over the idea as tears ran down her cheeks.

8

JOSH SAT BROODING at his desk at work. He hadn't seen Angela in two weeks. By any previous relationship standard he might have held that it was over. Done. Finite. Just chalk it up as a bad bet, and move on.

He stared at the phone. Of course, after two weeks, he'd usually gotten several tearful phone calls and at least one nasty message, all of which he usually dodged. He'd been careful to screen his calls all this week. It was a good thing he had, too—he was saved from an annoying sales pitch from someone asking him to change his long distance service, and two offers for new credit cards. The only thing it hadn't prevented him from being forced to deal with was Angela—and that was only because she'd given him nothing *to* deal with. She hadn't called, written, or stopped by.

She'd just vanished.

Josh fiddled with some papers. Several marathons wanted Solar Bars to sponsor them. *I don't know anything about these guys,* he thought as he looked over a brochure. *Maybe I could go down to the library…*

He stopped himself before he could continue with such an obvious and juvenile ploy. He had the Internet. He didn't have to deliberately do reconnaissance in enemy territory, just to see how Angela was faring during this cold war.

He ought to be thankful she was making it easy on

him. He ought to be thankful he'd found out about the
Italy trip in the first place. Otherwise, he might have
actually convinced himself that he was in love with her.
And that would have...

Come on, Josh. Who are you trying to kid?

He *was* in love with her. He didn't know how precisely that had happened, but just banging his head
against a wall trying to convince himself that he wasn't
was just as stupid as being in love and not doing anything about it. He'd made a grave tactical error by storm-
ing over to Angela's house and blasting her.

But it still hurt. It hurt that she hadn't told him she
was planning to leave for six weeks. He still wondered
when she would have let him know. A week or two
before? The night before? Or would she have let him
know that morning, because she needed a ride to the
airport?

*No, she wouldn't even ask for a ride. She'd have ar-
ranged for a shuttle or taxi—she's too self-sufficient to
need a ride from her not-quite-boyfriend.*

He was getting so bitter. This whole love thing sort
of sucked—he suddenly realized why he hadn't fallen
for it previously.

He couldn't go on like this, and he wasn't going to
just roll over and let her shut him out of her life because
he'd made a mistake. The last thing he should have done
was get angry with her for wanting to go to Italy. He
needed to *persuade* her...treat her so well, seduce her
so thoroughly, that she wouldn't even *want* to leave his
side for six weeks.

*Yeah. You've been doing a banner job of making her
crazy to stay with you thus far.*

He frowned. Dammit. He was losing his grip on this.

He needed to call in the big guns. He picked up his phone and hit the speed-dial.

"Hello?" a deep bass voice said.

"Hi, Dad."

"Josh! Haven't heard from you in a while. How's the company holding up?"

"Great. Manzanita has been a good move for us," he said. "So how's retirement treating you?"

"I get to play golf every day, I'm jogging on the beach, and I've been getting to those home improvements you know I've always talked about..."

Josh grinned. "Driving you nuts, huh?"

"Right out of my gourd." His father sighed deeply, and Josh laughed. "If your mother reminds me about my carbs and cholesterol levels one more time, I swear, I am going to Fat Charlie's Hamburger Hut and having a full-pound burger with a side of spicy fries."

"How's the diet thing going?"

His father grew quiet for a second. "It's a pain in the ass, that's for sure. And as much as I complain, if it weren't for your mother, I'd have gone really nuts by now. She's the only person who could have possibly kept me sane in all this." His voice went low. "Don't tell her I said so, though. Woman's got enough power over me."

Josh grinned. His father was the firm patriarch in the family, and everybody knew it.

"But, hey, enough about me. What's going on with you?"

"I've got this...problem."

He could picture his father hunkering down in his chair, a broad, crafty smile on his face. "What are we dealing with here? Marketing? Distribution? Your accountant giving you fits? Political trouble?"

"Let's call it more of a strategy issue," Josh said. Figures. His father hadn't been retired a year, and he got positively gleeful just thinking about somebody else's business problems and solutions.

"Now you're talking! So…strategy. What's your objective?"

What *was* his objective? He wanted Angela to see him again. He wanted her to love him. He wanted—well, he'd start with love. Getting her to love him was trouble enough to start with. "Let's say I've got a problematic potential partner. Likes me well enough, but not the way I do things."

"Well, that's managerial style, son," his father said, taking on a lecturing tone. He was obviously reveling in being useful again. "You've probably been pushing your way through things. You've got to learn when to be a hard-ass, and when to *finesse*."

Josh laughed.

"What? You think I don't know about finesse, is that it?"

"I think you could finesse your way out of Hell with an order for twenty air conditioners," Josh said. "It's just…this isn't really business, Dad."

"It isn't? Then what the heck are we talking about?"

Josh took a deep breath. "There's this woman…"

"Oh, *man*…" His father chuffed impatiently. "I thought this was gonna be *fun*."

"Hey, it's no picnic for me, either," Josh said. "I'm the one who's got to deal with her."

"Don't tell me—you've broken up with some girl who's not happy about the news, huh?" His father sighed. "Glad I'm not single anymore, and that's the damned truth. Well, it'll be nice to see you again. Come on down to the house, take a break for a few days, give her a cooling off period..."

"No, it's not like that. I didn't break up with this one."

"Really?" His father sounded a little more curious. "Huh. So when you say you've got to deal with her, what does that mean?"

"It means she's driving me crazy," Josh said, running a hand over his face. "She's got me so I don't know if I'm thinking straight from one day to the next. She's really affectionate one minute, then I blink, and it seems like she vanishes. She's beautiful, and brilliant, and..." He growled. *"And she pisses me off."*

His father was silent for a moment, then Josh heard the sounds of muffled laughter over the phone line.

"I don't find this funny," Josh complained.

"Sorry, son. It's just a case of what goes around, comes around." His laughter died down to chuckles. "Your mother drove me to fits by our third date. It was around then that I realized I'd either marry her or kill her, and I knew if I killed her I'd miss her too much."

"She's not even talking to me."

"Well, what are you doing talking to me, then? Go find the woman." His father let out a whistle. "How long has it been since your fight, then?"

"Two weeks."

"Two weeks!" his father yelped. "Good God, son. If she's anything like your mother, you'd better find her, and fast. I made the mistake of having a fight with your mother and waiting for her to come to her senses. By the time I lost my cool and went looking for her, she had not one but *three* guys, all prowling around her like wolves. Proposed to her that night," his father said nostalgically. "Among other things."

"T.M.I., Dad," Josh protested. "Too much information."

"Oh, grow up. So...when do I get to meet her?"

It wasn't a question. It was a command, and they both knew it. "I guess it depends on whether or not I can get her to talk to me."

"You're my son. If anybody could convince her, it'd be you."

Josh smiled, embarrassed. "Thanks, Dad."

"How does next weekend sound, then?" His father sounded cheerful. "I could always use another birthday gift, you know."

"All right then," Josh agreed. "Next weekend."

So what do you do when you're by yourself again?

Angela pushed her silverware around on the red-and-white checkered tablecloth, as she sat at DaVinci's Italian restaurant with the girls from work. She felt like one big ache, all over. She missed Josh—the way he stroked her cheek, the way he moved against her, pressing her into his mattress. The way his voice sounded, calling her late at night.

"Angela, are you all right?"

Angela shook her head quickly, as if shaking the thoughts out. "Sorry. What?"

"You've been staring off into the distance for the past two weeks," Tanya remarked. "You've gone out with us more, but you're basically playing with whatever you order, then bringing it home. I was just wondering if everything was okay."

"Looks like you've got man troubles," Ginny remarked, and the other two women nodded in commiseration.

Angela blinked. "Is it that obvious?"

"Listen, if I haven't heard a man-related blues story, I've lived through it." Ginny sighed, her gray eyes kind. "So what happened with you and Josh?"

Angela had come a long way in opening up to people, but so far, she'd just left a mildly weepy e-mail for Bethany and drank some very lightly rum-laden hot cocoa. She dived into her classes with a vengeance, but it wasn't quite helping. "There is no 'me and Josh.'"

The women murmured in unison. "I'm sorry, Angela," Ginny said. "But everybody knows about Josh Montgomery. He's just that kind of guy. He's incredible, but he never stays that long."

"How do you know that?" Tanya asked before Angela could.

Ginny shrugged. "He dated Jill, then Sabrina. They both said he was great in..." She stopped abruptly, obviously noticing Angela's shocked expression. "Whoops. Sorry. I just meant they both said he hadn't stayed around that long." She looked embarrassed, and bit her lip.

Angela still stared at her, silent.

"That didn't help much, did it?"

Angela shook her head.

"Well, at least you had a good time before he left," Ginny said with a resolute nod. "If he's got another reputation, it's for knowing how to treat women right."

Angela finally found her voice. "Why do you guys all think *he* left *me?*"

They all stopped and stared at her. "He didn't?"

"Oh, God," May said, her eyes wide. "He wasn't *cheating* on you, was he?"

"Of course he wasn't!" Angela said. "He just...he was..." She sighed, frustrated. "He was mad that I booked a trip without him."

They still stared. "You booked a trip without him?" Ginny finally said.

"Yes. Six weeks or so. I'm still going through the vacation paperwork on that one." Angela let out a huff of frustration. "But he had no right to make those kinds of demands."

Tanya's mouth dropped open. "You're kidding me, right?"

Angela frowned at her. "No, I'm not." They didn't understand how bad this was. It was a minor step, but it was an indication of things to come. Why weren't they getting it? "He even yelled at me," she said.

"Well, he shouldn't yell at you, but you were fighting, weren't you? And he was angry. I can see why. When you're in a relationship, you usually make plans like a six-week vacation *together,* you know?" Ginny smiled. "If I had a rich, good-looking boyfriend like Josh Montgomery, I'd probably invite him to come with me…"

"The thing is, he *isn't* my boyfriend—he *wasn't* my boyfriend. We were just seeing each other. We both agreed to just see each other."

Now the women stared at her with skepticism. "If you say so," Tanya said, then looked at her sympathetically. "Although I'll say this. If you were just 'seeing each other,' why do you look like your best friend just died now that he's gone?"

Angela couldn't come up with a response for that one. She took a sip of her iced tea instead.

Ginny smiled. "I wish I were young enough to still stick to principles," she said, with a slight shake of her head. "Now, I figure, if you can keep a guy happy and in your bed, you're ahead of the game."

"Amen, sister," Tanya said, clinking her soda with Ginny's.

"You don't really think that, do you?" Angela said, looking first at one of them, then the other. Even May was nodding her head sadly.

"It's just that you have to *compromise,*" May explained. "That's how Harry and I stay married. I love Harry with all my heart. Of course, I wouldn't complain if *he'd* pick the kids up once in a while—or do the dishes—or figure out what the vacuum cleaner is for besides taking up room in the closet..."

"Or what else the bed's for besides sleeping in," Ginny crowed, causing Tanya to laugh.

May smiled. "No, I remind him on that one," she replied, causing new peals of laughter. Even Angela giggled, feeling better. "And, he doesn't give me a hard time when I tell him 'listen, you are watching little Harry and Emily tonight. I am going out dancing, and that's that.' You've just got to pick one thing that you absolutely can't give on." She tapped on the tabletop for emphasis. "That's your line in the sand. I figure, Harry can forget certain points of women's liberation, as long as he remembers that every month, I get one night out with the girls."

"Well, is this Friday one of those nights? Because I'm going out," Angela said, with a firm nod. "I'm sick of feeling like this. I want to have some *fun.*"

"Whoo-hoo! I'll drink to that!" Ginny said, raising her soda in salute.

"You go, girl!" Tanya called.

"Ladies." Josh's smooth baritone emerged right behind her ear, and Angela jumped. She twisted in her chair quickly enough to hear her neck crack. "You looked like you were having so much fun, I couldn't resist coming over."

"Josh?" Angela couldn't believe it. "What are you doing here?"

"What I should have done two weeks ago," he said in a low voice. "Could I talk with you for a minute?"

She looked over at her lunch companions. They were a comedic mixture of hope and protectiveness. May was smiling at Josh encouragingly, while Ginny was frowning at him. Tanya looked like she didn't know which way she wanted to go with it.

"Sure." Angela stood up, carefully folding her napkin to get time to compose herself. She followed him outside the restaurant. "What...what did you want?"

"I..." He looked at her, his cobalt eyes deep and... unsure? "I...er, how have you been?"

She blinked at him. "Fine," she lied.

"That's good. That's...oh, hell with it." He leaned forward, and before she knew what he was doing he was pressing her against a wall and kissing her fervently. Her body started reacting before her mind could catch up. His tongue was in her mouth, and she welcomed it, gripping at his shoulders, bringing him closer. She moaned gently in the back of her throat.

She didn't know how long that went on...not long enough, though. He pulled back, leaning his forehead against hers, his breathing rough. "Let's try that again," he rasped. "So, how have you been?"

"Miserable," she whispered, unevenly. "You?"

"Worse."

She smiled. She couldn't help it. "That's nice."

He grinned, stroking her cheek. She curved into his hand like a cat, all but purring. "I missed the hell out of you."

She didn't want to admit any more than she had. "How did you find me?"

"One of the benefits of small-town living," Josh said, pointing at her car, parked in the restaurant's lot. "I wanted to apologize."

She pushed him away so she could look into his eyes. "Really?"

"Why do you sound so surprised?" He grinned at her, and despite his humor, his eyes seemed serious. He wasn't just trying to charm her. At least, she didn't think so. "I shouldn't have yelled at you. You made those plans ages ago. It just caught me by surprise." The look of frustration on his face comforted her. Probably because she knew how he felt. "To be honest, you always catch me by surprise. I haven't known quite what to do with you."

"I know the feeling," she murmured.

He grinned, that sexy, lightning grin that made his eyes glow. "So do you forgive me?"

"Well..." *Was she being too harsh on him?* The lunchtime conversation was still too fresh. "I suppose. But don't let it happen again," she added. As May said, she needed a line in the sand.

"You don't sound certain," he said, nuzzling her neck and making her heart race. "Why don't I make it up to you?"

"Wha...what did you have in mind?" He was starting to stroke her sides, nothing overtly sexual, but her eyes were still beginning to cross.

"Let me take you away this weekend. To San Diego. I told you I should take you there one of these days."

"San Diego?"

"I know this great hotel that has a view of the ocean, and the weather's great this time of year."

"Um..." It sounded lovely. And romantic. And she'd really, really missed him. "I guess so."

"I'll pick you up tomorrow, and we'll go to the air-port from your place," he said. Then his eyes smoldered. "I don't suppose you could bag class tonight, and stay with me?"

She shook her head. "Dance class. I always go to dance class. It's my favorite." But it was *tempting*.

He sighed, and she saw the frustration again. "I un-derstand," he said, then kissed her, slowly this time, until her head was swimming and she wanted to drag him to his car and ravage him. "I don't usually get this carried away in public," he said, apologetically. "I'll see you tomorrow."

"Okay," she said. Her lips felt swollen, and she was on the razor's edge of canceling her dance class—and taking the rest of the day off, for that matter.

"Angela," he added, before she could disappear back into the restaurant. "This means a lot to me. *You* mean a lot to me."

She smiled, then walked back into the restaurant on unsteady legs. When she sat down her co-workers stared at her like hawks.

"So? What happened?" Tanya asked eagerly.

Ginny laughed. "I think it's obvious what happened, from the look of her. Guess you're back together, huh?"

"Um, yes," Angela said, still dazed. "I think."

May sent her an indulgent smile. "Guess dancing is out this Friday, huh?"

Dancing! "Oh, no. I'm sorry! I completely forgot. I'm supposed to go with him to San Diego this weekend—I forgot about going out with you guys."

Ginny waved her statement away with one hand. "No problem. All women get their priorities whacked when a man enters the picture."

Tanya quirked an eyebrow at her. "Like you haven't?"

"Honey, if I could get Russell Crowe to enter my picture, I don't think anybody would ever see me again!"

They laughed, but Angela felt sobered, abruptly losing the high she'd felt from Josh's kisses. "I promise, no matter what, I'll go out with you guys next weekend," Angela said.

"It's okay," Tanya said. "Really. We understand."

"Well, I promise anyway." Angela said, and let them move on to other topics of conversation. Still, she could feel it…feel the slow sink of realization.

You've just broken your second rule to yourself.

She still had one more. She wasn't about to tell him anything—no professions of love. He had enough power over her as it was.

ANGELA SAT ON A big beige couch in Josh's parents' house, a small, blond-haired cherub sitting contentedly on her lap with her tiny fist in her mouth. She was drooling on it, Angela noticed. Glancing around to see if anyone else noticed this development, she saw Josh sitting with his parents at the kitchen table, talking animatedly. His youngest sister, Isabel, was standing by the grand piano in the living room with her boyfriend Drake. They were talking to some cousin or aunt, Angela couldn't remember which. Meanwhile, she heard clomping around upstairs.

"Robby, you get back here this instant!"

A small, naked and apparently wet boy made a dash down the stairs, paused just long enough to grin at everyone's laughing applause, then dash back up the stairs.

Robby's mother—Josh's middle sister, Harriet—was

also the mother of the blonde on her lap. She appraised
the child nervously. The drooling showed no signs of
abating. She took another glance around, then surrepti-
tiously wiped off the little girl's mouth and fist with the
corner of her frilly little dress. "There we go," Angela
said, relieved.

The child grinned toothlessly at her.

And this is how Josh decides to "make it up" to me.

San Diego was just as beautiful and peaceful as Josh
had described it. She'd felt very serene—right up to the
point when he pulled into his parents' crowded driveway.

"I have to do this," he said, his eyes trying to be
apologetic and failing. "It's my father's birthday."

Angela's first reaction had been shock. She was expecting this to be a romantic idyll, filled with lots of sun,
sand, and make-up sex that she'd kept reading about in
romance novels. Instead, she got blindsided by the stress
of meeting not just his parents, but his entire family, with
no prior notice. He just grinned at her as he ushered her
into the house and started introducing her around. She
managed as best she could with the absolute crush of
people swarming around her.

For a perceptive man, he'd been really dense about
this. She reluctantly admitted that they had an arrangement, something that far outstripped the "arrangement"
that they'd originally agreed on. But she was still getting
used to those emotions. For someone on shaky ground,
definition-wise, introducing somebody to their entire
family in one fell swoop was hardly the way to ease her
into this new status.

She thought of her khaki slacks, her white tank top.
Not that everyone else was dressed formally, but she
certainly would have dressed up if she'd realized she

was meeting his family. Darn it! Didn't he know women liked to be warned about these sorts of things?

If this is how he's going to apologize for last Sunday, how exactly is he planning to "make up" for this weekend?

The child tugged on her shirt, and she looked down.

"Ga," the baby said, solemnly. Then she yanked at the end of Angela's ponytail and grinned, a beatific baby smile.

Angela couldn't help it. She smiled back.

"She likes you."

Angela looked up to see Josh's parents. Josh stood safely a little behind him. She narrowed her eyes at him. He just grinned.

"Our Mindy doesn't take to many people," Josh's father said, sitting on her left side. "You must be pretty special."

To her dismay, Josh's mother sat on her right side. She was now neatly boxed in. Josh leaned against the opposite wall, his arms crossed in front of him, still grinning.

"So, Angela," his mother said. "I'm afraid Josh hasn't told us too much about you. How long have you two been seeing each other?"

Let the Inquisition commence. Angela suppressed a groan, and tried to look placid as the child settled herself in comfortably and started to doze. "Um…not very long at all, actually," she said, hoping that she could pass herself off as someone more casual, just a friend.

"Three months," Josh supplied.

She frowned at him.

"That's not too long," his mother mused, looking Angela over speculatively. "So, dear. How did you two meet?"

Josh's eyes gleamed with mischievous amusement. "Well, that's a funny story, actually...."

Angela panicked. "We met in the library," she improvised, interrupting him. "He was looking for something, and I helped him, er, find it."

His father grinned at him. They could have been brothers. "Really? What were you looking for?"

Angela glanced at Josh, her eyes imploring him for help.

"Actually, I was looking for her," he said, causing his father to laugh. "As you can see, she was very helpful."

His mother clucked her tongue, rolling her eyes a little. "Men," she said, with obvious disapproval.

"I couldn't agree with you more," Angela said, frowning at Josh.

"Uh-oh," his father said. "They're starting to take sides."

"Honestly," his mother said, scooping up the sleeping child off of Angela's lap. "Having you two around is like living in *Saturday Night Live*." She carried the girl upstairs, where the naked Robby had disappeared.

Angela wound up having a good time. She discussed books with Isabel, who had some interest in writing— "more as a hobby than a career," she'd said modestly— and then she'd talked about the kids with their proud mother, Harriet. She'd talked about Manzanita with his father, and about her old house with his mother. They had an early dinner, around a large table. It warmed her heart, to see such a big, strangely *normal* family enjoying time together.

They got to the birthday portion of the get-together. After frowning and bellyaching over his sugar-free carrot cake, Josh's father looked gleeful at the amount of presents he'd received, then tore into them like a five-year-old. New golf clubs were oohed and aahed over. After a while, they went back to separate, happy conversations. The kids were put to bed.

"Looks like it's time for us to go," Josh said. Although she'd been having a pleasant time, she still felt relieved.

She went over to Josh's father. "It was nice to meet you, Mr. Montgomery." She felt her face redden slightly. "I'm sorry I didn't bring a birthday gift. This was sort of a surprise for me." She glared at Josh, who just smiled back at her.

"Robert, please." He hugged her. "And don't worry about it—I think you were my gift." He winked at her, and he reminded her of Josh. She smiled back.

"I STILL CAN'T BELIEVE you did that."

Josh smiled at Angela's comment. He probably shouldn't have, but he couldn't resist. She kept trying to pigeonhole them in their "arrangement," or under the tepid guise of "friends," and it annoyed him. He wasn't going to hide her from his parents, when he wanted very badly for them to meet her—a woman who was finally worth bringing home. He wasn't about to pretend he was feeling anything other than what he was feeling, not in front of anyone. Including her.

He'd been charming Angela for the rest of the evening, taking her to the beach, for a romantic moonlight stroll, and even out dancing. She'd slowly thawed, but it had taken a measure of his considerable charm.

He wanted her charmed for what he had to tell her tonight.

The hotel was perfect: a view of the moonlight glinting off the crests of waves hitting the beach, a soft breeze, the murmuring crash of surf in the distance. He couldn't have planned it better.

I love you, Angela. I love you, Angela.

He'd never said the words before, so he supposed that was a good enough reason to be nervous. He wasn't nervous about her reaction to it. Okay, maybe a little nervous about that, but how badly could she take it?

I hate you, get away from me, I could never love you, his mind instantly supplied. *Or, even worse, "You're kidding, right?"*

All right. He was really, really nervous about her reaction.

She was wearing one of the small terry robes the hotel supplied, and her hair was loose and blowing slightly in the breeze. He walked up behind her, kissing her gently on the back of her neck and at the sweet indentation just behind her ear. She shivered and leaned back against him obligingly.

"I suppose I could forgive you for this afternoon," she said slowly, turning. She caressed his light cotton boxers, and he instantly went hard beneath her curious fingertips. "If you make it worth my while."

Don't get distracted, he scolded himself. "Maybe we should talk first."

She stroked his erection, coaxing it from its hiding place with satiny fingers. He groaned. "Talk." She chuckled, a low, sexy sound. "Is that what they're calling it these days?"

She started pushing insistent kisses against his bare chest, and he could feel the plush material of her robe against his hardness. This woman could drive him crazy with just a few touches. It was like putting a fire out with gasoline. "Angela, where are we going with all this?" he asked, moving back a little.

His mistake was that, in the hotel room, moving back from the balcony meant moving toward the bed. She drew the curtains and moved in on him. Her brown eyes glowed with golden highlights, and her full lips curved in invitation, with just a hint of humor. "You're the one who taught me where we could go with all of this." She nudged him, and he felt the bed hit the back of his knees. She was stroking him, pulling at the tie of the robe, letting it fall open to reveal the smooth nude body, hidden just inside. His breathing was getting quicker.

"I don't mean the sex," he said, trying hard to focus. "To start, I really missed you this week..."

To his surprise, she pushed him, hard. He tried to keep his balance, but his foot slipped on the smooth comforter and he fell on to the bed with a lurch. "I missed you, too," she said, with a hungry stare.

"I want to see you more often," he said, trying to lead into his statement, not drop it on her.

"You see me every weekend," she said reasonably, pressing moist little kisses down his stomach. His muscles clenched, and he gritted his teeth. "And stained glass will be ending soon...I guess maybe I could see you Wednesdays, too."

He was breathing hard now, and his blood roared through his head. He grimaced as she grabbed the waistband of his boxers and gently eased them down his legs, then shed her robe. "Angela, I really wanted to...ah..." he said, as she started breathing on him, inching lower, her full lips a mere smile away from his erection.

"Shh," she said, her finger caressing both him and her lips in a gesture of silence. "We don't need to talk about this right now..."

He wanted to protest, but her lips covered him, and it was all he could do to keep breathing. He let out an explosive groan, his hips rising off the bed as she moved up and down on him slowly, gently tracing him with her tongue. Her mahogany hair slid like a silk cloud over his stomach and his thighs. He gasped and moaned, his hands bunching in fists before finally skimming over her hair, inadvertently moving her farther down on him. *"Angela,"* he breathed, feeling his body shiver.

She pulled off of him with a long, slow caress, brushing him ever so slightly with the edge of her teeth and causing him to let out a startled "unh" of pleasure. She smiled at him, mischievously. "My turn."

This was his chance—his last chance at rational thought. "Angela, I love…having you around me," he said, chickening out as she started to kiss her way up his body, stroking him as she did so. "I love spending time with you. I love waking up with you." He took a deep breath. "Angela, I love…"

She covered his mouth with her own, before he could finish the sentence. Her kiss was insistent, passionate, making his blood sing and his head swim. She positioned herself over him, and before he realized what was going on, she drove him into her in one smooth motion.

"Josh," she moaned, and he felt enveloped by her moist, tight heat. "Talk later. Make love to me."

He felt her body clench around him. He couldn't help it. His body took over.

He felt her rock against him, and he held her hips, pushing gently down on her thighs, pulling her toward him. She closed her eyes, looking almost meditative as she threw her head back. Her breathing was shallow, and she moved slowly, her hips circling him. She wasn't rushing toward an end result—she was enjoying the feel of his body inside of hers, and the sensation was driving him mad.

She leaned down and kissed him, the new angle making him groan as she ground against him. He pushed up, hard, making her gasp in return. Her eyes flew open, and she smiled in sexual challenge. She pressed against him harder, drawing him deeper inside her, clenching him tighter, and he felt his control starting to slip. Her tempo increased. She was riding him, breathing in short, mewling little gasps, her breasts glistening lightly with sweat. She bit at her lower lip.

"Oh," she breathed, moving against him furiously. "Oh, oh…"

"Come on," he said, pushing into her.

She let out a cry and he felt her convulsing around him, gripping him like a fist. He pulled her hard against him, burying himself in her, feeling his own release coursing through him in powerful waves.

She collapsed alongside him, and he could still feel their mutual pleasure in their muted quivering of muscles, in the cooling of skin.

After several minutes, he rolled her over. Her eyes were closed, and she had a half smile. He grinned, seeing it. "Guess you showed me," he said, pulling the covers up over their naked bodies.

She didn't say anything.

He took a deep breath. Time to bite the bullet. "Angela, I think we'd better have that talk now."

He waited for a response. He only heard the soft sound of even, measured breathing. After a few moments, he realized that was all he was going to get.

"Angela?"

Still nothing. Finally, he nudged her. She turned over with an incoherent mumble, and curved into the pillow.

She was sound asleep.

He turned off the light, and lay there, awake, with

both hands behind his head. Wasn't it supposed to be the man who climaxed, then fell fast asleep? And wasn't it the woman who fumed because, yet again, they'd avoided any talk of love?

Hell. When did I get to be the woman in this relationship?

9

"So, how was San Diego? You haven't mentioned a word about your getaway all week." Tanya turned slightly from the driver's seat of her car. "Everything okay?"

Angela had finally begun to relax, but Tanya's casual question caused all the tension she'd been holding at bay to come back with a pinch between her shoulders. "San Diego was nice," she replied, staring out the car window but not seeing past the glass. It was nine o'clock on Friday night, and the sky was pitch-black. "How was the club?"

"The usual…loud music, May dancing her head off," Tanya said. Angela looked over and for a second caught Tanya's light-eyed gaze as she studied Angela in her rearview mirror. "Too bad you couldn't have been there, but then, I know how it is. Everything *is* okay between you and Josh, right?" Her voice was hesitant, as if she didn't want to pry, but couldn't help herself.

Angela squirmed against her seat belt. "We're fine."

Ginny, who was riding in the front passenger seat, craned her neck around to look at Angela. "Hmm. Nice? Fine?" She shook her head. "Bland adjectives spell trouble. Spill."

Angela peered into the darkness. "Where are we going, anyway? I'm starving."

Ginny glanced at Tanya. "Evasion. Definite sign. This is going to take drastic measures."

"Angela will tell us when she feels like it," Tanya said, and Angela let out a little sigh of relief. "We're going to dinner at this new restaurant. Well, not exactly new...remember that old diner out by the highway? Well, with the town growing and all these new businesses coming in, somebody bought it and is making it into this retro restaurant. They say the food's really good, too. Nouveau Californian." Tanya chuckled. "We'll see how long it lasts."

Angela fell quiet as Tanya and Ginny talked about the different restaurants in the outlying towns, trying to ignore the chill she suddenly felt. She knew that diner, all right.

Sweetie, I'm going to work, her mother would say all those years ago. Her mother would come back from her day job, maybe have a hasty dinner with Angela and her grandmother, then kiss her good-night at seven before working a shift at The Roadstop, as the diner was then known. Her mother would sometimes bring home food, which was good on the occasions when Gram had fallen ill and there was less money for food than usual. By the time her mother was the age Angela was now, she had been divorced for eight years, with a young daughter and her mother to take care of by herself.

Angela could still picture her mother, her faded mint green uniform so stiffly pressed it hurt to look at it, and her hair pulled back in a severe ponytail that had ended at the nape of her neck.

Angela reached up, feeling her own ponytail absently. *I'm not my mother.*

"Hello? You awake back there?" Ginny asked, ignoring Tanya's huff of impatience. "You know, sometimes it's better to get these things off of your chest…"

"I'm scared that I'm in love with Josh."

They sat there for a moment, and in the silence that followed, Angela could have bit her tongue off. The words had just jumped out. *I shouldn't have said anything. What will they think? What was I thinking?*

Before she could somehow try to retract the statement, Ginny nodded, her eyes sympathetic as she turned to her. "I thought it might be something like that. Angela, it's better for you to talk about it, believe me."

Tanya nodded, too. "Tell me…are you scared of being in love, or scared of being in love with Josh?"

Angela paused. "I hadn't thought of it that way. Both, I guess." She took a deep breath. She hadn't talked like this with anybody since Bethany, and just opening up was hard. "I thought when we started that it would just be casual. I don't exactly have a history of relationships."

"So it's really more love in general, then?"

Angela sighed. "Well, sort of. Josh is…complicated."

Ginny turned, looking over the back of her seat. "Is it his whole past track record with women?"

Angela frowned. "Not really his reputation," Angela said, thinking about it even as she said it. She hadn't even really thought about it since they'd started their arrangement. She'd never seen him "in action," as it were. "If anything, it's how much he's involved with me. I feel like he's calling all the shots…that I don't have time to really process what's going on. I keep thinking I don't want to do something, and the next thing I know, he's charming me or persuading me, or whatever, and suddenly I'm doing exactly that."

Strangely, they seemed to understand. "You've been together, what, eight months?" Ginny asked.

Angela thought about it. "More like four or five." Had it really been only that long? She was starting to lose track—she could barely remember what her life was like without him.

"Really? It seemed like longer."

"You're a couple that really seems to work well together," Tanya interjected. "He really cares about you. He might try to persuade or charm you, but that's probably just an aspect of his personality. He's not bossing you around or bullying you to get you to do what he wants, does he?"

"Of course not." As if she'd stand for that!

"And what you wind up doing…is it something that, in your gut, you really feel morally wrong about? Are you doing things you feel you shouldn't be doing?"

Angela paused. "I…no. Probably not really."

Tanya nodded again. "It's the love thing in general. You feel like he's edging you toward love, and you don't know if you're ready for it or not."

"I guess that's it." Angela closed her eyes, remembering Saturday—how panicked she'd felt when he'd started talking about love, and wondering what exactly he was going to confess to her. "No, that's not it. It's that he won't let me have time to come to these decisions my own way. I might love him," she said, and even the words made her palms sweat. "But I need to do things on my own time. He keeps rushing me. How can I make the right decision if he keeps rushing me?"

"Have you explained that to him?" Ginny said.

"I'm working on it."

"Well, I will say this," Tanya said gently. "I've seen how he looks at you, even when you're not looking at him. I've seen how he talks to you, and how he acts around you. The man obviously loves and cares about you deeply. He might be a little heavy-handed, and a little impatient, and the guy has enough charm to light up a city block. But he's also under *your* power a little. And that's what this is all about, isn't it? How much of yourself you're giving up?''

''I don't know,'' Angela said. ''It doesn't feel like it. It feels like I'm fighting to stay myself.''

''It's a Friday night, and instead of being with him, your *boyfriend,* you're out with us,'' Tanya pointed out. ''How did he feel about that? He didn't charm you out of that, did he?''

Angela thought about it. ''No. He didn't sound thrilled, obviously. It doesn't help that I've been dodging him all week, either.'' Angela smiled a little, finally. ''I think he's re-grouping.''

''The fact of the matter is, he loves you. And despite your skittishness, I think you love him. You might need to think about it, but to pretend you can just ignore what you're feeling until you're comfortable with it…it's not fair. It's not fair to him, and more importantly, it's not fair to you. You deserve to be happy.''

You deserve to be happy.

She'd been worried about her independence, about her dreams and how she would have to curtail them in an effort to stay in a relationship with him. He'd only been kind to her, and compassionate, and loving. Sure, he'd had that one bobble when he'd bolted from her arms, then yelled at her for making plans without him. They were just…fights. They happened from time to time. She'd just be deluding herself if she waited for a relationship that never had any problems, ever.

She liked—no, she *loved* the time she spent with this

man. She loved waking up with him, loved listening to him talk about work or his family or basically anything. She loved the way he thought about her.

I love Josh.

She waited for the fear to hit, and it did, but it was a muted echo compared to what she was used to feeling.

She smiled, and for a moment, she wished she hadn't promised that she would go out with the girls tonight. That thought didn't instill fear, either. Maybe she would call him later. Or stop by his house.

Maybe I'll just hijack a car and go over there as soon as we stop....

She grinned at herself. Her legendary reserve was crumbling with every passing mile.

They pulled up at the diner. It was packed with cars, and teenagers hung out in the parking lot, laughing and talking around the backs of trucks and jeeps. Several of them had lettermen jackets from Manzanita High. There were also more urban and upscale cars. Solar Bars' yuppie infusion, as it were. She remembered the semis that had regularly been parked up and down the street, and laughed to herself.

They made it to the doors, and Angela was practically tapping her toes with impatience. *I love Josh, I love Josh.* It was bouncing through her head, bubbling through her bloodstream. Of course she loved Josh. It seemed so obvious now. She had the chance of a lifetime—not repeating her mother's mistake, but learning from it. She had let her mother's experience cow her for far too long. He had never been anything but kind to her—insistent, yes, but kind. Why was she letting old ghosts stop her? It seemed silly, now, to be afraid.

They pushed their way through the crowd at the front of the diner, getting to a harried-looking waitress who informed them that the wait would be half an hour. Angela groaned, and Ginny laughed. "Hungry?"

"Yes." She was hungry to see Josh.

Tanya gave her a piercing look, and then smiled. "Go call him while we're waiting. I'll drop you off at his place right after we eat dinner."

Angela stared at her, then hugged her as she laughed. "I've been there," Tanya said, hugging back. "Go on. Call."

"I hope I feel that way some day," Ginny said as Angela started to leave. "And, Tanya, I hope you smack me for it."

Angela felt ridiculous, but happy. She pushed her way through the crowd. She knew the layout of this building by heart, and despite the changes to the decor, she still knew where everything was. She walked past tables, almost blindly, heading for the corridor that led to the rest rooms and the pay phones.

"Oh, Josh, you haven't changed a bit!"

Angela stopped for a second, and almost tripped as the person behind her bumped into her. Grumbling, the man walked around as Angela saw who was talking and stared, frozen.

There, in one red vinyl-covered booth, was Josh—smiling his winning grin at her talkative travel agent, Shelly.

Angela felt nothing for a second. The scene made no sense to her. That was Josh, she realized, her Josh, the one she was in love with. The fact that he was with another woman didn't quite compute. *I'll have to leave him a message, then,* she thought inanely.

Then she realized what was going on.

He's out to dinner. With another woman.

She had never felt jealousy before in her life, and the

force of it hit her like a brick. Her heart felt like it had imploded. She saw him smiling at Shelly, the same smile she was so used to receiving. He was talking animatedly.

She bet that Shelly would have never abandoned Josh to go out to dinner with her friends. Which could possibly explain why Josh was now out sharing a meal with Shelly, rather than waiting patiently by the phone for Angela.

She couldn't blame him, she supposed. She couldn't believe how much it hurt.

She didn't know how long she'd been standing there, or how long she would have stood there, until she saw his gaze move for a second from Shelly, meeting her surprised gaze, then move back to Shelly. His mouth dropped open and his eyes darted back to her.

She didn't have to think about what she was going to do. Her body started moving—she whirled on her heel and bolted.

"Angela!"

She plowed through the crowd, shouldering her way through the throngs of people. She just had to make it to the door, to get some fresh air. She needed time to *think*. She didn't want his explanations when she couldn't even make sense herself of what she was feeling.

She moved through the rest of the group like a needle through cloth, strategically hitting each empty pocket and threading toward the door. She could hear some angry voices behind her, sounds of a scuffle. She didn't dare turn around. The diner was large enough, but now it seemed like a football field. She was practically sprinting.

"Angela?" Tanya began, looking at her with shock. "What's wro…"

Angela bolted past Tanya and Ginny, pushing the doors open and almost tripping down the steps. The night air was a blessedly cool relief, but she didn't stop running. She'd made it past the crowd of teenagers, off to the dark side of the road. She didn't want to see him. She just wanted to go home and think. Was that so much to ask...to not be overwhelmed by a man who had an explanation for everything?

A car's headlights flashed in front of her, and for a moment, Angela was blinded. She stopped then, colliding with the brush at the side of the road. She breathed in gulping, gasping breaths, holding the stitch in her side. To her consternation, the car slowed, then stopped. She tried to get ready to run again, but heard May's voice in the darkness. "Angela? Is that you?"

Suddenly, Angela had the energy. She bolted over to the car, ignoring May's look of shock as she tugged at the passenger side of the car. May unlocked the door, and Angela all but flung herself inside. "Please take me home."

"What's wrong?"

Angela thought she could see people coming out of the diner. "Just please!"

May stomped on the gas, and with a screech her station wagon tore across the pavement. Within seconds, the diner was disappearing rapidly in the side view mirror. Angela breathed a sigh of relief, and pressed her forehead against the cool window. She started shaking.

"I was just going to join you guys for dinner before going home for a night alone with my husband," May said. "You're scaring me. What happened?"

Angela thought about it. "I figured out I'm in love with Josh," Angela said, with a little tremor in her voice. "Things pretty much went to hell from there."

JOSH WATCHED AS THE station wagon drove off with Angela inside.

This was not how I'd planned this night to work out.

"Mister, I'm talking to you." The young man Josh had inadvertently knocked over in his haste to get to Angela had followed him outside. He was a high-school linebacker, and surrounded by his football buddies. He obviously had something to prove, and Josh was in no mood.

"Josh, what happened?" Josh recognized Angela's two co-workers, who were eyeing the scene in amazement, and were looking for Angela amongst the crowd.

"You think you can just run into people that way?" the kid continued. "Not around here, pal. I don't care who you work for."

The owner of the diner stepped out, looking horrified. He straightened his plum-colored suit nervously. "If there's going to be trouble," he warned in a prim tone, "I'm calling the police."

"Where's Angela?" Angela's friend asked. He was pretty sure her name was Ginny.

"I said, you can't just…"

"I'm sorry," Josh said to the kid. "I didn't mean to. I was in a hurry to catch my girlfriend. She just drove off in a station wagon," Josh said, to answer Ginny's question.

"Where did she go?" Angela's other friend asked, her voice filled with concern.

"I don't know," Josh said.

The kid half shoved him. "That's not good enough," he said, glancing at his friends. "You want to get your girlfriend…"

"Josh," a new voice drawled from the doorway, "is everything okay?"

Everyone turned to check out this new development. Shelly stood framed in the doorway. She was wearing a very short skirt, a very low-cut blouse, and a small smile.

Josh sighed in exasperation. "Does everything *look* okay?"

Angela's two friends looked at her, then at him, and he could almost hear the mental click. "It's not what you think," he said immediately.

"You *bastard*," Ginny said. The other one couldn't say anything, apparently.

"Please…" he said, trying to stop them, but they were beyond hearing him. They stormed off toward their car, and drove off.

He turned to the linebacker, feeling poisonous. "So? You want to do something about all this?"

The kid, who had seen the whole exchange, grinned sheepishly and shook his head. "Nope. Looks like you've got your hands full." He glanced at Shelly, and to Josh's disgust, he elbowed him. "Way to go, man. Two chicks!"

Josh shook his head. Still, it got him out of trying to reason and or battle with this kid, so he supposed he ought to count his blessings. It might be the only thing that went his way tonight.

He looked at the owner. "Could you do me a favor, and put our meal on my account? You've got me down for a few corporate parties this year. I'm Josh Montgomery, with Solar Bars, Inc."

The man blinked. "Oh. Of course, Mr. Montgomery."

Josh looked at Shelly, who still wore that small smile. "I think I'm going to have to take you home, Shelly."

Shelly frowned a little, then shrugged. "Okay. I understand."

They got into his car, and were halfway to her house,

and he hadn't said a word since. He was too intent on
the road, on getting rid of Shelly so he could drive over
to Angela's and explain the circumstances before she
blew it out of proportion. He knew her. She'd been
dodging him for a week, and he was already afraid of
losing her. Now what was going to happen?

"She'll get over it, believe me."

Josh had pretty much forgotten Shelly was sitting
there. "Sorry?"

"She'll get over it. Trust me. Women want to believe
the best of the men they're with," she said, and her
voice was bitter. "You pretend he wasn't whispering
into his cell phone. You ignore the fact that he was out
till two o'clock in the morning with the boys. You just
keep building these little justifications for him, until one
day he says he's leaving you for another woman. Up to
that point, you listen." She sighed. "By then, you can't
believe what you're hearing."

Josh shifted uncomfortably in his seat. "I would never
cheat on Angela."

"Then why were you out to dinner with me?"

He glanced over at her, surprised. She was looking at
him, her eyes low-lidded.

He shook his head. "I'm sorry your husband was a
jerk, and I know how hard it's been for you, moving
back to town and all. I just wanted to be nice." He
glanced at her, a little more sharply. "That's all."

She turned away from him for a second, looking out
the window. When she turned back he could see she was
hurt and more than a little bit angry. "Just nice."

"Did you really think it was more than that?"

"I thought about it," she said slowly. "Once we
started talking, though, it was 'Angela this' and 'Angela

that.' I figured you probably cared a lot about her, and that you were probably trying to warn me off.''

He heaved a mental sigh of relief.

"Either that, or you were just feeling guilty for cheating on her," she said, making him feel even worse. "I figured I'd know one way or the other by the end of the night."

They arrived at her house, and he pulled into the driveway. He kept the motor running. "Well, I've got to go back to Angela," he said quickly. "She's really angry, and she's probably hurt."

Shelly didn't move, just looked at him for a second. "I guess asking you in for a nightcap is out of the question."

He looked back at her, unwavering. "It is for me," he said quietly. "Sorry, Shelly."

She shrugged again. "Can't blame a girl for trying." With that, she got up and walked into her apartment.

He waited until she was safely inside, then broke speed records getting to Angela's house. Her lights were out. He rang the doorbell. Several times. Then he pounded on the door. Still nothing. He peered into her garage. Her car was there, so he pounded a little more, until he was afraid the neighbors would call the cops. Then he realized—she hadn't taken her car tonight. She was probably still with her friends.

He waited for two hours, and she still didn't show up. He called her number on his cell phone. "Angela? If you're home please pick up." No answer—not that he was really expecting one. "Okay, if you're not home, please give me a call as soon as you get in. Please. It wasn't what you think at all. Just let me explain. I want to talk to you. We need to talk." He thought about saying "I love you," but didn't want to drop that on her in addition to everything she was probably thinking about. If he was trying to drive her away, that'd be the smartest plan. "Just...call me."

He hung up, waited a little more, then drove home. He'd catch her tomorrow. Then they'd talk.

THREE DAYS LATER, he was going out of his mind. He had not heard from nor seen Angela the entire weekend. Manzanita was growing, but it wasn't that damned big, he reasoned. He'd invited Adam over, and they sat in his home office.

"She's being childish about this." Josh prowled around the room. Adam, sitting on the overstuffed chair, just listened to him rant. "I wasn't doing anything wrong, and if she isn't going to listen to me, then she deserves whatever she's going through right now. You know she's just blowing it out of proportion somewhere. If she'd just *talk* to me, we wouldn't be in this mess! It'd be cleared up in a matter of five minutes!"

"You've got a five-minute explanation of why you were out to dinner with another woman?"

Josh glared at him. "It wasn't like that and you know it, Adam."

"Maybe you should try it out on me," Adam said placidly, "because right now, you're in no state to talk to Angela. You need to cool down, see things from her side. I'm not saying you did anything wrong," he hastily added as Josh's expression turned more fierce, "I'm just saying that she'll be fine. When she's ready to talk to you, she'll talk to you."

"Yeah," Josh said, rubbing at his eyes. "To tell me we're finished."

Adam snorted. "You're my best friend, Josh, but

you've got to admit that you get…*impatient,* shall we say? You want things to run on your timetable. You get these plans, and when problems crop up, you go for any way to just work around them. Sometimes, you've got to sit back, and see where things take you. Relax.'' He smiled, an approximation of a Zen calm. ''It'll all work out.''

Those words were no comfort whatsoever, Josh thought.

He'd barely made it through the weekend by hanging out with Adam, going over reports, working on the new product line launch, going over the media plan for the next two quarters. It was no use. He'd tried to work, read, watch TV, but all he could see was Angela's face, and her shocked look in the diner before she'd turned and made a break for it.

Now that it was Monday morning, he was at the Manzanita Public Library, bright and early, waiting for her. He'd give her a piece of his mind, making him worry like this. Angry or not, she could have at least let him know she was okay. She could have yelled at him. She could have *faced* him.

He saw a car drive up. It wasn't her white Honda, but he did recognize the occupants. Two of the women had been with Angela on Friday night. He watched as they walked up to the door, ignoring him as they spoke in concerned tones.

''I'm worried about her,'' the one he recognized as Ginny said in a hushed voice.

''It would be easier if she'd just open up a little more,'' the other one, with the dark hair, said. Josh strained to catch the rest of her sentence, but she was speaking too softly. She looked up, then recognized him.

Ginny obviously recognized him, too. "You've got some nerve, showing up here," she hissed.

"I just wanted to see Angela." He might have expected this. "She hasn't been in contact with me all weekend. Do you know when she'll be in?"

The dark-haired one was more sympathetic. "She's feeling very hurt, Josh," she said, in a quiet voice.

"And if you'd thought with the head on your shoulders instead of the one in your pants, she wouldn't be!" Ginny added, her eyes blazing.

"I wasn't cheating on her," Josh said sharply, then took a deep breath. He didn't need to do this. The only person he owed an explanation to was Angela. "I want to talk to her about this. Do you know when she'll be in?"

They looked at each other. Ginny's mouth was set mutinously.

"She's taking a few days off," the dark-haired one explained, obviously sensing trouble and trying to avoid it. "Possibly all week."

"She's not feeling well," Ginny added. "And don't try going to her house, either. She's not there."

"Where is she, then?" Josh demanded.

Ginny stepped toward him pugnaciously. "I need to tell you because…?"

The other woman spoke up. "Ginny, stop it."

"Tanya, he's hurt her." Ginny turned her angry gaze toward the dark-haired woman. "He's a player! You're not going to just…"

"I'm not going to 'just' anything," Tanya said gently. "But he's obviously concerned."

"Ha." Ginny glared at him. "Guilty's more like it."

Josh gritted his teeth. "I just want to talk to her."

"Well, when she's ready, maybe she'll get in touch

with you. *Maybe.*'' Ginny stomped past him and into the library.

Tanya was looking at him apologetically, ready to walk past him, but he put a gentle hand on her arm, stopping her. "Please," he said. "I...maybe I made a mistake. I know that I never meant to hurt her, and I would never do anything intentionally to make her this unhappy. I just don't see how her spending time away from me is going to resolve the situation at all. Where I come from, we work through things. I want to work through this with her." He looked at Tanya, wondering how he could convince her. "I love her, Tanya. Please, help me out here."

Tanya sighed, and he could see her crumbling a little. "I can't tell you where she is, Josh," she said, her eyes still apologetic. "She just needs some time to herself. She'll get in contact with you."

Tanya hastily went into the library.

Josh leaned heavily against his car, running his hands through his hair. At least he knew she was alive, he thought. He then rubbed his hands over his face. But now he was supposed to wait until she decided to talk to him?

Who knew what she'd think of, what she'd reason, while she was away from him. No. He couldn't afford to relax and let things fall where they may. He needed to figure out a way to see her.

He glanced through the window of the library, then squinted. Then he walked in. Ignoring Ginny's glare, he pulled a flyer off of the wall.

Flamenco dancing. Offered Thursdays at the Community Center, from 7 to 9.

Angela took flamenco dancing. It was her favorite class, the one she'd stuck with when Chinese cooking finished and yoga had been cancelled. Hadn't she always said how important her classes were to her?

He'd find her there.

"ALL RIGHT, LADIES…turn. Clap clap. Turn." The flamenco instructor wore a long, swirling skirt, and her heels clicked loudly on the wooden floor in the dance room at the community center. Angela's attention was only half there.

It was the Thursday after that disastrous night at the diner, and Angela still didn't know how she was going to deal with what she'd seen. More importantly, she didn't know how she was going to deal with what she felt.

Turn turn clap. She had spent the better part of the week at a bed-and-breakfast in Napa. Ginny had recommended it to her. She hadn't really done much of anything except think. She had returned this afternoon to go to her class, and because the midweek rates at the B & B shot up for the busy weekend trade. Still, she had needed the time to sort out what had happened.

She didn't think he was cheating on her, even after what she'd seen. Ginny would probably call her foolish, but in some way, she felt like she knew Josh. He wasn't that sort of person. If he'd grown tired of her, then he would have done something or said something, and dissolved their "arrangement" months ago.

No. He would have *broken up* with her. That's what people did in relationships. Besides, he was an honorable man. And she genuinely felt like he loved her. That wasn't the problem.

It wasn't what he'd done, anyway—she knew that. It was her own reaction that had scared her the most.

She had just realized that she loved him…was dancing with the euphoria of that fact just moments before facing the image of him with another woman. And that was when it had hit her—what being in love with someone really meant. Being in love didn't mean that she accepted the fact that he was in love with her. It meant that she wanted to be with him, that she wanted it more than anything on earth. And to her shock, the first thing that had crossed her mind on seeing him sitting and laughing with Shelly was *what did I do to make him unhappy?*

She shook, and misstepped. She quickly looked around, correcting herself, trying to match the other dancers.

She had been scared to death by the fact that, in that second, she regretted going out with her friends—that she would have done anything to be sitting there with him. That she didn't want to lose him, and didn't want him to leave her. She had never wanted anything the way she wanted Josh Montgomery. And she was terrified of what she'd give up, just to be with him.

And what if I gave all that up, just to lose him anyway?

She misstepped again, almost stumbling. She decided to get a drink of water from the fountain in the corridor, ignoring the instructor's look of concern. She felt her long skirt swish against her ankles as she walked out of the room.

She leaned down to the fountain, feeling the cold water spill across her lips as she took several long sips.

"You looked great in there."

She jerked her head up, a little water splashing on her chin. She quickly wiped off her face. "Josh? What are you doing here?"

He looked strange. His eyes were shadowed, and he

looked really tired. Her heart immediately ached for him. He looked good besides that. She'd been tossing restlessly in her strange hotel bed for the better part of the week, and her body longed to just snuggle beside his, feel his warmth and the soft whoosh of his breath.

"I came here to see you, Angela," he said. "I came here to talk to you. I hoped you would still come to class."

She had almost considered skipping it, but knew it would help take her mind off him, if only a little. Besides, it bothered her that thinking of him had made her miss so much already. "I wasn't ready to talk to you."

"I was hoping you'd be ready now."

She heard the low note of pleading in his voice, and saw the weary look in his eyes. He looked so unhappy.

"All right."

"Will you come with me?"

She nodded, grabbing her jacket and purse from where it was hanging in the hallway nearby, and let him lead her out to his car.

"There's someplace I'd like to take you," he said, as the car cruised quietly along the darkened road. There was a sliver of moon in the sky.

"You don't need to take me anywhere special. We just need to talk."

"I want to take you here," he demurred. "I haven't taken anybody else here."

Setting the scene meant so much to him, she thought, as he drove silently. "Josh, I agreed to talk to you. I was really upset..."

"Here we are," he said, and the low tone of his voice surprised her. They were up by his house. The car bumped along a dirt road, and pulled out between some trees. She peered out with apprehension. There was a grove ahead of them, but it was shadowy and dense. "This is my thinking place. I used to come up here a lot, when I was a senior in high school, trying to figure out what I wanted to do."

She gritted her teeth, fighting her impatience. "I'm trying to say something here."

"I am, too." He unbuckled his seat belt, and turned a little to face her. "I've thought here a lot in the past week. And I realized I'd never taken anybody else here, ever."

She glanced around. It was secluded, completely shaded in by trees. "Not even some girl?" she said, skeptically, then could have bitten her tongue.

He took her hand, lacing it with his. She didn't make any move to clasp his back. His palm was warm. "I know what you must think of me, Angela. I can only say that I wasn't there with Shelly in any sort of romantic way. I was out to dinner with her, yes. But I thought of you the whole time."

She tugged her hand away. "That's not a great excuse, Josh."

He let out a weary breath. "That didn't come out right. Yes, I was a little mad. I think I was trying to get even a little, or prove something to myself. I'm not proud of that."

She turned to him, relaxing a little. She was glad he was being honest, at least. "I can understand."

"I was angry that you'd been avoiding me that week after San Diego, but only because I had something really important to tell you."

"I know," she whispered. "Josh, I didn't think— well, no. I *did* think that maybe you were cheating on me with Shelly. At least, I did at first."

"I wasn't."

She nodded. "I know. Now. I figured that out on my own." She took a deep breath. "But it *hurt*..."

She didn't know how she was going to get through this, when he reached over, not kissing her, just pulling her against his chest. She felt the warm strength of him, and buried her head against his shoulder. "Honey, I'm sorry, I'm so sorry."

"I know. I just..."

"Angela, I know that you're probably afraid to trust me, or anybody, but I have to tell you." He nudged her away from him, and she looked at him with eyes rimmed with tears. "I love you, Angela. I've never loved anybody as much as I love you."

She felt her heart catch in her throat. She had trouble speaking.

"I love you, too."

His eyes glowed like Christmas lights, and he smiled. Then he crushed her back against his chest, and she could feel heat pouring off him like a furnace. He was so happy he radiated with it.

He nuzzled her hair, kissed her neck, then kissed her mouth, hungrily. She kissed him back with equal ardor.

"I love you," he whispered again, against her flesh.

"I love you, Josh," she murmured back, clutching his shoulders.

That's why I'm so scared.

10

ANGELA LOOKED UP at Josh, who was getting ready for bed. She put her book down next to the bed, on top of a growing pile of her books. While waiting for him, the herbal tea she'd been sipping had cooled and was sitting on the nightstand. She'd wash the cup out tomorrow, she thought, when she made breakfast.

In a surprisingly short time, the little actions had become routine.

"Rough day?" she asked.

He looked over at her, and her stomach felt sugary at the heat in his eyes. "Better now," he said, stripping down to boxers.

Her eyes devoured him. She'd been all but living with him for the past three weeks, had seen him naked at various points for the past five and a half months, and she still couldn't get over the sight of him. He climbed into bed next to her. He smoothed his hand over the silky nightgown she was wearing. "Why do you still wear nightgowns?"

She shrugged. "I don't know. They always seem like a good idea."

He nuzzled her neck, and she felt her synapses shorting out, one by one. "You're so cute," he murmured. "You continually wear something that you know you'll only keep on as long as I'm not home. Sometimes, I just don't get you."

His nuzzling was getting a little more purposeful, and her breathing went shallow. "I think you're figuring me out," she said, around a little gasp.

He paused momentarily in his goal, angling up on one arm to look at her. "If only," he said, and though he was grinning, his eyes were serious. "I've been trying to figure out how to ask you this, but I don't know how you're going to react."

She froze, like a startled cat. *Please, please don't ask about Italy.* She hadn't made up her mind, herself.

He had to notice the tension shoot through her—curled as he was around her, it'd be hard to miss. "Relax," he muttered, with a tiny edge of annoyance in his voice. "It's not like I'm proposing murder or something."

"What did you want to ask me?"

He paused for a moment, then let out a deep breath. "I've got this big party for Solar Bars on Friday. It's for our sales team...they've busted tail, and we're doing twice our target for this quarter. It's going to be a big blowout. I'm having it over at that new Moroccan restaurant they just opened."

She finally relaxed. "That doesn't sound so horrible."

"I'd like you to go with me." He pinned her lightly to the bed, pushing wayward locks away from her face with gentle fingers. "It would mean a lot if you would go with me."

She paused, a little tension creeping back into her muscles. "Friday—that's..."

"That's the night you and the girls were going to go over to San Francisco, stay at that hotel. See the Asian art exhibit on Saturday."

She could feel the pressure increasing, like a spring. His eyes didn't waver.

"Why didn't you tell me about this earlier?"

"I forgot," he said, and his eyes darted away, then darted back to her full of guilt. "I'm really sorry. I meant to, I swear. Besides, I only planned it about two weeks ago, when the numbers came in, and I wanted to do something while it was still fresh in their minds. I wanted them to know how much I appreciate their efforts."

She squirmed beneath him. There was only a thin nightgown and boxers and tons of heat between their bodies. She felt him starting to get aroused, and her body started responding characteristically. She focused on the conversation, frowning. "It's not like you'll miss me," she started to point out. "You'll be with all of your company people, you'll need to talk to a lot of them...you know, power-mingle or whatever. I don't see how my being there will do you any good."

His eyes were intense. "Don't you?" He laughed, and it had a ragged little edge. "It's an important night for me. And if it's important to me, I instantly think of you."

She felt a pang in her heart. How could she argue with logic like that?

"I can't...I mean..."

He started kissing her throat, up behind her ear, and her body made the smallest of writhes before she stopped herself. "You guys haven't made the reservation for that room yet," he murmured. His voice against her skin sent a tickling thrill up her back.

"Well, no."

"You could always schedule for another weekend..."

"Josh, that's not the point."

He retreated again, and there it was—the plea in his eyes, that masculine plea that was not begging or even conceding, but full of need nonetheless. "Angela, please. I promise I'll make it up to you. But this means a lot to me. Please, please come."

His voice positively rang with it.

This means so much to him.

"Let me talk it over with the girls, see what I can do."

His smile was like winter sunshine—brilliant and warming. "Thank you, Angela," he said.

He moved down, with purpose, and kissed her intently. "I said I'd talk it over," she said, although she figured they both knew she'd agreed.

"I know," he said, trailing down her neck, coursing over her shoulders. His fingers turned clever, using the silky nightgown against her, rubbing it across her breasts. "And now I'm thanking you for trying."

"Well, then," she said, then gasped as he edged the nightgown up her body. "As long as we both know that."

He tugged the nightgown over her head, smiling as the straps got caught on her arms. "This is why I advocate sleeping in the nude," he said. He stroked her sides, ignoring the obvious jutting tips of her breasts, kissing the flat of her stomach, around her navel, along the top edge of her panty line. His hands continued to move in long, gliding strokes. It was like being memorized by hand, she thought, as he moved back up, kissing her face gently as his hands ran through her hair. She arched her hips up to meet the hard point of his erection, and felt him back away.

"Not so fast," he murmured, and she caught a glimpse of his smile before he nuzzled her breasts and simultaneously started edging her panties down her legs. "I'm not through thanking you."

She let him take off her panties, feeling herself go wet before he'd removed them completely. He eased between her legs, moving lower...

She shot up, her hand going out toward his head. "That's okay. You don't have to..."

He pressed her back down, gently but firmly. "Of course I don't have to. I do this because I *want* to." He moved forward, giving her right breast, then her left breast a quick suckle that had her arching her back and moaning. "There. Now just lie back and let me do what I want."

She felt like one big, boneless, shivering mass of nerves as his head retreated down between her legs. She felt his fingers part her, probing tenderly at her entrance, and she moaned and bit her lip to stop from yelling. He was gentle—he seemed to know every single sensitive spot on her. She felt one of his broad fingers enter her as another toyed with her clitoris, and a whimper escaped despite her efforts.

"That's it, Angela. Just relax." She felt as well as heard the words, his breath warming her most sensitive spot.

"Josh," she said, half warning, half plea. Before she could go any further, she felt his mouth close on her. His tongue circled where his finger had been playing, moving in loving strokes. "Oh...*oh.*"

He was relentless in his attention, and she was pushing up against him insistently, ignoring her previous reluctance as she moved greedily to get more. She was panting now, feeling her body throb and ache. It was just his mouth, but it was full of warmth and tantalizing strokes. She felt the pressure build, and was begging mindlessly for release.

He obliged her. She felt the orgasm hit her like a fist, and she arched off the bed, screaming his name.

She was lying there, dazed, when he sat up, grinning. "Like I said. I can't believe you still wear nightgowns."

She felt him move up toward her, vaguely recognized that he was taking his boxers off. Then he was moving on top of her, hovering there for a moment, seeming so big and substantial that he was sure to crush her. "Josh," she said, breathless.

He moved inside her easily, her previous orgasm making his entrance a smooth glide. She still felt him, large and insistent, as he pushed in to the hilt. She put her hand up on his shoulder. "Let me get on top. Your turn. I want to make love to you…"

"I think we're doing just fine," he said instead, supporting his own weight so she wasn't crushed, but rather circled by his arms, again lightly pinned to the bed.

"But really…"

"Shh." To continue to quiet her, he moved inside her, circling slightly. To her amazement, her body started to feel aroused again, when by all rights she should have been exhausted, wrung out.

"Oh," she breathed, and her hands traced the hard muscles of his chest. "Oh, Josh. Right there."

He withdrew, slowly, moving his hips just enough so she felt every inch of him. She raised her hips to meet him as he buried himself again. His slowness was delicious, torturing.

Still, she felt like he was the one calling the shots, from his vantage point above her. His eyes were closed, his face set in fierce concentration. She felt her body taking over, moving against his, feeling the rhythm he set.

"That's it," he murmured, and she felt him moving against her, inside her.

She moaned as he kept stroking inside of her, moving against her spot unerringly. She murmured incoherently, spreading her legs further, wrapping them around his waist. The corresponding pressure was almost unbearable.

He lowered his head against her, and his breathing was that of a predator, harsh and fast. She was breathing the same way, she thought, but the combination of his very mass, his animal sexuality, made her feel a moment of excitement just bordering on fear. Her body was jumping with sensation, overloading her system.

The second orgasm was followed by a third, then a smaller, echoing fourth, all in quick succession. She felt sure she screamed, and clawed her nails down his back—in that moment, just as animal-like as he was.

He groaned in response, and pumped against her, hard. Then he let out a deep, shuddering breath.

"It keeps getting better," she heard him mutter from the tangle of her hair beside her right ear. "How does it keep getting better?"

"I don't know," she murmured, and she wasn't humoring him. It had somehow moved past what they'd started with. "I thought maybe you'd get bored with me, after all this time. It's not the variety you're used to…"

He rolled over, putting her on top of him. He put a finger on her lips, gently tracing them. "*You're* what I'm used to," he said, silencing her. "I love you, Angela."

She sighed. "I love you, too."

She saw a shadow in his eyes, just for a moment. "I'm not just saying that, either. I've never said that to any other woman." He paused. "And if you're not sure, you shouldn't say it, either."

"Of course I'm sure," she said, stung. "I don't say things I don't mean."

He studied her for a moment, then closed his eyes. "Sorry. I...sorry. I guess I'm just a little anxious lately."

He didn't have to say why. He'd all but circled in red: their six month was coming up.

Italy, she thought, feeling a pang of guilt.

"Well, *you* should relax," she said, nuzzling his chest. "It's not like I'm going anywhere."

She immediately regretted the choice of words, and bit her lip.

"I guess not," he said, and his voice sounded relieved. "Thanks, Angela. For agreeing to come to the party."

She was about to protest, yet again, that she'd only said she'd talk to her friends, but he edged her gently over to the side. She turned over to shut out the light. By the time she'd snuggled against the pillows, he was spooned companionably behind her, his breath warming the nape of her neck. His fingers moved beneath the pillow her head rested on, reaching for and finding the hand she habitually tucked under it. Their fingers laced.

Within minutes, it seemed, he'd fallen asleep.

Angela lay awake for a long time afterward, thinking. *I love this man.*

She'd been living with him for three weeks, seeing him for five and a half months, and she felt like the idea of being apart from him would be like driving a stake through her chest.

That hadn't stopped her from seeing a subtle trend.

She'd only set up three rules: no staying at each other's houses, no breaking plans for him, and not ever saying "I love you." Systematically, she'd broken each one. Now, it was as if the floodgate had broken. She couldn't say no to him. Didn't want to say no.

He'd suggested that he wanted to spend more time with her, and somehow, she'd dropped the intermediate stained glass class that she'd recently signed up for. She'd planned to sign up for part two of Chinese cooking, too, but that hadn't happened. She kept flamenco dancing, but that was it. And she'd spent less time than usual with her friends. Not that they had complained— if anything, Tanya had been encouraging. But she felt it, the distance that was growing steadily.

Yet every time she went to do something about it, it seemed like he'd come up with some new plan to be with her—and there was something in his eyes that made her want to stay, do anything to make him happy.

What would I do if I lost him?

The idea of him unhappy—the idea of him *gone*— was beyond unpalatable. It was intolerable.

Italy came back in her mind, sharply. Five weeks, max. That was all the time she could manage away for her trip, after her little ''sickness'' when she'd vanished for a week.

She'd been getting happy, buzzing calls from Bethany on her voice mail at the library, and had heard her on her machine at home when she called in to retrieve messages.

But that would be five weeks away from him.

Maybe you could bring him with you.

He couldn't—she knew that. He had all that business stuff to attend to, things he couldn't just leave alone while he wandered around somewhere for several weeks on a whim.

He'd asked you to go to this party, with only a few days' notice.

It was different, she justified. Then she felt her grip on his fingers tighten. She deliberately relaxed them.

What's happening to me?

She didn't know what she would do if she lost him, but at this rate, she was rapidly losing herself.

JOSH LOOKED AROUND the room. It was dark in the restaurant. The walls were painted a deep midnight blue and covered here and there with exotic-looking tapestries. His salespeople were having a great time, he could tell. Everyone was seated at low tables, sitting on pillows on the floor. They were laughing, talking loudly, nipping various dainty pieces of meat-filled pastry or roasted chicken off of plates with their fingers. Belly dancers would periodically come out. Men and women alike both cheered and caroused in response.

All of them, he noted, except for Angela.

He had seated her next to Adam, trusting him to entertain her. She barely cracked a smile, he noticed. And he continually checked for one, as he made his rounds to the crowded tables, exchanging a joke or a word of congratulations.

She hadn't gone into specifics, but he got the feeling that her friends had given her a rough time about breaking her plans with them. She had gone tight-lipped, and said that it didn't matter. In Angela-speak, that meant it had been difficult, painful, but she was blocking it out as best she could. He hated that, and felt guilty that he had been the cause of it.

In retrospect, maybe this party thing wasn't such a good idea. But he hadn't known what else to do, and it was starting to wear him down.

He'd been ecstatic when she'd admitted that she loved him, in his car that night, now almost four weeks ago.

He had insisted on bringing her home, and repeating the experience, several times—first the lovemaking, then the profession of love. He couldn't get enough of it, or her. And slowly, he'd convinced her to keep staying at his house. Spending more time with him. He would see her toothbrush sitting companionably next to his in the toothbrush holder on his sink, and it would make him smile. There were signs of woman all over his house, now—her pink razor crouched in the shower next to her shampoo, her clothes were hanging tentatively in a corner of his closet. He'd spent almost every night with her, spoke with her every day. She made coming home a welcome relief.

All of this was marred by only one tiny problem, and he wasn't even sure if it was in his head or not.

He would come home, and she would be reading a travel magazine, and look up at him, her face carefully blank. He would nuzzle her, talking of some future plan, and even though she was listening, it seemed like she wasn't there. She was spending more time with him physically. He just wasn't sure where her mind was.

Or her heart, for that matter.

He realized he was scowling, and carefully schooled his face into a nonetheless strained smile as he got his hand pumped by an eager sales executive. "Congratulations. Great quarter."

"Wait till next month!" the man said, already a bit red-faced from the champagne being served.

Wait till next month.

Their six-month anniversary was coming up. That was yet another source of tension.

He couldn't believe that she would just walk away…she'd acted like she wasn't, but he couldn't be sure. And he knew he couldn't go through with this sick feeling of worrying, wondering if he'd made the cut somehow or not. What was he going to say? That he didn't want to go month-to-month anymore…he was sick of renting, and now finally wanted to buy? Not temporary anymore, but permanent?

He paused, midstride, and almost got run over by two enthusiastic dancers.

He moved to one side, stepping halfway behind a curtain. He studied Angela. She smiled politely at Adam, her eyes darting around the room. *Looking for me,* he thought, with a surge of warmth.

Permanent. That was exactly what he wanted. And that was exactly what he'd do. He'd ask her to marry him.

Suddenly, he felt lighter, as if his tension were a suit of armor that he'd finally been able to remove. He moved toward her, sitting down next to her. The relief was visible on her face.

"Having a good time?" he asked, taking her hand and kissing the back of it gently.

He ignored Adam's amused expression, choosing instead to focus on how her eyes glowed in response. "I am now," she whispered, leaning closer to his collar. He leaned forward and kissed her, not caring what the rest of the table thought. This was the woman he loved and was going to marry. A few public displays were allowed.

He rested an arm around her, watching the dancers, not really paying attention. He stroked her shoulders, feeling the tension there. "Thank you, again."

She glanced over at him. "For what?"

"For canceling your San Francisco plans for me."

She looked uneasy. "Well, that's okay."

"No, really," he said, tipping her chin up. "I mean

it. It was important to you, and I really, really appreciate it.''

He didn't let go until her darting gaze finally focused on him. "You're welcome," she said slowly, with a small smile.

"How about I make it up to you?" A plan was starting to take shape in his head. He'd have a whole week to make the arrangements. "I'll take you into San Francisco next weekend, instead. We'll do whatever you want."

She made a skeptical face. "I don't know, Josh. It's not quite the same."

He leaned in close to her ear. "Trust me. It'll be even better."

He was satisfied when she shivered. "Okay, Josh."

He kissed her again, then turned back to the dinner conversation. His mind wasn't really on it—it was swarming with ideas. A hotel with a view of the bridge, he thought, top-notch with room service and a deep hot tub. Candles, everywhere, and flowers. Lots of flowers.

And a ring, he thought. Something unusual, something beautiful, like her.

It was a perfect plan—in theory. He glanced over at her, once again unplugged from the conversation.

Now, if only he could guarantee that she would say yes.

WHAT ARE YOU DOING?

Angela was hiding in the rest room of the Moroccan restaurant Josh had persuaded her to go to, dodging the party he'd wanted her to attend...blowing off her friends in the process.

They had taken it well—that is, Tanya had taken it well. Ginny had simply crossed her arms.

"You're getting that in-over-your-head look, Angela. You might want to evaluate why you're always breaking plans for him these days. And what would happen if you decided not to do it anymore?"

Ginny had a point there. What *would* happen, Angela mused?

He would be hurt. She would hate to see him hurt, she thought. At this point, she hated even seeing him uncomfortable.

But that wasn't the real reason, was it?

He might leave.

Just the thought made her uneasy enough to fiddle with something, fidget, do anything but dwell on the supposition. She glanced around the bathroom instead. Actually, this wasn't even the bathroom…it was an adjoining sitting room, away from the stalls and the sinks. There was a large cushioned couch against one wall, and a brightly lit mirror obviously meant for use by women touching up their cosmetics. It looked very much like a boudoir, done in royal blue velvet.

"Angela. I should have known you'd be here."

Angela glanced over, and saw Shelly, wearing a lipstick-red dress, obviously a signature color of sorts. She looked at odds with the cool blue of the room. She sat on one of the chairs in front of the mirror, studying Angela in the reflection rather than head on. From her small purse, she pulled out a small compact, an eye shadow duo, a blush and a lipstick, and proceeded to apply them with the precision of a portrait painter. Angela wasn't sure why Shelly bothered—her face looked porcelain perfect to begin with.

Angela knew nothing had happened between Josh and Shelly on the night they'd had dinner together. She trusted him enough to know that. Still, seeing the woman who had managed to cause not one but two of the major fights between herself and Josh was enough to make her uneasy. She started to get up, walk away, but Shelly's next question stopped her.

"So...are you looking forward to Italy?"

Angela frowned. And now, hitting her with the twenty-million-dollar question. "My ticket is fully refundable," she murmured. "Isn't that right?"

Shelly's hazel eyes widened. "You're still considering canceling?"

"Rescheduling," Angela hedged. "I'm thinking of rescheduling. Maybe something later. Now isn't the best time..."

Shelly's eyes narrowed. "This has to do with Josh, doesn't it?"

Angela felt her temper blossom like an icy explosion. "Does the Travel Center always include relationship therapy with its services, or did I get that thrown in when I asked for business class?"

Shelly didn't rise to the bait. Instead, she sighed, philosophically. "You must hate me."

"I don't hate you," Angela said, although she was feeling closer to it than she'd thought possible. "I just wonder what business it is of yours what my relationship to Josh is. Afraid of losing your commission?"

"No. Just speaking as a woman who's been there."

Angela felt a muscle in her neck tighten to the point of snapping. "You've been there with Josh?" Her voice was low, frigid.

"Hmm? Oh, no. Not for want of trying, I'll have to admit. Josh is a very good-looking man, and a wealthy one. He's got a reputation for treating women well."

"He doesn't have women, plural, anymore." Angela

felt her hands balling into fists. That this woman would *dare*...

"I know that. You're an incredibly lucky woman, Angela."

Angela paused, wondering what Shelly's angle was. "Yes, I know."

"No, I don't think you do," Shelly said, surprising her. "I moved back to Manzanita because I got divorced, did you know that?"

"Um, no." Angela shifted her weight, unsure where this conversation was going. "I'm sorry," she added awkwardly.

"So am I," Shelly said. "We lived in Oregon. He spent most of our money, left me in debt and desolate. I had to move back in with my parents. I had just moved into my own apartment not long before the night Josh and I had dinner." Angela saw the lines creasing the corners of her eyes—worry lines, that no expensive makeup could erase. The bitterness in Shelly's voice was palpable. "I had always insisted on being an independent woman, when we got married. Had my own life, my own friends. I married my husband in a rush, but I let him know exactly what I wanted. I thought he was okay with that. I think he even was, for a while."

Shelly shifted, staring at herself in the mirror, as if she were telling the story to the face in front of her and not a riveted stranger like Angela. "But then he changed. He started getting jealous and demanding. I thought we'd work it out. Next thing I know, he's divorcing me. Leaving me for a waitress in a Mexican restaurant. When I asked him why, he said..." She took a deep breath. "He said he wanted a wife, and I 'sure wasn't being one.'"

Angela took a quick inhalation of breath, a surprised hiss.

"I was shattered when he left. When I got back here, I vowed that I was looking for a man who'd take care of me, and that I would do everything I could to make him happy. If he wanted me to focus on him, then that's damned well what I was going to do. I'd screwed it up once, and I'm not going to do it again."

Angela swallowed hard. "Why are you telling me this?"

Shelly finally looked back at her. Her eyes were almost emotionless, glassy, like a doll's. "I'm telling you this," she said patiently, "because Josh Montgomery is just what I'd be looking for in a man. He's what every woman looks for in a man. And if it's going to be a choice between Josh and a trip to Europe, I'd say you're out of your mind if you leave."

Angela blinked. Of all the advice she could receive, from all the people she could receive it from, she had hardly been expecting this.

"One more thing," Shelly said, dabbing one last puff of powder on her forehead before shutting her compact with a click. "If you choose to leave Josh alone, I guarantee you, while you're gone, a lot of other women *won't*. And men don't like to be alone for long, I've discovered."

"Josh isn't like that," Angela stated flatly.

"All the more reason you ought to weigh your choice carefully, don't you think?"

"I've wanted this for a long time," Angela said, slowly. "If he really loves me, he should understand that. He should be supportive. I can't be the one that keeps bending."

Shelly looked at her, shaking her head. "Believe me.

Men don't bend. They break. And they break you with them."

Shelly left, leaving only a dusting of spilled powder and a trace of floral perfume in her wake.

Angela leaned back against the deep blue couch cushions, thinking hard.

She'd given up so much, already. She'd given in. She felt like she was always giving in.

Was it really that bad?

She rubbed her eyes, suddenly weary.

She had a ticket for two weeks from now in a drawer in her apartment, and a lover who was no doubt growing impatient in the other room.

What am I going to do?

11

IT HAD TO BE PERFECT.

Josh realized that he was tapping his finger nervously on the table he was sitting at, on the top floor of the San Francisco Marriott. From atop the imposing glass structure that rather reminded him of a jukebox, he could see the city stretching out, cloaked here and there with clouds. The sun was setting, a deep cerulean blue edging into green, yellow and crimson before plunging gold into the bay. It was beautiful, serene.

Where the hell was she?

He had told Angela that he had a late meeting in Sacramento on Friday, which was true—he was late, working with the jeweler. He'd already set up restaurant reservations, and had everything ready. He was going to seduce her, tonight...and then propose to her.

His palms were sweating. Absently, he wiped at them with a cocktail napkin. He hadn't been this nervous during his first year running Solar Bars. Had never been this nervous in his recollection.

What if she says no?

The ring—a simple affair of yellow gold and tiger eye flanked by diamonds that reminded him of her eyes—sat heavy as lead in his pocket, nestled in its black velvet box.

She wouldn't say no. Not if he had any power to

convince her otherwise…and he'd never had an incentive to persuade anyone like he did tonight.

He glanced at his watch, noting the time still hadn't changed. She'd been very cagey about tonight. He wasn't sure if she were looking forward to it or dreading it. He was figuring her out, as she'd said, that was true, but it didn't extend far enough. He'd know tonight for sure. At the very least, when he saw her he'd know what sort of obstacles he was up against. Maybe she'd be dressed in jeans, ready to hit the wharf. Or in something drop-dead sensual, ready to show him what she wanted was more sex than talk. It was, he'd discovered, her none-too-subtle way of avoiding him. A neat trick, too, he noted. He was rarely able to resist it.

"Josh."

He glanced up sharply, and it was all he could do to keep his jaw from dropping.

She was wearing a dress. Not a sexy, low-cut and high-cut number, nothing overt. It was simple, a warm peach that made her skin color glow. She'd put on contacts and makeup, he noticed, and her hair was up in a gentle knot that let tendrils curl gently around her face. It looked sort of gauzy, and sensual.

It looked romantic.

His heart did a quick double-pump in his chest, and for the first time that night, he allowed himself to hope that this wasn't going to be a pitched battle. In fact, it was starting to look like he'd won before he even took the field.

He stood up, and she walked over to him, her eyes twinkling gently. She looked at him like he was a superhero and her best friend all rolled into one. She leaned up and kissed him, gently.

"I went shopping," she said, doing a slow twirl. Her

skirt fell to midcalf, and she wore peach heels. She looked like some glamorous forties movie star.

"I approve." He took her hands, brushed kisses across each knuckle. "I made reservations at Charles of San Francisco."

Her eyes glanced down at his suitcase. "Why don't we get you settled in first?"

He shifted uneasily. He sort of wanted to get this over with.

Is that any way to look at your marriage proposal?

She must have read some of his intention, because she smiled, cozying up to him. "What time is the reservation?" she whispered.

The proximity of her body wasn't making this any easier. "Um, eight-thirty, I think."

"It's only seven. Why don't you go up, take a shower? You look really tired from your meeting."

It wasn't the meeting. He grasped at the straw, anyway. He certainly looked and felt like he'd been through a meat grinder. Maybe a shower wasn't such a bad idea.

He walked with her up to their room, watching as she unlocked the door. She'd just gotten her nails done, he noticed. She'd really gone all out on her day in San Francisco. He breathed a little easier. A woman like Angela didn't go to all this trouble if it weren't something really important. And certainly not if she were going to try and let a guy down easy.

Of course, Angela wasn't like anybody else.

He took off his tie with a sigh of relief, and pulled out his suit. "I'd ask you to join me," he said, kissing her gently, enjoying the way she lingered. "But you look so beautiful, I wouldn't feel right to spoil it."

"That's okay. You take a long, hot shower." She

smiled, a mysterious smile that reminded him of the first time he'd met her. "I'll be here when you get out."

He kissed her again, as if to assure himself that she really meant it.

He walked into the bathroom, shutting the door behind him, and stripped. Stepping into the steaming hot jet of water was a blessing. He wanted to wash all the stress and tension off of himself. After what seemed like forever, he finally shut the water off. He wasn't relaxing, at this point. He was stalling.

Come on, Josh. You're just asking her to marry you.

Sure, he told the bit of his reflection he could make out under the fogged-up glass. *Easy for you to say.*

After a moment, he grabbed the suit from the back of the bathroom door where it was hanging. He pulled his clothes on, and hurriedly combed his hair. He heard noise, then some low music playing out in the room. *Angela, probably trying to kill time,* he thought, putting on his shoes. *I've been in here forever.*

He stepped out, and immediately stopped, surveying the room as steam from the bathroom crept out around him.

The room was lit by the warm glow of what looked like dozens of candles, all in that same peachy color as Angela's dress. The small table by the suite's kitchenette was set for a candlelit dinner, complete with a long-stemmed rose that went from pale peach to flame orange, sitting beautifully in a cut crystal vase.

He goggled. "What's all this?"

"This," she said, sidling up to him, "is a surprise."

He felt pushed off balance. He had been in control of the situation. Now, he was careening out of control. *Angela? Setting up a romantic seduction scene? Since when? And what's going on here?*

"Um, Angela," he said, trying to recoup. "Honey, we've got dinner reservations…"

Her eyes were wide and almost mischievous. "We're not going to make them. I wanted to keep you to myself tonight. Is that all right?"

Her voice was tentative, as if she weren't sure if he'd be angry. That, also, wasn't quite like Angela. He found himself nodding. "I suppose it's…"

There was a knock at the door, and her smile was brilliant with delight. "That'd be dinner."

She glided over to the door, opening it to reveal a white-jacketed server with a wheeled cart. Delicious aromas emerged from the covered silver trays. After silently and efficiently setting out a beautiful meal that looked like prime rib and various side dishes, he disappeared out the door with a barely audible "enjoy your meal."

Angela shut the door behind him and locked the dead bolt.

Whatever it was, she obviously meant business. And she wasn't going to let him follow through with his carefully laid plans.

For the first time that night, possibly that week, he wasn't worried. *New outfit, hair done, nails done. Romantic setting, ordered in food.*

Maybe he'd been worried for nothing. Maybe, just maybe, what she had in mind ran parallel with what he'd intended. He would just ride this out, and see where she planned to go with this.

Her eyes glowed a warm brown-amber in the candle-light. "Are you hungry?"

He smiled, gesturing to the table. "After you."

ANGELA SAT, SIPPING her wine gingerly. She'd ordered his favorite food, had all but kidnapped him. She was going to show him how much he meant to her—open up in all the ways she'd been afraid to in the past. She was going to tell him how much she loved him. She was going to *show* him how much she loved him.

And then she was going to tell him she was leaving for Italy. For six weeks. Without him.

He put his napkin down on the table, sighing. "That was great." He studied her curiously. "So. We've had a wonderful meal, and some very pleasant conversation. What did you have in mind next? I'm completely at your disposal."

She nibbled her lower lip. "I thought maybe…dancing."

He got up, stretched a tiny bit. "Dancing. I could be up for dancing. Preferably something a little slower, though. Where did you want to go?"

She glanced at the living room floor. She felt ridiculous, but… "I was thinking we could improvise."

He frowned. "Improvise?"

"Here," she said. "I thought we could dance here."

He smiled then, and she eased a fraction. He walked over to the CD player. They were listening to something rich, jazz-inspired, with a sexy saxophone overlay. He reached for her, gracefully circling her in his arms.

"How's this?"

"Just what I was thinking of," she whispered, leaning her head against the lapel of his suit.

They moved like that for a few minutes, swaying gently, easily to the music. She felt the hand at her waist flex, pulling her closer. The hand that held hers was warm, comforting.

"Do you have any idea how much I love you?" she said, looking up at him.

He blinked, then rested his forehead against hers. "If

it's anywhere near as much as I love you," he said, "then I think we're both pretty lucky."

"I know I'm lucky. I was lucky to find you. Lucky that you're more than I expected." She leaned up on tiptoe, kissed him gently.

He kissed her back, more intently. They stopped dancing. He framed her jaw with his hands, kissing her with a series of soft, soulful kisses that teased warmth out of her as well as arousal.

She stroked her hands up the front of his suit, clinging to him. *He had to understand.*

She pulled back a little, looking at him, almost willing him mentally to understand her intentions. *I love you, I need you. But I still need space.* "You've been so understanding, and so gentle with me."

"I'll always be gentle with you," he said, pressing slow, careful kisses on her neck. He pulled back, too. "I promise. I'll always care about you, and I'll always want to be with you."

She stroked his face, concerned slightly by that last remark. "But you've also given me the room to be myself."

He smiled, and his hands moved to her waist, tugging her to him. "Of course. I love who you are, Angela. You're like nobody I've ever met. I don't think I could make you anything other than what you are." He stroked up her sides lightly, brushing the sides of her breasts and making her gasp, involuntarily, with pleasure. "I don't think anything could change you."

"Oh, you'd be surprised," she murmured, then pressed a little more insistently. She felt his erection beginning to firm, and sighed, a little smile on her face. "I just wanted to show you how much you mean to me. Tonight."

She kissed him, then started unbuttoning his shirt.

Minutes moved by slumberously. It was like making love for the first time—or the last time. She paid loving attention to every detail, from the spicy scent of his cologne to the way his muscles felt, firm and sleek. He turned her, undoing the zipper on the back of her dress with the same careful slowness. He kissed her from the nape of her neck, down the path the zipper had revealed, the long length of her spine unhindered by any bra strap.

She shivered, and let the dress fall to the floor, until she was only wearing her garter belt, stockings and shoes.

She turned, tugging off his suit jacket and tossing it over a chair, then kissing his chest down where the buttons of his shirt were opened. He removed his shirt, groaning slightly as she paid attention to his flat nipples, the planes of his stomach. The shirt went the way of the jacket. He kicked off his shoes, and she stepped out of hers.

He pulled back the heavy cover on the king-sized bed, leaving only taupe blankets and cream-colored sheets. She went and stretched out on it, her butt firm and pert beneath the peachy-cream-colored garter belt. She still wore the stockings. They had delicate lace at the top and one single crimson rose in the front, and she thought he'd enjoy them. The flare of his blue eyes proved her theory correct.

"I love you," he murmured, sliding out of his trousers and pulling off his socks. He was only left in black silk boxers. She smiled.

"I love you," she answered, and reached for him.

They just lay there, still for a few moments, heating each other's skin with the close proximity of their bodies. The silk felt wonderful against her naked stomach.

She smoothed herself over him, and he reached up and kissed her. She smiled against his lips, then pulled away, and removed the pins from her hair. It fell in mahogany curls, framing her face, tickling down her back. He fisted his hand in it gently, bringing her back down for a longer kiss, more lingering. His tongue came into play with hers, tasting the rim of her lips, giving gentle suction. He nibbled at her mouth. She felt as well as heard her breathing start to speed.

Always so wonderful, she thought, distracted by the feel of him, the taste of him. *I love this man.*

He turned, angling so she lay flat against the cushiony softness of the bed. She braced herself for another deliciously forceful kiss, but he paused. His eyes were wide, wondering. He moved her hair away from her face, then caressed her cheek gently with his fingertips. He traced the arch of her eyebrows, ran a fingertip playfully down her nose.

''You're beautiful,'' he said, his voice a reverent hush. ''Every day I see you, you get more and more beautiful.''

It made her heart ache. She swallowed, hard, and her hand came up to do the same, tracing the hard planes of his face, the chiseled line of his jaw, the angle of his cheekbones.

I love you. I love you. I love you.

And on a lower counterpoint:

Please, please understand.

She reached for him, and he lowered his head for a kiss that made her heart beat frenetically. She felt it, the stirring need that he always called forth. It had an edge of desperation, of love and fear and intensity. She needed him. She needed space.

She needed both, desperately.

He was pressed against her side, and one hand reached down, feeling for the feathery curls between her legs. She gasped as he found her clitoris, and started teasing her, no more than gentle taunts. She breathed in small harsh gasps. "Josh."

"We've got all night," he murmured against her skin, and the tickling pleasure redoubled. He started to dip one finger inside of her, and she pressed her hips against him. He laughed.

"I can take it," she said, remembering their first night together, "if you can."

He laughed again, and pulled away. He stripped off the boxers, and his penis was erect, huge with need. "I've got a lot of patience tonight," he said, and began toying with her again. The look on his face wasn't mischievous, however—on the contrary, it was filled with a passionate tenderness. "I want it to be very, very special."

He started kissing her breasts, first one, then the other, suckling gently until she was writhing beneath him, murmuring incoherent words of love and need. She felt the orgasm hit, and narrowed her eyes at him as he chuckled with uneven breath. "Two can play at this game," she muttered, starting to reach for him.

He stopped her, his eyes surprisingly serious. "It's not a game, Angela," he said, his voice low. He studied her.

She paused. "I know, Josh. I won't play with you," she said, her own voice serious. Then she smiled. "But I will make tonight special."

With that, she gently held him, feeling the heat coming off of his penis against the palm of her hand. She grinned as he leaned his head back and closed his eyes, groaning softly. She carefully moved her fingers around him, cupping the weight of his balls, feeling the tension in his thighs. Then she started tasting him, and his hands bunched up in fists against the bed sheets. She licked, gauging his reaction, taking him with slow, loving suction. He was breathing harder now, his body tense as a bowstring.

She was waiting for him to snap.

He pulled her up against him, and kissed her, not gently, but ferociously. She kissed him just as hard, their tongues mating as he rolled on top of her. Abruptly, he stopped, his breathing hard and ragged against her neck.

"Slow, Angela." His voice was muffled by her hair, and she smiled and rubbed his back as he leaned down and positioned himself at her entrance, readying her as he usually did, lightly probing her with the head of it. "I want to remember this."

She sighed as he pushed in inch by inch. He filled her completely, then lay still inside her. Putting pressure at the juncture of her thighs, he kissed her, simultaneously nudging her against her most sensitive spot.

The second orgasm surprised her, and she gasped against his lips in shock.

He only kissed her more fiercely, and his hips began to move in earnest. She lifted her hips to meet him. Each slow retreat, and slower entrance gliding inside her, making her feel the heat radiate from between her legs up to her heart. She was gasping, tugging at him, wrapping her legs around his. He was breathing harder, and a thin sheen of sweat covered his torso. He still continued his relentlessly slow pace, moving inside her like the ocean's eternal rhythm.

"Josh," she said, as impossibly the pressure began to build again, this time in gradual and escalating increments. "Oh, Josh..."

"Angela," he murmured, and finally his speed began to increase. "Yes. Yes..."

Her hips rose to meet his, and they were suddenly straining against each other, pistoning to meet each other, still graceful but full of sexual fire. She could feel him, full and hard, inside of her, and she...

"Josh!" she screamed, and her legs wrapped around his waist. The orgasm was more powerful than anything she'd ever felt. Aftershocks rocked through her system, and her head pounded against the pillow as her body shuddered.

He continued pumping against her, his pace a frenzy of passion. He was still wrapped in her, and she felt the orgasm belt through him as he emptied himself inside of her with three long, shuddering releases.

They were silent and still, lying in each other's arms for a long time afterward as the sweat cooled on their bodies and their breathing evened out.

Angela clutched him almost protectively, running her fingers through his hair. *This is a man who understands me. A man who wouldn't hurt me, or leave me, or make me be something I'm not.* She wondered why she had ever even worried. Of course he'd be supportive of her trip to Italy. Josh had made demands on her time, true. But he'd been so giving. She could trust him. Maybe when she got back from her trip, she'd think about living with him. They could take their time, just as they had tonight. It would be special. She'd be ready by then. She loved him.

Now was the perfect time to explain all of this.

She cuddled against him. "I love you," she said. "Josh, I..."

"Shh. I wasn't expecting this, and you know how I

like plans,'' he said, and she giggled. ''But this couldn't be more perfect. I love you, Angela.''

''I know,'' she said.

He stared at her. ''Angela, will you marry me?''

At first, the words didn't even make sense. ''Sorry?''

''Marriage. You know. Matching rings, white dress, one place of residence. Possibly kids, but I don't want to push.''

''Marriage?'' She sat upright, catching his chin with her forehead. She rubbed at it, even as he groaned and laughed, rubbing his jaw. ''You mean, *that* was what this was all about?''

''Of course,'' he said. ''And you had me sweating, believe me. I don't think I've been this nervous in all my life.'' He took a deep breath. ''Incidentally, I haven't heard a yes yet.''

He watched her and she hurriedly pulled a blanket over herself. ''It's so fast,'' she hedged. *Even her mother had known her father seven months before they got married. Oh, no.* ''Don't you need to think about it a little more?''

''I know,'' he said, in that quiet, serious voice. ''Sometimes I think I knew when I first met you. You challenge me. You make me happy.'' He got under the blanket as well, nuzzling up against her.

She felt panic, sick and queasy, in her stomach. Her mind raced. She loved him, more than she thought she'd ever love anything. But marriage was something else. If anything could turn love to hate, it was that. ''I love you, too,'' she said, firmly. ''You know I feel the same.''

''Then you'll marry me?'' His voice was confident, but she sensed the underlying tension.

''I didn't say that.''

She felt all his muscles tense, and he turned her to face him, his blue eyes cold. "So you're saying no?"

"I didn't say that, either," she said, hating that pain, the beginnings of his anger. "I'm just saying it's terribly fast. You know how I am, Josh...what I am. You know I need time to think."

"How much time?" he asked, and she took a relieved breath as she felt a possible reprieve in her grasp.

"I would think about...five weeks," she said. Then took another deep breath to steady herself. "When I get back from Italy, in fact. I can tell you then."

The silence hit her like a fist. He stared at her, and she could see the vein pulsing in his neck. "Italy. You never cancelled the tickets."

"Why would I, Josh?" She tried to ask it as gently as possible, but the assumption gnawed at her. *He'll understand, he'll understand...*

"Because you're going to spend a month away from me, on another continent, and again, you hadn't mentioned any plans that you were going," he said, and his voice was edged in frost. "A separate vacation for that long a time period, without even discussing it with me, your boyfriend, the guy who wants to marry you. A month with your friend..."

"Bethany," she said. "My very best friend from college. Practically family. And I'd still been thinking about it..." She realized she was pleading, and clamped her mouth shut.

"For a month." He said, leaning back. He closed his eyes.

For a brief, painful moment, she felt like taking it back—taking it all back, saying she loved him, she'd cancel the ticket, she'd marry him. Anything to wipe that pain from his face.

Please, please understand!

"Fine." He sighed. "It'll be a little problematic, but I'll go with you."

She blinked. "No," she said, then winced as his eyes opened and his gaze pinned her like a bug.

"Why not?"

"Because this is for me," she said, struggling miserably. "Because I need time. I need some space, to think this out."

"You need *space*." His voice was now frigid, and she saw something had tipped the balance over...something had broken the camel's back. "I see."

She feared he didn't. "Josh, let me try to explain."

"Oh, you don't need to explain." He rolled off the bed, gloriously naked, his muscles rippling dangerously. "I think I get the picture now."

"Josh, please..."

"It's always been about you," he said sharply. "I have tried to make you happy, Angela. I've tried to make you love me. I see that's where I made the most grievous mistake."

"I do love you!"

"Do you?" His eyes blazed. He tugged his boxers back on with a vicious yank, then reached for his trousers. "You care for me, I'll give you that. But dammit, Angela, I've been doing all the work, making all the moves. Do you realize that tonight was the first time you've ever planned something for us? I thought I could work past that fear of commitment you've got going. Make you see that I wasn't going to hurt you, that you could trust yourself to love me. But you just keep dancing away. Then tonight, seducing me, just so I wouldn't be ticked off that you were leaving for another continent in a month, which you naturally neglected to mention until a week before departure.'' He pulled on the trousers, cursing under his breath as one leg got fouled up in the process. ''But I'm done. I'm sick of banging my head against a wall for a woman who cares about me deeply *but doesn't love me enough to stay with me.* I'm sick of being the one who does all the work.''

That hit, and hit hard. She felt her own temper flare as she got to her feet. ''Of course you do all the work. You're the one calling all the shots, aren't you? You make all the plans, and I'm the one who has to cancel mine. You're the one who has to be in control all of the time. Well, here's a news flash, Josh—you can't control love. And I'm not going to let you control me!''

He growled at her. ''I do *not* try to control you!''

''Oh, you're subtle about it. You charm me, seduce me…love me. But I need to have my own space, Josh. I need to be my own person. If I lose that, then I'll lose all the qualities that you claim to love. I'll lose myself!''

''So you'll get to be your own person if I happily agree to let you romp around Europe for a month?'' he spat out, and she almost hit him. Fury pulsed through her like lightning. ''If you were half as invested in this relationship as I am, you'd understand why that isn't an option.''

''If you understand me half as well as you think you do,'' she countered levelly, ''you'd see why this is the only option I've got.''

They stood, squared off against each other, him in trousers, her in garters and stockings. Each with matching frowns of love turned hurtful.

''I thought I understood you,'' Josh said, quietly, reaching for his shirt and pulling it on haphazardly. ''Now, I realize you're not the woman I thought you were.''

He tugged on his suit, grabbed his briefcase. "Stay the weekend if you like. Do whatever you feel you have to. But if you get on that plane to go to Europe, I'll know your decision."

"Why are you making this so hard on me?" she said around a sob, stepping between him and the door.

"You're making it hard on yourself," he said, stepping around her. He paused at the doorway. "I still love you. That's what hurts most of all."

With that, he stepped out the door, leaving her in stockings and tears.

12

"JOSH, I'M WORRIED about you," his father said, his thick silver eyebrows all but knitted together in their concern.

Josh toyed with the eggs his mother had placed in front of him on the kitchen table. "I'll be fine."

"Really?"

Josh almost groaned when he saw the gleam of stubbornness in his father's eyes. Blue eyes, startlingly like his own. Everybody said so. "Really."

"How often have you called the office, in the four days you've been down here?" his father asked casually.

Josh winced. "I trust Adam, Dad. It's not like I can keep my eye on every little thing."

His father pointed at him with his fork. "Good grief. You're worse than I thought."

"Dear, you might want to ease up on Josh," his mother said, sitting down at the table and frowning. "And you don't want to work yourself up."

"I just want to see the extent of the damage, here, Margaret," he said firmly. "God. To think I liked that girl."

"There's no reason why you shouldn't. She's a good woman." Josh shrugged, underscoring the pain he felt. "She just didn't love me, that's all." He took a swallow of coffee to wash down the lump of bitterness in his throat.

His father shook his head, baffled. "That's where you lose me. You weren't running around on her, were you? Yelling at her? Doing...I don't know."

"Dad, you know me better than that."

"Yes, I do. Which is why I can't understand how this happened."

You'd have thought his father was the one this had happened to, Josh thought wryly. He bit into a strip of bacon. "It came as a surprise to me, too."

"What in the world were her reasons?"

"Dad, do we have to go into this?"

His dad's jaw muscles clenched, making him look fierce. "When my only son comes to me, looking like he's gone fifteen rounds with Muhammad Ali, then yes, we have to go into this."

Josh sighed. He'd already replayed the scene, hell, the whole six months he'd been with Angela, over and over. Wondering what he'd done, or what he hadn't done. Where he was lacking.

"All I know is, I spent six of the best months of my life with her. Well, six of the toughest, too," he said, smiling a little as he remembered the uphill battle he'd undergone. "I did everything I could to make her happy. I swear, Dad...well, you know how you get when you're planning to take over a company?"

His father grinned wolfishly. "Boy, do I ever."

"Well, that's what I was like. I planned it down to the last detail. I thought I had every base covered. In fact, I thought we were on the exact same page. I asked her to marry me." He pushed his plate away. "Then she yanked the rug out from under me."

"What did she say?" his father pressed. "What reason did she give to say no?"

"That was just it," Josh said, slowly. "She didn't

even have the guts to say no. She just withdrew. Said she'd go to Italy for six weeks and think about it.'' He closed his eyes. ''Only I knew what she was really saying. It finally hit me. All this time—all this work. And all of it was on my side. I was always the one who initiated. I was the one who pushed for a relationship. I thought I was getting her to trust me, getting her to love me. And all I was doing was wasting my time.''

''Why do you say that?''

His mother's tone was sharp, and it surprised him. ''Mom, how would you feel if you loved somebody, did everything you could think of to make them happy, make them want you—and all of a sudden, instead of rushing to be with you, they make a run for it? Does that say that someone's as invested in the relationship as you are?''

She finally looked up from her plate. To his surprise, her gray-green eyes blazed.

''So she never made any show of loving you?''

His mother rarely lost her temper—barely had one to begin with. Josh saw his father staring at her, equally mystified. ''I'm not going to say Angela didn't care about me. I know she did. But she didn't love me.''

''I'm sorry, son,'' his father rumbled, his voice filled with sympathy.

''So am I.'' His mother stood up, her chair dragging along the floor with a harsh shriek. ''Sorry I had to hear this.''

She stalked off from the table. *Stalked.* His gentle, smiling mother walked out like a gambler who'd just lost a high-stakes poker match.

His father's jaw dropped. ''Holy cow. What was *that* about?''

Josh rubbed his hands over his face. ''Could you

please tell me what I've done that suddenly makes me vile to women? Please? So I can stop doing it?''

"Beats the hell out of me." His father started to stand. "I'd better go find out what's the matter…"

"No, Dad. Whatever she's mad at, it's something I said. I'll go see if I can fix it," he said.

He walked through the house, looking for her. He finally found her in the attic office. "Mom?"

His mother was sitting at the small writing table that was set up by the window. She looked out into the sunlight, her back to him.

He walked up, shut the stairs behind him. "Mom, what is it?"

She didn't say anything, but pushed the window open a little further. He felt the cool breeze on his face, like a whisper.

He was always closer to his father, granted, but his mother had always been comforting—had always supported him, been on the bleachers cheering while his father had been on the sidelines, coaching. To have her be like this, act like this, was a one-two punch following Angela's refusal.

"Come on, Mom," he said, using the charming voice he often employed when he was younger, trying to stay up past bedtime. He thought it would cheer her, make her start talking. "How am I supposed to fix it if you won't tell me what's…"

"Don't game me, Josh." Her voice was cold, and he stopped. "I'm your mother. Don't you dare try to con me."

He blinked. Then his anger stepped to the fore. "All right. What is this?"

She turned to him. Her cheeks were wet, and it hit him like a fist in the gut. "Mom?"

"I thought I'd raised you better than this."

His world had spun out of control when Angela didn't say yes to his marriage proposal. With that perspective, he supposed this attack shouldn't have surprised him. Still, he was stunned. "Mom, what did I do?"

"It sounds like you did everything, from what you've told me," she said, her words mocking his. "You charmed her. You planned things for her. You did everything in your power to show her why she should be with you."

"Is that what made you angry? That I was trying too hard?"

"No," she said, with an exasperated tone. "I'm angry because you didn't do the one thing she needed. You didn't ask her what *she* wanted."

He bristled at this. "Mom, you're off base here. She wasn't exactly forthcoming. I did everything I could to find out what she liked, what she dreamed about..."

"Just so you could use it, Josh," she said strongly, her eyes rimming with tears again. "Don't you hear what you're saying?"

He stopped.

"Josh, I've known you all your life," she said, with a small smile that reminded him more of the mother he knew, and he calmed fractionally. "I've seen you admire your father, with his determination, his drive, and his ability to plan or charm his way into just about anything. Goodness knows, I found him hard to resist."

"Mom, what are you saying?"

She looked at the attic stairs almost furtively. "I love your father. More than I've ever loved anyone. But sometimes, I've resented the hell out of him."

"What?"

"I didn't hate him," she said quickly, frowning at

him. "I'm not saying that. But he did what you're doing. He loved me because I stood up to him—he'll tell you stories, I know. But slowly, he wore me down." She took a deep breath. "Did I ever tell you I wanted to be a writer?"

Josh sat down on the daybed, feeling stunned. "I remember you majored in English lit."

"Your father needed help with his store. Then, as he got bigger, more successful, he needed my support. I loved him so much, it never occurred to me not to give him all my attention, all the time I could spare. Then you kids came along."

"Mom," Josh said, wounded.

She shook her head. "You were a joy to me. Don't ever think you weren't. But it was more time, and more attention. The writing just never seemed as important. So I let it go."

She leaned back in her chair, her eyes going a misty, dreamy blue-green-gray. "I remember once, I was taking you and your sister shopping. I guess my car was broken down—we had to take the bus. We hadn't moved to Manzanita yet. We were still in—I think we were in San Francisco." She smiled at the memory. "So there I was, trying to ride herd on you while I was lugging your sister and a bag full of who knows what. And I remember looking up, and seeing a billboard of Sandra Rossi."

Josh frowned. The name sounded familiar.

"She's a feminist author," his mother explained. "I went to school with her. We used to sit around, drinking really cheap wine and talking about our careers. And there she was, doing what we'd dreamed about. And there I was."

"With nothing." Josh's voice was flat.

"Not with nothing!" she countered. "I'm not trying

to tell you I made the wrong choice. I didn't. I made the best choice I knew, at the time." She got up, walked over to the bed, sat next to him. "But I will say this— if I had to do it all over again, I would have saved a little more for myself, Josh. Not that I love you or your father or your sisters any less. But somewhere along the way, I lost a part of myself. A part I am just now, after all of these years, starting to get back. And that, I have regretted."

"And you think I was trying to make Angela make that choice?" he asked, turning the scene over in his mind.

"No," she said. "I think you were trying to give her no choice at all."

ANGELA SAT IN THE airport terminal in San Francisco. In a few short minutes, she was going to get onto a plane that would take her over the North Pole, drop her off for a stopover in London, then take her to Milan. From there, she'd take a train to Florence.

From Florence, she'd go anywhere and everywhere.

She looked down at her carry-on.

Of course, she'd be going alone.

She tried to call Josh, leaving messages at Solar Bars and at home.

Josh, please pick up. We can't just leave it like this.

But that, apparently, was precisely what he wanted.

Tanya nudged her. "Hey. You okay?"

Angela nodded, then shrugged. "As okay as I'm going to be."

"You'll be fine, believe me," Ginny said staunchly. "He was being an asshole."

"He was being scared," Angela corrected, gently. "I can understand that. I've been there."

Tanya smiled from the other side of her, giving her a little shoulder-hug. "We've all been there."

Ginny stared at her, eyes narrowing. "You're not thinking of giving in, are you?"

Angela shook her head, feeling guilty. She'd considered it. As she packed her suitcases, she'd thought about it. Every time she left a message for Josh that never got returned, it nagged at her. And especially as she cried herself to sleep in her too-large and empty bed, she'd considered it.

What would I be giving up, really? Just a trip to Europe.

Just a trip. Right. *And the Superbowl is just a friendly football game.*

She couldn't. For her own sake, and ultimately for Josh's sake, she couldn't. She'd resent him if she gave up her plans to see Europe for the first time, just because he couldn't see how much she loved him—and how much she needed this. What's more, she'd learn to hate herself.

"Maybe he'll change his mind," Tanya said, her voice sounding dubious but obviously trying to be encouraging.

Ginny snorted. "Oh, sure."

"Ginny, you're not helping."

"Like you are, with comments like that?"

"You're both helping," Angela said, stopping their mini-squabble before it could get heated. "I really appreciate it. If I'd had to wait around here by myself, I don't know what I would have done."

They both hugged her this time, and Angela let them, relishing the warmth.

"Now boarding, British Airways Flight 1506, San Francisco to London, out of Gate 9."

Angela couldn't help it. She made one last sweeping glance over the airport lobby. She didn't know what she was expecting. Josh, standing there with an armful of flowers, saying he was sorry? Telling her to have a good trip?

She didn't see him. Didn't see anyone but travelers like herself.

She got up, got her bags with trembling hands. "Guess this is it."

They hugged her again, maternally. "You have a good flight," Tanya said. "And enjoy your trip."

"Italian men, baby. They're like *Esquire* models with dark coloring. And if you don't go for that—the food, oh my word, the food." Ginny sighed dramatically. "If that doesn't cheer you up, nothing will."

"I love you guys," Angela said quietly. "Thank you, so much."

With a little wave, she made her way to the gate, watched as the man tore off her boarding pass and returned the rest of her ticket. She made her way down the tunnel-like walkway that led to the plane. It felt like going through a pipeline.

This is it.

She was finally getting on with her life. She wasn't just reading about something—she was doing it. In a strange way, being with Josh had helped her gain that courage. If nothing else, she had him to thank for that.

No. You have yourself *to thank for that.*

But she did have him to thank for so many other wonderful things in her life. She had a wealth of opportunity in front of her. This year, Italy—next year, who knew what? The options were unlimited.

She thought, briefly and painfully, of her last meeting with Josh.

Well, there's one limit.

She didn't want to take off crying. She quickly shifted thoughts to stuffing her rolling bag in the overhead, tucking her smaller carry-on in the space in front of her. She had a window seat. She wanted to see the view.

Why can't I get more excited by this?

She buckled her seat belt. She couldn't get more excited because a part of her still expected Josh to somehow fix this. He was a planner, someone who fixed things. He'd always been so understanding. She couldn't believe that he wasn't doing something elaborate to try and get her back, to show her he loved her. To somehow make this work.

She still felt that as she stared, sightless, at the paperback novel in front of her. It was a horror novel, by one of Josh's favorite authors. She closed the book as they prepared the cabin, and kept her eyes shut as they started down the runway.

He didn't do anything.

The realization hit, and hit hard. She stared out the window, looking at nothing, feeling the pressure of the plane as it blasted down the runway and turned into the dreamy floating of takeoff. She didn't cry, and as long as she stared and fought it, she wouldn't.

It's all over.

She didn't know how long she sat like that, frozen, staring.

"Angela? Angela Snowe?"

She glanced over, glad her eyes were dry. Maybe she'd get some sleep. It was the stewardess.

"Yes?" Her drink order. She considered getting the strongest drink they offered. Maybe it would help her sleep through the flight, take the edge off for a while.

She just needed to hold on until she could reach Bethany in Florence. Then she could completely fall apart.

The flight attendant handed her an envelope. "This is for you."

Angela stared at it blankly. "What is it?"

The woman simply smiled. "It's for you," she repeated.

She looked at it for a moment. *Angela Snowe,* sure enough, printed on the front of the cream-colored envelope.

Her heart started to pound.

Don't hope, you idiot.

She opened it, slowly. She glanced over the words, recognized Josh's bold, clear handwriting.

Angela,

I asked the stewardess to give you this once you were in the air, because I knew if you changed your mind on the ground, it wouldn't be right. I also knew that if you wavered, even a little bit, I would probably crack and change my mind. So this is for both of us.

I'm sorry for what I did.

I didn't realize what I was asking—I could only think about how much I loved you, and that, if you loved me, you'd naturally want what I want, when I wanted it. I didn't take into account how different you are. Pretty dumb, considering you were right— it's those very differences that make me love you as much as I do.

Angela swallowed hard at that. She could picture him, writing it slowly and thoughtfully. And he was right— if she'd read this anywhere but on the plane, she'd be canceling her ticket and going to him, with all the possibilities of resentment that it would have created.

I've been doing a lot of thinking. I didn't want to get hurt in this relationship, and I thought, if I just kept it under control, I wouldn't be. I was wrong. Looks like the only way I can be with you isn't by planning it out, or putting in more effort. It's by letting go and trusting things to work out.

Now she was more than swallowing hard. She felt her eyes rim with tears, brushed them away impatiently with the back of her hand.

I love you. That's true no matter how you feel, or where you are. Take all the time you want in Italy—don't worry about calling or writing. Do what you need to do to decide. I'll be waiting when you get back.

By the time she got to his signature—"All my love, Josh"—she was crying steadily.
I could hijack the plane. Make it turn around.
She laughed at herself, hiccuping slightly through her tears. No. That wasn't the point of this, was it?
He loved her.
He was willing to wait for her.
She sat back, finally feeling the first twinges of excitement coursing through her. He loved her. He'd wait.
She could do anything.

TWO WEEKS. It had been two weeks since he'd given that stewardess the envelope for Angela. He had no idea how it had panned out. Or if she'd even gotten it at all.

He was doing pretty well, for an insane person. He'd managed to get a lot of business traveling done. At least it was slightly easier to sleep in a bed that was strange to him, rather than in his now eerily quiet house. He wasn't comfortable there. If he wasn't working late, then he was out with Adam, or out by himself.

He left his Palm Pilot at home for these outings, like tonight at the Cable Car. He hadn't scheduled anything, and women who approached him for whatever reason got the most polite brush-off he could manage.

You're not her.

What was she thinking? Was she thinking of him? Had she forgiven him?

He ran his fingers through his hair, and glanced at the bartender. Without a word, the bartender studied him, shook his head, and popped open another beer for him.

"Man, you're one sorry guy," Adam said, walking up next to him. "Everybody in town's noticed it. Josh Montgomery, finally falling in love. And finally getting dumped."

"I haven't officially been dumped," Josh said, hoping he was joking. He took a long draw off the beer bottle. "She just needed some space."

Adam patted his shoulder in male sympathy. "Needing some space. If you say so, Josh... No. I'm really sorry, man. That's right up there with washing her hair when it comes to brush-offs. It's not great, but it's a definite breakup."

"I don't believe that. I can't believe that," Josh said. "This is what she needs, and dammit, I'm going to trust her on this."

Adam sat on the bar stool next to him, and sighed. "I'm sorry. I've been where you are, and I know what it's like. But if you suddenly feel the need to start beating on some random stranger who wanders in here, for no good reason, give me a holler. I'll back you up."

Josh smirked at him. "That's why you're my partner, Adam."

"And here I thought it was my God-given biochemical acumen—hello, what's this?"

A pretty young woman with black hair and a short skirt sauntered by, giving them both a quick study. She smiled, indicating interest.

Adam raised his eyebrows, then he glanced guiltily at Josh. "Never mind. There are plenty of fish in the sea, right? I'll just hang out with you. You've been alone too often lately."

"Are you crazy? Did you see the way she smiled at you?" Josh shook his head. "Get over there."

Adam glanced over to where the girl was now sitting, and openly eyeing him. "You sure?"

"What are you waiting for? An engraved invitation?"

"Thanks." Adam stood up, got ready for his come-on saunter, then stopped. "Call me later. If you need to talk."

"I'm fine." Josh lifted his beer in salute, then smirked as Adam walked over and struck up a conversation with the woman.

At least one of us'll be happy.

He wasn't going to think about it. Angela had not left him. She really had loved him—she still did. At least, that's what he was betting on.

The jukebox was going full blast now. The music was loud, heavy on guitar, with a pulsing beat. There was no mistaking the Cable Car for some country honky-tonk bar these days. It was too bad—he could have used the quiet. And while he wasn't a country fan, songs about it being a fine time to be left would probably suit his mood perfectly.

He didn't want to go back to his empty house, but he didn't think he could stay here.

Maybe I could hit a movie...

"Josh?"

He barely made out the female voice. *Definitely can't stay here,* he thought, finishing his beer in one long swallow.

"Hello?"

He turned to see who was talking.

She was wearing her long mahogany hair, loose and tumbling around her shoulders. Compared to the short skirts, flirty dresses or skintight jeans the other female patrons were sporting, she was wearing a pair of loose-fitting cotton khakis and a T-shirt. Both were fairly rumpled. Her familiar pair of glasses were slightly askew, and she pushed them up unconsciously, moving a lock of hair away from her face at the same time. She was the most beautiful woman he'd ever seen.

He didn't speak. He barely breathed.

"Do you know how long I've been looking for you?"

He shook his head slowly.

"I went straight to your house from the airport," she said, taking off her glasses and tucking them carefully in her back pocket. "I waited for about an hour. Then I cruised by your office. Then I cruised by every restaurant in town. I decided to try here next. It was lucky that I saw your car."

"Angela," he finally said, leaning close so she could hear him. "What are you doing here?"

She smiled, and it was the sweetest smile he'd ever seen. "Well, I've got this...situation. I was hoping you could help me with it."

"You don't say." He felt his heart start to beat again, and a tentative sense of relief crept over him. "Well, I like to think of myself as a helpful guy."

Her hands touched his shirtfront, ran up his chest until they linked behind his neck. He got the vague sense that people were watching, and quickly brushed it aside. "See, I went on this trip to Italy. I had a terrific time." She paused.

"And?" he prompted, trying for patience.

"I saw everything I'd only ever read about—the Duomo, St. Peter's, the Uffizi," she said, with a small smile. "Everything was one fantastic adventure. There was just one problem—I missed you."

He swallowed, hard, not wanting to interrupt.

"It wasn't as fantastic as you are," she said, her eyes never leaving his. "I realized that I wasn't afraid anymore. Of anything. So I told Bethany that she'd be hearing from me soon, and left."

"What'd she say to that?" Josh asked, wondering if he could take her into his arms now. He waited, wanting her to make the first move.

Angela leaned forward, and he rested his forehead against hers as his heart felt like it would explode. "She said that she hoped I realized she was doing my wedding photography. Then recanted when I told her she was going to be my maid of honor."

He felt his heart beat faster. "So what do you need my help with?"

"I'm planning a wedding," she said, slowly. "But I need somebody who loves me, and who still wants to marry me." Her doe eyes stared at his, full of hope…and nervousness. "Do you think you can help me?"

He studied her, this woman who had changed his life. Then, slowly and with purpose, he leaned down and kissed her with all the love and passion he felt in his heart. She responded eagerly, urgently.

Finally, he pulled away, seeing his own emotion mirrored in her eyes.

"You're in luck," he said, his voice thick with emotion. He held her close. "When it comes to that, I'm a sure thing."

Hugh Blake, soon to become stepfather to the Maitland clan, has produced three high-performing offspring of his own. But at the rate they're going, they're never going to make him a grandpa!

There's *Suzanne*, a work-obsessed CEO whose Christmas spirit could use a little topping up....

And *Thomas*, a lawyer whose ability to hold on to the woman he loves is evaporating by the minute....

And *Diane*, a teacher so dedicated to her teenage students she hasn't noticed she's put her own life on hold.

But there's a Christmas wake-up call in store for the Blake siblings. Love *and* Christmas miracles are in store for all three!

Maitland Maternity Christmas

A collection from three of Harlequin's favorite authors

Muriel Jensen
Judy Christenberry
&Tina Leonard

Look for it in November 2001.

Celebrate the season with

Midnight Clear

A holiday anthology featuring
a classic Christmas story from
New York Times bestselling author

Debbie Macomber

Plus a brand-new *Morgan's Mercenaries* story
from *USA Today* bestselling author

Lindsay McKenna

And a brand-new *Twins on the Doorstep* story
from national bestselling author

Stella Bagwell

Available at your favorite retail outlets in November 2001!

Silhouette®
Where love comes alive™

HARLEQUIN®
makes any time special—online...

eHARLEQUIN.com

shop eHarlequin

- ♥ Find all the new Harlequin releases at everyday great discounts.
- ♥ Try before you buy! Read an excerpt from the latest Harlequin novels.
- ♥ Write an online review and share your thoughts with others.

reading room

- ♥ Read our Internet exclusive daily and weekly online serials, or vote in our interactive novel.
- ♥ Talk to other readers about your favorite novels in our Reading Groups.
- ♥ Take our Choose-a-Book quiz to find the series that matches you!

authors' alcove

- ♥ Find out interesting tidbits and details about your favorite authors' lives, interests and writing habits.
- ♥ Ever dreamed of being an author? Enter our Writing Round Robin. The Winning Chapter will be published online! Or review our writing guidelines for submitting your novel.

All this and more available at
www.eHarlequin.com
on Women.com Networks

HINTB1R

CALL THE ONES YOU LOVE OVER THE HOLIDAYS!

Save $25 off future book purchases when you buy any four Harlequin® or Silhouette® books in October, November and December 2001,

PLUS

receive a phone card good for 15 minutes of long-distance calls to anyone you want in North America!

WHAT AN INCREDIBLE DEAL!

Just fill out this form and attach 4 proofs of purchase (cash register receipts) from October, November and December 2001 books, and Harlequin Books will send you a coupon booklet worth a total savings of $25 off future purchases of Harlequin® and Silhouette® books, AND a 15-minute phone card to call the ones you love, anywhere in North America.

Please send this form, along with your cash register receipts as proofs of purchase, to:
In the USA: Harlequin Books, P.O. Box 9057, Buffalo, NY 14269-9057
In Canada: Harlequin Books, P.O. Box 622, Fort Erie, Ontario L2A 5X3
Cash register receipts must be dated no later than December 31, 2001.
Limit of 1 coupon booklet and phone card per household.
Please allow 4-6 weeks for delivery.

I accept your offer! Please send me my coupon booklet and a 15-minute phone card:

Name: _____

Address: _____ City: _____

State/Prov.: _____ Zip/Postal Code: _____

Account Number (if available): _____

---

097 KJB DAGL
PHQ4012

WITH HARLEQUIN AND SILHOUETTE

There's a romance to fit your every mood.

Passion
Harlequin Temptation

Harlequin Presents

Silhouette Desire

Pure Romance
Harlequin Romance

Silhouette Romance

Home & Family
Harlequin
American Romance

Silhouette
Special Edition

A Longer Story With More
Harlequin
Superromance

Suspense & Adventure
Harlequin Intrigue

Silhouette Intimate
Moments

Humor
Harlequin Duets

Historical
Harlequin Historicals

Special Releases
Other great
romances
to explore

Harlequin Romance®
Love affairs that
last a lifetime.

HARLEQUIN *Presents*~
Seduction and passion
guaranteed.

Harlequin® **Historical**
Historical
Romantic
Adventure.

HARLEQUIN®
Temptation.
Sassy, sexy, seductive!

HARLEQUIN® *Super*ROMANCE™
Emotional,
exciting,
unexpected.

HARLEQUIN® AMERICAN *Romance*®
Heart, home
& happiness.

HARLEQUIN®
Duets™
Romantic comedy.

HARLEQUIN®
INTRIGUE®
Breathtaking
romantic suspense.

HARLEQUIN® *Blaze*™
Red-Hot Reads.

HARLEQUIN®
Makes any time special®

Visit us at www.eHarlequin.com   HSERIES01

Look to the stars
for love and romance
with bestselling authors

JUDITH ARNOLD
KATE HOFFMANN
and GINA WILKINS

in

WRITTEN
IN THE
STARS

Experience the joy of
three women who dare to
make their wishes for love
and happiness come true in
this *brand-new* collection
from Harlequin!

Available in December 2001
at your favorite retail outlet.

HARLEQUIN®
Makes any time special ®

Visit us at www.eHarlequin.com

PHWS